W. P. KINSELLA

now joins the distinguished company of such great writers as Robert Penn Warren, Philip Roth, Willie Morris, and Robert Stone—all winners of the prestigious Houghton Mifflin Literary Fellowship Award.

SHOELESS JOE

Universally acclaimed by critics and readers alike, here is a heartwarming, hilarious, and enchanting novel about the power of dreams to transform reality...

"ANY BOOK THAT HAS SHOELESS JOE JACKSON, FENWAY PARK AND MOONLIGHT GRAHAM IN IT ALMOST BEFORE YOU CAN PAUSE TO CATCH YOUR BREATH HAS GOT TO BE MORE FUN THAN REGGIE JACKSON UNDER A HIGH FLY..."
Los Angeles Times

...and that's only the beginning. Please turn the page for more rave reviews of

SHOELESS JOE

"AN UTTERLY DISARMING, WHIMSICAL KNUCKLER OF A NOVEL...
Create a world of compelling whimsy... the nostalgic world of the American pastime and American times past. With rare skill, Kinsella turns his obsession into metaphors of memory and emotion."

Los Angeles Times

"AS CURIOUS, COMPELLING, ARTFUL, AND MYSTERIOUS AS THE GAME IT CELEBRATES. SURELY A STRONG CANDIDATE FOR ANY LITERARY HALL OF FAME."
George Plimpton

"FRESH AND BELIEVABLE...
Baseball becomes a metaphor for religion, a symbol of the need to hold onto something, anything, in a faithless age... From the small details of memory, love, and family... to the larger themes, Kinsella has got it right."

Miami Herald

"MYTHIC...FANCIFUL...
The novel attests to the timeless game and the power of love."

Publishers Weekly

SHOELESS JOE

W. P. KINSELLA

WINNER OF A HOUGHTON MIFFLIN LITERARY FELLOWSHIP AWARD

BALLANTINE BOOKS • NEW YORK

Library of Congress Catalog Card Number: 81-19196

ISBN 0-345-34226-7

This edition published by arrangement with Houghton Mifflin Company

Manufactured in the United States of America

First Ballantine Books Edition: April 1983
Fifth Printing: July 1986

For Olive Kinsella and Margaret Elliott;
for Ethel Anderson. In memory of
John Matthew Kinsella (1896–1953).

"Some men see things as they are,
and say why, I dream of things
that never were, and say why not."
—BOBBY KENNEDY

Contents

I

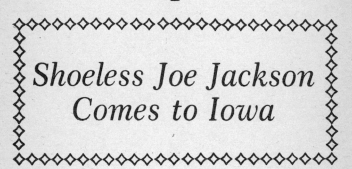

Shoeless Joe Jackson Comes to Iowa

My father said he saw him years later playing in a tenth-rate commercial league in a textile town in Carolina, wearing shoes and an assumed name.

"He'd put on fifty pounds and the spring was gone from his step in the outfield, but he could still hit. Oh, how that man could hit. No one has ever been able to hit like Shoeless Joe."

Three years ago at dusk on a spring evening, when the sky was a robbin's-egg blue and the wind as soft as a day-old chick, I was sitting on the verandah of my farm home in eastern Iowa when a voice very clearly said to me, "If you build it, he will come."

The voice was that of a ballpark announcer. As he spoke, I instantly envisioned the finished product I knew I was being asked to conceive. I could see the dark, squarish speakers, like ancient sailors' hats, attached to aluminum-painted light standards that glowed down into a baseball field, my present position being directly behind home plate.

In reality, all anyone else could see out there in front of me was a tattered lawn of mostly dandelions and quack grass that petered out at the edge of a cornfield perhaps fifty yards from the house.

Anyone else was my wife Annie, my daughter Karin, a corn-colored collie named Carmeletia Pope, and a cinnamon and white guinea pig named Junior who ate spaghetti and sang each time the fridge door opened. Karin and the dog were not quite two years old.

"If you build it, he will come," the announcer repeated in scratchy Middle American, as if his voice had been recorded on an old 78-r.p.m. record.

A three-hour lecture or a 500-page guide book could not have given me clearer directions: Dimensions of ballparks jumped over and around me like fleas, cost figures for light standards and floodlights whirled around my head like the moths that dusted against the porch light above me.

That was all the instruction I ever received: two announcements and a vision of a baseball field. I sat on the verandah until the satiny dark was complete. A few curdly clouds striped the moon, and it became so silent I could hear my eyes blink.

Our house is one of those massive old farm homes, square as a biscuit box with a sagging verandah on three sides. The floor of the verandah slopes so that marbles, baseballs, tennis balls, and ball bearings all accumulate in a corner like a herd of cattle clustered with their backs to a storm. On the north verandah is a wooden porch swing where Annie and I sit on humid August nights, sip lemonade from teary glasses, and dream.

When I finally went to bed, and after Annie inched into my arms in that way she has, like a cat that you suddenly find sound asleep in your lap, I told her about the voice and I told her that I knew what it wanted me to do.

"Oh love," she said, "if it makes you happy you should do it," and she found my lips with hers. I shivered involuntarily as her tongue touched mine.

Annie: She has never once called me crazy. Just before I started the first landscape work, as I stood looking out at the lawn and the cornfield, wondering how it could look so different in daylight, considering the notion of accepting it all as a dream and abandoning it, Annie appeared at my side and her arm circled my waist. She leaned against me and looked up, cocking her head like one of the red squirrels that scamper along the power lines from the highway to the house. "Do it, love," she said as I looked down at her, that slip of a girl with hair the color of cayenne pepper and at least a million freckles on her face and arms, that girl who lives in blue jeans and T-shirts and at twenty-four could still pass for sixteen.

I thought back to when I first knew her. I came to Iowa to study. She was the child of my landlady. I heard her one afternoon outside my window as she told her girl friends, "When I grow up I'm going to marry . . ." and she named me. The others were going to be nurses, teachers, pilots, or movie stars, but Annie chose me as her occupation. Eight years later we were married. I chose willingly, lovingly, to stay in Iowa. Eventually I rented this farm, then bought it, operating it one inch from bankruptcy. I don't seem meant to farm, but I want to be close to this precious land, for Annie and me to be able to say, "This is ours."

Now I stand ready to cut into the cornfield, to chisel away a piece of our livelihood to use as dream currency, and Annie says, "Oh, love, if it makes you happy you should do it." I carry her words in the back of my mind, stored the way a maiden aunt might wrap a brooch, a remembrance of a long-lost love. I understand how hard that was for her to say and how it got harder as the project advanced. How she must have told her family not to ask me about the baseball field I was building, because they stared at me dumb-eyed, a row of silent, thickset peasants with red faces. Not an imagination among them except to forecast the wrath of God that will fall on the heads of pagans such as I.

"If you build it, he will come."

He, of course, was Shoeless Joe Jackson.

Joseph Jefferson (Shoeless Joe) Jackson
Born: Brandon Mills, South Carolina, July 16, 1887
Died: Greenville, South Carolina, December 5, 1951

In April 1945, Ty Cobb picked Shoeless Joe as the best left fielder of all time. A famous sportswriter once called Joe's glove "the place where triples go to die." He never learned to read or write. He created legends with a bat and a glove.

Was it really a voice I heard? Or was it perhaps something inside me making a statement that I did not hear with my ears but with my heart? Why should I want to follow this command? But as I ask, I already know the answer. I count the loves in my life: Annie, Karin, Iowa, Baseball. The great god Baseball.

My birthstone is a diamond. When asked, I say my astrological sign is hit and run, which draws a lot of blank stares here in Iowa where 50,000 people go to see the University of Iowa Hawkeyes football team while 500 regulars, including me, watch the baseball team perform.

My father, I've been told, talked baseball statistics to my mother's belly while waiting for me to be born.

My father: born, Glen Ullin, North Dakota, April 14, 1896. Another diamond birthstone. Never saw a professional baseball game until 1919 when he came back from World War I where he had been gassed at Passchendaele. He settled in Chicago, inhabited a room above a bar across from Comiskey Park, and quickly learned to live and die with the White Sox. Died a little when, as prohibitive favorites, they lost the 1919 World Series to Cincinnati, died a lot the next summer when eight members of the team were accused of throwing that World Series.

Before I knew what baseball was, I knew of Connie Mack, John McGraw, Grover Cleveland Alexander, Ty Cobb, Babe Ruth, Tris Speaker, Tinker-to-Evers-to-Chance, and, of course, Shoeless Joe Jackson. My father loved underdogs, cheered for the Brooklyn Dodgers and the hapless St. Louis Browns, loathed the Yankees—an inherited trait, I believe—and insisted that Shoeless Joe was innocent, a victim of big business and crooked gamblers.

That first night, immediately after the voice and the vision, I did nothing except sip my lemonade a little faster and rattle the ice cubes in my glass. The vision of the baseball park lingered—swimming, swaying, seeming to be made of red steam, though perhaps it was only the sunset. And there was a vision within the vision: one of Shoeless Joe Jackson playing left field. Shoeless Joe Jackson who last played major league baseball in 1920 and was suspended for life, along with seven of his compatriots, by Commissioner Kenesaw Mountain Landis, for his part in throwing the 1919 World Series.

Instead of nursery rhymes, I was raised on the story of the Black Sox Scandal, and instead of Tom Thumb or Rumpelstiltskin, I grew up hearing of the eight disgraced ballplayers: Weaver, Cicotte, Risberg, Felsch, Gandil, Williams, McMullin, and, always, Shoeless Joe Jackson.

"He hit .375 against the Reds in the 1919 World Series and played errorless ball," my father would say, scratching his head in wonder. "Twelve hits in an eight-game series. And *they* suspended *him*," Father would cry. Shoeless Joe became a symbol of the tyranny of the powerful over the powerless. The name Kenesaw Mountain Landis became synonymous with the Devil.

Building a baseball field is more work than you might imagine. I laid out a whole field, but it was there in spirit only. It was really only left field that concerned me. Home plate was made from pieces of cracked two-by-four embedded in the earth. The pitcher's rubber rocked like a cradle when I stood on it. The bases were stray blocks of wood, unanchored. There was no backstop or grandstand, only one shaky bleacher beyond the left-field wall. There was a left-field wall, but only about fifty feet of it, twelve feet high, stained dark green and braced from the rear. And the left-field grass. My intuition told me that it was the grass that was important. It took me three seasons to hone that grass to its proper texture, to its proper color. I made trips to Minneapolis and one or two other cities where the stadiums still have natural-grass infields and outfields. I would arrive hours before a game and watch the groundskeepers groom the field like a prize animal, then stay after the game when in the cool of the night the same groundsmen appeared with hoses, hoes, and rakes, and patched the grasses like medics attending to wounded soldiers.

I pretended to be building a Little League ballfield and asked their secrets and sometimes was told. I took interest in the total operation; they wouldn't understand if I told them I was building only a left field.

Three seasons I've spent seeding, watering, fussing, praying, coddling that field like a sick child. Now it glows parrot-green, cool as mint, soft as moss, lying there like a cashmere blanket. I've begun watching it in the evenings, sitting on the rickety bleacher just beyond the fence. A bleacher I constructed for an audience of one.

My father played some baseball, Class B teams in Florida and California. I found his statistics in a dusty minor-league record book. In Florida he played for a team called the Angels and, according to his records, was a better-than-average catcher. He claimed to have visited all forty-eight states and every major-league ballpark before, at forty, he married and settled down in Montana, a two-day drive from the nearest major-league team. I tried to play, but ground balls bounced off my chest and fly balls dropped between my hands. I might have been a fair designated hitter, but the rule was too late in coming.

There is the story of the urchin who, tugging at Shoeless Joe Jackson's sleeve as he emerged from a Chicago courthouse, said, "Say it ain't so, Joe."

Jackson's reply reportedly was, "I'm afraid it is, kid."

When he comes, I won't put him on the spot by asking. The less said the better. It is likely that he did accept money from gamblers. But throw the Series? Never! Shoeless Joe Jackson led both teams in hitting in that 1919 Series. It was the circumstances. The circumstances. The players were paid peasant salaries while the owners became rich. The infamous Ten Day Clause, which voided contracts, could end any player's career without compensation, pension, or even a ticket home.

The second spring, on a toothachy May evening, a covering of black clouds lumbered off westward like ghosts of buffalo, and the sky became the cold color of a silver coin. The forecast was for frost.

The left-field grass was like green angora, soft as a baby's cheek. In my mind I could see it dull and crisp, bleached by frost, and my chest tightened.

But I used a trick a groundskeeper in Minneapolis had taught me, saying he learned it from grape farmers in California. I carried out a hose, and, making the spray so fine it was scarcely more than fog, I sprayed the soft, shaggy spring grass all that chilled night. My hands ached and my face became wet and cold, but, as I watched, the spray froze on the grass, enclosing each blade in a gossamer-crystal coating of ice. A covering that served like a coat of armor to dispel the real frost that was set like a weasel upon killing in the night. I seemed to stand taller than ever before as the sun rose, turning the ice to eye-dazzling droplets, each a prism, making the field an orgy of rainbows.

Annie and Karin were at breakfast when I came in, the bacon and coffee smells and their laughter pulling me like a magnet.

"Did it work, love?" Annie asked, and I knew she knew by the look on my face that it had. And Karin, clapping her hands and complaining of how cold my face was when she kissed me, loved every second of it.

"And how did he get a name like Shoeless Joe?" I would ask my father, knowing the story full well but wanting to hear it again. And no matter how many times I heard it, I would still picture a lithe ballplayer, his great bare feet white as base-balls sinking into the outfield grass as he sprinted for a line drive. Then, after the catch, his toes gripping the grass like claws, he would brace and throw to the infield.

"It wasn't the least bit romantic," my dad would say. "When he was still in the minor leagues he bought a new pair of spikes and they hurt his feet. About the sixth inning he took them off and played the outfield in just his socks. The other players kidded him, called him Shoeless Joe, and the name stuck for all time."

It was hard for me to imagine that a sore-footed young outfielder taking off his shoes one afternoon not long after the turn of the century could generate a legend.

I came to Iowa to study, one of the thousands of faceless students who pass through large universities, but I fell in love with the state. Fell in love with the land, the people, the sky, the cornfields, and Annie. Couldn't find work in my field, took what I could get. For years, I bathed each morning, frosted my cheeks with Aqua Velva, donned a three-piece suit and snap-brim hat, and, feeling like Superman emerging from a telephone booth, set forth to save the world from a lack of life insurance. I loathed the job so much that I did it quickly, urgently, almost violently. It was Annie who got me to rent the farm. It was Annie who got me to buy it. I operate it the way a child fits together his first puzzle—awkwardly, slowly, but, when a piece slips into the proper slot, with pride and relief and joy.

I built the field and waited, and waited, and waited.

"It will happen, honey," Annie would say when I stood shaking my head at my folly. People looked at me. I must have had a nickname in town. But I could feel the magic building like a gathering storm. It felt as if small animals were scurrying through my veins. I knew it was going to happen soon.

One night I watch Annie looking out the window. She is soft as a butterfly, Annie is, with an evil grin and a tongue that travels at the speed of light. Her jeans are painted to her body, and her pointy little nipples poke at the front of a black T-shirt that has the single word RAH! emblazoned in waspish yellow capitals. Her red hair is short and curly. She has the green eyes of a cat.

Annie understands, though it is me she understands and not always what is happening. She attends ballgames with me and squeezes my arm when there's a hit, but her heart isn't in it and she would just as soon be at home. She loses interest if the score isn't close, or the weather's not warm, or the pace isn't fast enough. To me it is baseball, and that is all that matters. It is the game that's important—the tension, the strategy, the ballet of the fielders, the angle of the bat.

"There's someone on your lawn," Annie says to me, staring out into the orange-tinted dusk. "I can't see him clearly, but I can tell someone is there." She was quite right, at least about it being *my* lawn, although it is not in the strictest sense of the word a lawn; it is a *left field*.

I have been more restless than usual this night. I have sensed the magic drawing closer, hovering somewhere out in the night like a zeppelin, silky and silent, floating like the moon until the time is right.

Annie peeks through the drapes. "There *is* a man out there; I can see his silhouette. He's wearing a baseball uniform, an old-fashioned one."

"It's Shoeless Joe Jackson," I say. My heart sounds like someone flicking a balloon with his index finger.

"Oh," she says. Annie stays very calm in emergencies. She Band-Aids bleeding fingers and toes, and patches the plumbing with gum and good wishes. Staying calm makes her able to live with me. The French have the right words for Annie—she has a good heart.

"Is he the Jackson on TV? The one you yell 'Drop it, Jackson' at?"

Annie's sense of baseball history is not highly developed.

"No, that's Reggie. This is Shoeless Joe Jackson. He hasn't played major-league baseball since 1920."

"Well, Ray, aren't you going to go out and chase him off your lawn, or something?"

Yes. What am I going to do? I wish someone else understood. Perhaps my daughter will. She has an evil grin and bewitching eyes and loves to climb into my lap and watch television baseball with me. There is a magic about her.

"I think I'll go upstairs and read for a while," Annie says. "Why don't you invite Shoeless Jack in for coffee?" I feel the greatest tenderness toward her then, something akin to the rush of love I felt the first time I held my daughter in my arms. Annie senses that magic is about to happen. She knows she is not part of it. My impulse is to pull her to me as she walks by, the denim of her thighs making a tiny music. But I don't. She will be waiting for me.

As I step out onto the verandah, I can hear the steady drone of the crowd, like bees humming on a white afternoon, and the voices of the vendors, like crows cawing.

A ground mist, like wisps of gauze, snakes in slow circular motions just above the grass.

"The grass is soft as a child's breath," I say to the moonlight. On the porch wall I find the switch, and the single battery of floodlights I have erected behind the left-field fence sputters to life. "I've tended it like I would my own baby. It has been powdered and lotioned and loved. It is ready."

Moonlight butters the whole Iowa night. Clover and corn smells are thick as syrup. I experience a tingling like the tiniest of electric wires touching the back of my neck, sending warm sensations through me. Then, as the lights flare, a scar against the blue-black sky, I see Shoeless Joe Jackson standing out in left field. His feet spread wide, body bent forward from the waist, hands on hips, he waits. I hear the sharp crack of the bat, and Shoeless Joe drifts effortlessly a few steps to his left, raises his right hand to signal for the ball, camps under it for a second or two, catches it, at the same time transferring it to his throwing hand, and fires it to the infield.

I make my way to left field, walking in the darkness far outside the third-base line, behind where the third-base stands would be. I climb up on the wobbly bleacher behind the fence. I can look right down on Shoeless Joe. He fields a single on one hop and pegs the ball to third.

"How does it play?" I holler down.

"The ball bounces true," he replies.

"I know." I am smiling with pride, and my heart thumps mightily against my ribs. "I've hit a thousand line drives and as many grounders. It's true as a felt-top table."

"It is," says Shoeless Joe. "It is true."

I lean back and watch the game. From where I sit the scene is as complete as in any of the major-league baseball parks I have ever visited: the two teams, the stands, the fans, the lights, the vendors, the scoreboard. The only difference is that I sit alone in the left-field bleacher and the only player who seems to have substance is Shoeless Joe Jackson. When Joe's team is at bat, the left fielder below me is transparent, as if he were made of vapor. He performs mechanically but seems not to have facial features. We do not converse.

A great amphitheater of grandstand looms dark against the sky, the park is surrounded by decks of floodlights making it brighter than day, the crowd buzzes, the vendors hawk their wares, and I cannot keep the promise I made myself not to ask Shoeless Joe Jackson about his suspension and what it means to him.

While the pitcher warms up for the third inning we talk.

"It must have been . . . It must have been like . . ." But I can't find the words.

"Like having a part of me amputated, slick and smooth and painless." Joe looks up at me and his dark eyes seem about to burst with the pain of it. "A friend of mine used to tell about the war, how him and a buddy was running across a field when a piece of shrapnel took his friend's head off, and how the friend ran, headless, for several strides before he fell. I'm told that old men wake in the night and scratch itchy legs that have been dust for fifty years. That was me. Years and years later,

I'd wake in the night with the smell of the ballpark in my nose and the cool of the grass on my feet. The thrill of the grass . . ."

How I wish my father could be here with me. If he'd lasted just a few months longer, he could have watched our grainy black-and-white TV as Bill Mazeroski homered in the bottom of the ninth to beat the Yankees 10–9. We would have joined hands and danced around the kitchen like madmen. "The Yankees lose so seldom you have to celebrate every single time," he used to say. We were always going to go to a major-league baseball game, he and I. But the time was never right, the money always needed for something else. One of the last days of his life, late in the night while I sat with him because the pain wouldn't let him sleep, the radio picked up a static-y station broadcasting a White Sox game. We hunched over the radio and cheered them on, but they lost. Dad told the story of the Black Sox Scandal for the last time. Told of seeing two of those World Series games, told of the way Shoeless Joe Jackson hit, told the dimensions of Comiskey Park, and how, during the series, the mobsters in striped suits sat in the box seats with their colorful women, watching the game and perhaps making plans to go out later and kill a rival.

"You must go," Dad said. "I've been in all the major-league parks. I want you to do it too. The summers belong to somebody else now, have for a long time." I nodded agreement.

"Hell, you know what I mean," he said, shaking his head. I did indeed.

"I loved the game," Shoeless Joe went on. "I'd have played for food money. I'd have played free and worked for food. It was the game, the parks, the smells, the sounds. Have you ever held a bat or a baseball to your face? The varnish, the leather. And it was the crowd, the excitement of them rising as one when the ball was hit deep. The sound was like a chorus. Then there was the chug-a-lug of the tin lizzies in the parking lots, and the hotels with their brass spittoons in the lobbies and brass beds in the rooms. It makes me tingle all over like a kid on his way to his first double-header, just to talk about it."

The year after Annie and I were married, the year we first rented this farm, I dug Annie's garden for her; dug it by hand, stepping a spade into the soft black soil, ruining my salesman's hands. After I finished, it rained, an Iowa spring rain as soft as spray from a warm hose. The clods of earth I had dug seemed to melt until the garden leveled out, looking like a patch of black ocean. It was near noon on a gentle Sunday when I walked out to that garden. The soil was soft and my shoes disappeared as I plodded until I was near the center. There I knelt, the soil cool on my knees. I looked up at the low gray sky; the rain had stopped and the only sound was the surrounding trees dripping fragrantly. Suddenly I thrust my hands wrist-deep into the snuffy-black earth. The air was pure. All around me the clean smell of earth and water. Keeping my hands buried I stirred the earth with my fingers and I knew I loved Iowa as much as a man could love a piece of earth.

When I came back to the house Annie stopped me at the door, made me wait on the verandah and then hosed me down as if I were a door with too many handprints on it, while I tried to explain my epiphany. It is very difficult to describe an experience of religious significance while you are being sprayed with a garden hose by a laughing, loving woman.

"What happened to the sun?" Shoeless Joe says to me, waving his hand toward the banks of floodlights that surround the park.

"Only stadium in the big leagues that doesn't have them is Wrigley Field," I say. "The owners found that more people could attend night games. They even play the World Series at night now."

Joe purses his lips, considering.

"It's harder to see the ball, especially at the plate."

"When there are breaks, they usually go against the ball-players, right? But I notice you're three-for-three so far," I add, looking down at his uniform, the only identifying marks a large *S* with an *O* in the top crook, an *X* in the bottom, and an American flag with forty-eight stars on his left sleeve near the elbow.

Joe grins. "I'd play for the Devil's own team just for the touch of a baseball. Hell, I'd play in the dark if I had to."

I want to ask about that day in December 1951. If he'd lived another few years things might have been different. There was a move afoot to have his record cleared, but it died with him. I wanted to ask, but my instinct told me not to. There are things it is better now to know.

It is one of those nights when the sky is close enough to touch, so close that looking up is like seeing my own eyes reflected in a rain barrel. I sit in the bleacher just outside the left-field fence. I clutch in my hand a hot dog with mustard, onions, and green relish. The voice of the crowd roars in my ears. Chords of "The Star-Spangled Banner" and "Take Me Out to the Ballgame" float across the field. A Coke bottle is propped against my thigh, squat, greenish, the ice-cream-haired elf grinning conspiratorially from the cap.

Below me in left field, Shoeless Joe Jackson glides over the plush velvet grass, silent as a jungle cat. He prowls and paces, crouches ready to spring as, nearly 300 feet away, the ball is pitched. At the sound of the bat he wafts in whatever direction is required, as if he were on ball bearings.

Then the intrusive sound of a slamming screen door reaches me, and I blink and start. I recognize it as the sound of the door to my house, and, looking into the distance, I can see a shape that I know is my daughter, toddling down the back steps. Perhaps the lights or the crowd have awakened her and she has somehow eluded Annie. I judge the distance to the steps. I am just to the inside of the foul pole, which is exactly 330 feet from home plate. I tense. Karin will surely be drawn to the lights and the emerald dazzle of the infield. If she touches anything, I fear it will all disappear, perhaps forever. Then, as if she senses my discomfort, she stumbles away from the lights, walking in the ragged fringe of darkness well outside the third-base line. She trails a blanket behind her, one tiny fist rubbing a sleepy eye. She is barefoot and wears a white flannelette nightgown covered in an explosion of daisies.

She climbs up the bleacher, alternating a knee and a foot on each step, and crawls into my lap silently, like a kitten. I hold her close and wrap the blanket around her feet. The play goes on; her innocence has not disturbed the balance. "What is it?" she says shyly, her eyes indicating she means all that she sees.

"Just watch the left fielder," I say. "He'll tell you all you ever need to know about a baseball game. Watch his feet as the pitcher accepts the sign and gets ready to pitch. A good left fielder knows what pitch is coming, and he can tell from the angle of the bat where the ball is going to be hit, and, if he's good, how hard."

I look down at Karin. She cocks one green eye at me, wrinkling her nose, then snuggles into my chest, the index finger of her right hand tracing tiny circles around her nose.

The crack of the bat is sharp as the yelp of a kicked cur. Shoeless Joe whirls, takes five loping strides directly toward us, turns again, reaches up, and the ball smacks into the glove. The final batter dawdles in the on-deck circle.

"Can I come back again?" Joe asks.

"I built this left field for you. It's yours anytime you want to use it. They play one hundred sixty-two games a season now."

"There are others," he says. "If you were to finish the infield, why, old Chick Gandil could play first base, and we'd have the Swede at shortstop and Buck Weaver at third." I can feel his excitement rising. "We could stick McMullin in at second, and Eddie Cicotte and Lefty Williams would like to pitch again. Do you think you could finish center field? It would mean a lot to Happy Felsch."

"Consider it done," I say, hardly thinking of the time, the money, the backbreaking labor it would entail. "Consider it done," I say again, then stop suddenly as an idea creeps into my brain like a runner inching off first base.

"I know a catcher," I say. "He never made the majors, but in his prime he was good. Really good. Played Class B ball in Florida and California . . ."

"We could give him a try," says Shoeless Joe. "You give us a place to play and we'll look at your catcher."

I swear the stars have moved in close enough to eavesdrop as I sit in this single rickety bleacher that I built with my unskilled hands, looking down at Shoeless Joe Jackson. A breath of clover travels on the summer wind. Behind me, just yards away, brook water plashes softly in the darkness, a frog shrills, fireflies dazzle the night like red pepper. A petal falls.

"God what an outfield," he says. "What a left field." He looks up at me and I look down at him. "This must be heaven," he says.

"No. It's Iowa," I reply automatically. But then I feel the

night rubbing softly against my face like cherry blossoms; look at the sleeping girl-child in my arms, her small hand curled around one of my fingers; think of the fierce warmth of the woman waiting for me in the house; inhale the fresh-cut grass smell that seems locked in the air like permanent incense; and listen to the drone of the crowd, as below me Shoeless Joe Jackson tenses, watching the angle of the distant bat for a clue as to where the ball will be hit.

"I think you're right, Joe," I say, but softly enough not to disturb his concentration.

II

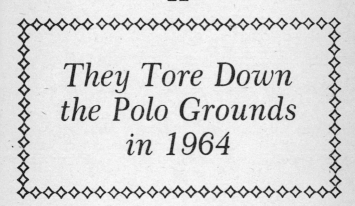

*They Tore Down
the Polo Grounds
in 1964*

We have been trading promises like baseball cards, Shoeless Joe and I. First I had to keep my rashly given vow to finish the baseball field. As I did, Shoeless Joe, or whoever or whatever breathed this magic down onto my Iowa farm, provided me with another live baseball player each time I finished constructing a section of the field: another of the Unlucky Eight who were banished for life from organized baseball in 1920 for supposedly betraying the game they loved.

I completed the home-plate area first. In fact I was out there the very next morning digging and leveling, for besides being the easiest part to do, it was the most important to me. Home plate cost $14.95 at my friendly sporting-goods store in Iowa City. It surprised me that I could buy a mass-produced home plate, although I don't know why it should have, considering that one can custom-order a baby nowadays. But somehow I had pictured myself measuring and cutting a section from a piny-smelling plank, the sawdust clinging like gold to my jeans. I installed it carefully, securely, like a grave marker, then laid out a batter's box and baselines.

But nothing happened.

I continued to work on the rest of the field, but less enthusiastically. Bases cost $28.95 for a set of three, starched and glazed white as the smock of a fat baker. It was weeks before the stadium appeared again in the cornfield. Each evening I peered surreptitiously through the kitchen curtains, like a spinster keeping tab on her neighbors, waiting and hoping. All the while Annie kept reassuring me, and I would call her a Pollyanna and tell her how I hated optimists. But I find it all but impossible to be cross with Annie, and we would end up embracing at the kitchen window where I could smell the sunshine in her snow-and-lemondrop curtains. Then Karin would drag a chair close to us, stand on it, and interrupt our love with hers, a little jealous of our attention to each other. Annie and I would stare in awe at the wonder we had created, our daughter.

Karin is five going on sixty; the dreamer in me combined with the practicality and good humor of Annie. We would both kiss her soft cheeks and she would dissolve in laughter as my mustache tickled her.

"Daddy, the baseball man's outside," Karin said to me.

It was still daylight, the days longer now, the cornfield and baseball diamond soaked warm with summer. I stared through the curtains where Shoeless Joe softly patrolled the left field I had birthed.

I swept Karin into my arms and we hurried to the bleacher behind the left-field fence. I studied the situation carefully but nothing appeared to have changed from the last time. Shoeless Joe was the only player with any substance.

"What about the catcher?" I call down.

Joe smiles. "I said we'd look at him, remember?"

"I've finished home plate. What else do you need?"

"I said *we*," reminds Joe. "After the others are here, we'll give him a tryout. He'll have a fair chance to catch on."

"All the others?" I say.

"All the others," echoes Joe. "Get the bases down and sand and level that ground around first base. It'll deaden the hot grounders and make them easy for old Chick to field."

But I have more questions than a first grader on a field trip: "Why have you been away so long?"; "When will you come back again?"; and a dozen more, but Joe only shifts the cud of tobacco in his cheek and concentrates on the gray-uniformed batter 300 feet away.

I did sand the first-base area, sometimes cursing as the recalcitrant wheelbarrow twisted out of my hands as if it had a life of its own, spilling its contents on the rutted path leading to the baseball field. My back ached as if someone were holding a welding torch against my spine, turning the flame on and off at will. But I sanded. And raked. I combed the ground as I would curry a horse, until there wasn't a pebble or lump left to deflect the ball. And as I finished I ignored my throbbing back, triumphant as if I'd just hurled a shutout. I'd stand on my diamond, where just beyond the fence the summer corn listens like a field of swaying disciples, and I'd talk to the sky.

"I'm ready whenever you are," I say. "Chick Gandil, you've never played on so fine a field. I've beveled the ground along the baseline so that any bunt without divine guidance will roll foul. The earth around the base is aerated and soft as piecrust. Ground balls will die on the second bounce, as if they've been hit into an anthill. You'll feel like you're wearing a glove ten feet square." I wave my arms at the perfect blue Iowa sky, and then, as I realize what I'm doing, I turn sheepishly to look at the house. Annie has been watching, and she flutters her fingers at me around the edge of the curtains.

The process is all so slow, as dreams are slow, as dreams suspend time like a balloon hung in midair. I want it all to happen now. I want that catcher to appear. I want whatever miracle I am party to, to prosper and grow: I want the dimensions of time that have been loosened from their foundations to entwine like a basketful of bright embroidery threads. But it seems that even for dreams, I have to work and wait. It hardly seems fair.

It was a Sunday afternoon the next time my wonderful mirage appeared. Annie's relatives were visiting. Her mother, face pink as wild roses, dentures a perfect white, silver-rimmed glasses flashing glints of disapproval at everything in sight, sat ramrod straight in an antique rocking chair. When there were lulls in the conversation she read her Bible, sneering a little in her perfection.

Annie's brother and his wife were also present. Mark is a

professor at the University of Iowa in nearby Iowa City. His area of expertise is the corn weevil. He and a business partner own apartment blocks and several thousand acres of farmland. He has designs on my farm. He also has brothers named Matthew, Luke, and John.

"Daddy, the baseball game is on," says Karin as she runs breathless into the living room.

"Now?" I say.

Karin smiles broadly, reaching her arms out to be picked up. She scissors her legs around me at belt level and, hugging my neck, whispers into my ear.

"Hot dogs."

"Excuse us for a few minutes," I say and head for the kitchen and out to the verandah. My relatives assume that we are going to watch television. They know that I am a baseball freak and despair that I have corrupted their daughter and am in the process of converting their granddaughter. They wish I had a more serious vice: that I would perhaps drink excessively and abuse Annie, or be arrested for some unspeakable act. They never mention my eccentricities to me, but they think I am crazy, and take turns pulling Annie aside and offering her all sorts of incentives to leave me. They all hope Mark will be successful in buying the farm. Then I will be forced to go back to selling life insurance, and perhaps Annie will come to her senses and leave me. When she does, they will all be waiting with a gaggle of Christian suitors ready to court her and bring her back into the fold, poor lamb.

My heart jumps as we hurry toward our bleacher in left field, for as we skirt the shadows on the third-base side I see Chick Gandil stomping around first base, like a bull pawing the ground. His intense face with its hollow cheeks and bullet eyes glares in at a batter, daring him to hit the ball past him.

"You see," Joe hollers up as Karin and I take our seats, "the others are waiting..."

"I'll have the infield ready in a month," I promise, my back twitching in anticipatory pain, "except you'll all have to be careful of the infield grass for a while, keep your spikes off it except to make a play. The outfield will take a little longer."

"Happy Felsch can wait a little longer," says Joe. "One thing we got is plenty of time."

He is able to wait. They are able to wait. It sounds as though I am conjugating a Latin verb in some obscure case. *I* can't wait. My blood blazes around my circulatory system like Cale Yarborough on an asphalt straight-away.

"Rome wasn't built in a day," my own mother would say if she knew of my plight, which she doesn't. She lives with her sister, my maiden aunt, in a high-rise in Great Falls, Montana, with a cat and a Bible. She occasionally watches a World Series game on TV, often forgetting which team she is cheering for, unless the Yankees are involved. Even though my father has been gone for over twenty years, she recalls how he loathed them, and as she sips her tea says things like "Oh, you Yankees, I hope you break a leg," and then looks to me for approval.

Reluctantly I continue to wait, and as I finish each area of the field a new player springs to life. The cornstalks are now toast brown in the orangeade sunshine of October; the ballpark smells of burning leaves and frost. The ever-listening corn rustles like crumpling paper in the Indian-summer breeze.

They've all come now—Chick Gandil and Shoeless Joe Jackson; the pitchers, Eddie Cicotte and Lefty Williams; the rest of the infield: Fred McMullin the utility player at second, Swede Risberg at shortstop, Buck Weaver at third. Happy Felsch stalks center field. Only the right fielder and the catcher are ghost-gray in the afternoon sun.

The magic grows and grows. As I walk with Karin and Annie toward the bleacher, the crowd hums lazily and the chatter of the infielders swoops across my baseball park like gull calls.

I keep asking about the catcher.

"Be patient," Shoeless Joe says.

"Keep your shirt on," Chick Gandil advises, "we've kept our promise so far, haven't we?"

And I have to admit they have.

My catcher will come too, someday—I'm sure of it.

I've taken to keeping stats on the games. After each one I sit at the kitchen table late into the night translating my inky scorecard into batting and fielding averages, roaming through the pages of the *Baseball Encyclopedia*. I write wild and sometimes incoherent letters to the White Sox Baseball Club and to the historian at the Hall of Fame in Cooperstown, asking for stats on the 1921 and 1922 seasons. But when the results come back nothing quite fits. The whole situation is mysterious and ethereal, reminding me of animals in a thicket that you can't quite be sure you've seen. The averages for opposing teams are subtly different from existing records, a few points lower or higher, an error or two more or less. It is as if in another, fairer climate the Black Sox Scandal never happened, and the Unlucky Eight play on, several of them earning baseball immortality. I stare in awe at the acres of figures in front of me; to translate this situation to reality would be like trying to stuff a cloud in a suitcase.

In the meantime, Karin and I are out every time there's a game, munching hot dogs, sharing Cokes, cheering Shoeless Joe and the phantom White Sox. I'm teaching her the finer points of the game and she is learning fast. At the last game, in the late innings, as a desperate situation developed in the field, Karin lay cuddled in my lap, apparently sleeping. Suddenly she sat up and said, "Daddy, why wasn't the hit-and-run on?" And she was right, it should have been. I was astounded.

Even Annie is excited about the game now. She is more comfortable here in our ballpark than she is in the big-city ones. If she's bored or too hot or too cold she can go back to the house. But as the summer has turned to fall and we have been gifted more and more often with this kaleidoscope of wonder, Annie has stayed longer and longer; occasionally she even leans toward the dark green fence to question or converse with Shoeless Joe.

This afternoon I kiss Karin's nose, which is covered in freckles the color of toasted coconut. "You have the most beautiful nose in the world," I tell her. She giggles.

"Kiss *my* beautiful nose," says Annie, leaning toward me. "Who do you think she got her freckles from?"

And I do kiss her nose and hold her close to me; her breath is scented faintly with orange drink, her hair is warm against my cheek and smells of sunshine.

And it was at about this time that the ballpark announcer spoke another brief parable for my ears alone. I stiffened and strained toward the sound like a hunting dog. Annie rattled her bag of peanuts, and I reached down automatically to stifle the small noise.

"What's the matter?" she said.

"You didn't hear?" I replied.

"Hear what?" said Annie.

I looked at Karin. She nibbled her hot dog, squinting her eyes slightly against the bright sun. She was daydreaming, humming to herself, tapping one sneaker-clad foot to some imaginary music.

"I just heard something," I said.

"Oh Lord," said Annie. "You're not going to build a football field or a racetrack?"

"No, I'm not," I say.

But it was two weeks before I was able to tell her what I was going to do. Two weeks of pacing the house, prowling the ballpark like a caged beast, sniffing the air, crunching leaves beneath my feet, the specter of winter hovering like a pale-winged bird. I knew that the season was over, that promises remained unkept.

In the delicious warmth of our bed, after making love, with Annie's head on my chest, her breath soft as a bird's, I tried to explain.

"In the spring I have a job to do."

"Seeding, and the house needs painting."

"No. I mean, yes. But this is the other thing. About what I heard at the game that day."

Annie raises her head slightly to look at me. Her eyes are clear and green as outfield grass after rain. She pushes some damp red curls from her forehead.

"Oh, that," she says, as if it hasn't been on her mind too, crowding her senses like a fat lady squeezing into a checkout line.

"I have to . . . I have to . . ." But the right words won't come. What I have to say is so simple yet so complicated, like explaining the concept of baseball to a primitive man in an age just about to discover fire.

"What did the announcer say this time?"

I take a deep breath, like a pitcher before a critical delivery. "Ease his pain."

"That's all?"

"That's all."

"And you know who *his* is?"

"Yes."

"Well?"

"I'm afraid you'll laugh. All I can say is I was right before, about building the park and all."

"Is it Joe Jackson?"

"No."

"One of the other ballplayers?"

"No."

"Then who?"

I feel as if I am about to suggest an unnatural sex act to a total stranger in a supermarket. "J. D. Salinger."

"The writer?"

I nod.

"What has this got to do with baseball?"

I remain silent. I know, but I can't tell her. The story floats within me, tenuous as a spider web, impermanent as dew.

Annie might well continue with a spate of questions: "You don't know him, do you? He lives in the East somewhere, doesn't he? Isn't he a hermit or something? What kind of pain does he have? Does he want it eased?" But she too remains quiet. She lowers her head to my chest. Our breathing becomes audible, then ominously loud. The ticking of the old alarm clock on the nightstand sounds like a convict rhythmically pounding rock.

"Oh, love," Annie whispers into my neck, "you do what you have to do."

"I'll tell you everything, Annie, just as soon as I can. As soon as I really know."

"Ray, it's so perfect here. Do whatever you have to, to keep it that way."

How do I feel about this? Annie's question is indeed pertinent: What has my new assignment to do with baseball? Even while laboring in the baseball park, while sweat pours into my eyes and my blue work shirt is soaked to the color of a bruise, I tingle as if looking forward to a first date. It is like when I was given the option of building the baseball diamond: I know what I have to do, I'm just not certain of how to go about it.

A vision of what I have to do flashed in front of me as I heard the announcer's instructions; a scene that might have been projected by a shadow box was outlined on one of the clouds that hung over the stadium. The picture was of me and J. D. Salinger seated at Fenway Park in Boston watching a baseball game, our hands busy with hot dogs, soft drinks, and scorecards. The scene was in black and white, Salinger silhouetted so I could not see his physical features. I have only seen one photograph of Salinger, taken in 1951. It showed a dark-eyed young man with brilliantined hair and eyebrows the black-green color of crow wings.

Now, as the pallid winter sky lowers over Iowa like a gray dome, I wonder again and again how I am ever going to accomplish such a miraculous feat.

Salinger, almost everyone knows, has been holed-up like a badger, on an isolated hilltop in New Hampshire, for over twenty-five years. He has published nothing since a story in *The New Yorker* in 1965. He virtually never gives interviews, guards his privacy as if it were a virgin bride, even refuses to let his stories be anthologized.

Sometimes as I stare out my window at the snow swirling across the cornfield, ticking like sand against the tall green fence of the ballpark, I feel my problem is hopeless. In the spring I must leave the loving warmth of Iowa behind, abandon this magic place, forsake Annie and Karin, drive over a thousand miles to a New Hampshire mountain, and convince the most famous American recluse of the century to attend a baseball game with me at Fenway Park in Boston.

Annie's family is right. I am quite mad. Why can't I settle for watching the baseball results on TV at 10:30 each evening, and close-reading the box scores in the peach-colored sports pages of the *Des Moines Register* each morning? Then, like any normal baseball fan, I could talk trades and averages with the mechanics at the John Deere dealership in Iowa City, and develop a permanent squint from studying the sky, worrying about rain or lack of it. But then the excitement races through me like minute corks bobbing in my blood, and I know I have to follow the instructions I've been given.

Over the winter, as the days contracted with cold and the cornfields lay folded under a blanket of snow, I spent my time at the library in Iowa City reading and rereading everything by and about J. D. Salinger. As I read, I discovered some uncanny coincidences. Or are there ever coincidences?

I found an article, an interview I'd read some years before in the *Des Moines Register*, in an obscure literary magazine. The interview with Salinger was about baseball, and it saddened me as it excited me. It left me with a feeling of vague anxiety, of nameless fears snuffling about me like cold-nosed rodents; like reading of a favorite baseball player whose star has descended to the point where he parks cars at a restaurant or sits in a room above a delicatessen in Indianapolis, drinking vodka and waiting for his pension.

Salinger, the article stated, was a devout baseball fan, a man who kept a copy of the *Baseball Encyclopedia* in a prominent place on his bookshelf; a knowledgeable fan with a predilection to the Boston Red Sox, but one who avidly watched whatever baseball was available on television.

So at least he knew of baseball. The interview established a vague kinship between us; perhaps we could be called ninth-inning cousins, for I have always been a little eccentric where baseball is concerned.

I advocate the establishment of shrines in recognition of baseball greats: Ty Cobb, Tris Speaker, Shoeless Joe Jackson, Ruth, Gehrig, Mantle, Mays, DiMaggio, and a few dozen others. Not just at Cooperstown, but at roadside shrines, like the cairns that commemorate cavalry battles, treaty signings, and Indian uprisings. Sites where bleary-eyed travelers could rest for a moment, drink clear water, fill their radiators on broiling afternoons, and study the highlights of their heroes' careers, recorded in bronze and granite.

Grottoes perhaps. Explosions of magnificent folly. A bronze of Al Gionfriddo flying like Peter Pan high over the Yankee bullpen, as he gloves a drive off DiMaggio's bat at the 415-foot mark. Or of Willie Mays sprinting toward the bleachers, back to the plate, arms outstretched, hauling in Vic Wertz's drive in the 1954 World Series.

For days after I read that interview I was more restless than usual, dreaming of Salinger exiled for twenty-five years, living like a guru on a mountaintop. Something seemed about to happen. The air was thick with anticipation.

The interview saddened me so because it radiated loneliness. He hadn't, the article stated, been to a live baseball game since 1954, when he went to the Polo Grounds in New York to watch Sal Maglie pitch—even though, in 1965, in his last published story, Salinger had Seymour Glass describe baseball as "perhaps the most heart-rending, delicious sport in the Western Hemisphere."

"If you hadn't become a writer, what would you have liked to be?" the interviewer asked.

"When I was a kid," Salinger replied, "I wanted more than anything else in the world to play at the Polo Grounds. But I've seen myself grow too old for that dream—seen the Giants moved across a continent to San Francisco, and finally, they tore down the Polo Grounds in 1964."

Those words deepened our kinship. I admit that I am overly sentimental about baseball. The interview touched my heart and made what I did next seem completely incongruous.

I bought a gun. I have never owned a gun. Once, as a child of ten in Montana, I took my father's single-shot .22 and fired into a row of sparrows that sat like tufted pegs on my mother's clothesline. I watched a dozen spring airward as if tossed by a juggler, and one fell. The feathered droplet on the ground looked so small; it shivered like an old woman's hand as I picked it up. I actually felt its heart stop beating as I carried it in to show my mother. I was as proud as our yellow cat when she dragged home a snake or mouse to prove her ability as a huntress.

"Bring it back to life," my mother said, looking up from her ironing board. The scent of scorched cloth drifted about the room, dark to my eyes after the blazing sky of outdoors.

My mouth dropped open. I was expecting praise.

"Bring it back to life," my mother said again, holding the iron's dull silver base toward me as a knight might hold a shield.

I stood dumfounded for a moment. "I can't," I whispered, feeling small as the bird cooling in my hand.

"Well, until you can I don't think you should shoot anything unless you need it for food."

I have never again fired a gun.

But now in the dormant months of the new year, I drive the hundred miles to Des Moines and spend a day frequenting pawnshops in an area of the city where store windows are covered in rusted metal mesh. Grit crunches underfoot on the unswept sidewalks. Unshaven men with sunken eyes dog my steps. I look at handguns, all heavier than I anticipate, cold as fish, smelling blue and oily. I flinch as if burned when a swarthy proprietor drops a half-dozen bullets into my extended hand.

"You're not used to handling a gun, are you?" he says, smiling as he might at a child, his large lips dry and peeling, the orange-brown color of sweet potatoes. "It'll grow on you," he whispers. "It gets warm after you carry it for a while; the weight hangs right here by your heart," and he pats his stained, vertically striped shirt.

"With a gun you're never alone." He smiles again, showing long twisted teeth.

"That's real literature," I say. "I bet you didn't just make that up."

"Came from an NRA bulletin. You belong to the NRA?"

"Not yet," I say, winking conspiratorially. He lowers his price by fifteen dollars.

"Suppose you want it for protection?"

"Doesn't everyone? The neighborhood's changing. You know what I mean." I smile slyly.

As the winter passes, a plan of action begins to form, at first as misty as dawn rising on the cornfield. But as I discern and dissect each new nugget of information—something that adds to my arsenal of ideas—I hear sounds, eerie, unusual sounds, like ball bearings—smooth, silver, cold—being plopped into an unseen pool, sending out ripples in ever-widening circles. I sense that when the sounds stop, my plan will be complete. I will be able to begin my journey.

"You don't know him, do you?" Annie's imagined question hangs like music in my thoughts.

I don't know Salinger. But Salinger *does* know *me*.

I discover this in a stale-smelling copy of the May 1947 issue of *Mademoiselle* from the Bound Periodical Room at the University of Iowa Library. Inside those yellowed pages, among Studebaker advertisements and ads featuring women who all look like the Andrews Sisters, is a story called "A Young Girl in 1941 with No Waist At All." It is one of Salinger's uncollected stories and not a very good one, but while reading it I discover that the young man in the story, Salinger's character, is named Ray Kinsella. My name.

Suddenly a thought shoots through my mind. In *The Catcher in the Rye* there is a character named Richard Kinsella, a schoolmate of Holden's who gives long and ambiguous answers to questions. Richard Kinsella is my identical twin brother. Salinger has used us *both* as characters in his fiction. If that is not a sign, an omen, a revelation, I don't know what is.

Where did Salinger find us? How did he decide to use such an unusual and obscure name? Did he know someone by that name? Did he pick it out of the phone book or just make it up?

There are not many of us around. A few in New York, Florida, California. My father's family once lived in New York, then part of it, including my grandfather, moved to the Black Hills of North Dakota. My father was born there, in a sod hut, on the open prairie not far from Bismarck, North Dakota, in 1896.

Except for my twin brother, I am an only child. One of my uncles also produced two sons, twins I think, whom I have never met. They keep bees somewhere in Florida. I have fantasies of them one day appearing on my Iowa doorstep, dressed in pith helmets and gauze, shaking hands while wearing huge leather gauntlets.

For me it is an alarming experience to discover someone else with my name. But the idea that it is J. D. Salinger who has created the fictional me fills me with a warmth, the same kind I feel as I stand in the dark in my daughter's bedroom watching her sleep. I feel proud and very brave, but very scared.

I study my map of the United States; it is red-veined as a bloodshot eye. And as I do, I hear a few more ball bearings plop into my imagination. I realize that I cannot go directly there, like some missile programmed and locked into specific coordinates. I cannot land in New Hampshire like a rock thrown through a window.

I lay out a schedule. I imagine a little man with bifocals sitting in an office that smells of furniture polish and floor wax, charting out a baseball schedule. I study the homestands of the teams, draw red circles like vermilion lakes on the map, connect them with snaky yellow lines—Chicago, Cleveland, Pittsburgh, New York, Boston.

I have to absorb the new season like sunlight, letting it turn my winter skin pink and then brown. I must stuff myself with lore and statistics until my fingers ooze balm with which I can staunch *his* wounds—whatever form they may take. He hasn't seen a live game in over twenty-five years; he needs my memories. And I will arrive like Little Red Riding Hood with a basketful of them, like crustless sandwiches under a cool tea towel. I'll tell him of the warmups, of the home team in their white uniforms doing calisthenics and wind sprints like fast-flying sailboats on a green sea. I'll make him smell the frying onions and hear the sizzle of the hot dogs, and I'll tell of baseballs scattered like white oranges on the outfield grass. I'll walk beside him as if I am a bottle of blood swinging from a gray enamel standard; I'll pierce a vein and feed him the sounds, smells, and sights of baseball until he tingles with the same magic that enchants me. Then we'll ride off together, as in the happy ending of a western movie, drifting toward the closest baseball stadium.

My journey will be like going out to hunt stars with a net on a stick. I have to make certain that there is plenty to share. I have to do all the right things, at all the right times, in all the right places; fill my pockets with string and stones, a jack-knife and a frog, have my suitcase bulging; arrive in New Hampshire as if I have been on a long road trip and am now moving in for a homestand.

April arrives, tender and personal as the breath of animals in a barn; snow shrinks from the sun. The fields puddle. The sun drinks away the standing water, and the land is ready for seeding.

Each spring I hire a retired corn farmer from Iowa City to help me. Machines of all kinds are mysteries to me. I regard them as minor deities and attempt not to understand them but to please them. The farmer's name is Chesty Seidlinger, and he farmed all his life until his children moved him bodily to an Iowa City apartment three years ago. If I didn't want to, I wouldn't have to pay him; he would do the job for the love of it. In that respect we understand each other. He wears a floppy brown felt hat, bib overalls several sizes too large, and black gum boots with ocher-colored soles, even though the land is dry. For two days we drive the great green machines with their clashing gears and phalluslike planting arms. It doesn't take long to seed a quarter-section.

"What have you got there?" Chesty asks, eyeing the ballpark fence.

"I've built myself a baseball diamond," I answer honestly.

"Been told you had, but I wanted to hear it from you," he says. Chesty is stocky as a well-packed sack of chop and walks with his toes turned out.

"Must take up an acre or more." He shifts the cud of tobacco in his cheek. His tone tells me that I can't afford to part with an acre. "What do you plan to do with it?" Chesty, I'm sure, has never intentionally done an impractical thing in his life, and I can hear him saying to his pale, housedress-clad wife, "He always seemed like such a sensible young man—I wonder if it runs in his family. Poor little Annie. I've known her all her life—such a pretty thing."

I consider telling him outrageous lies about importing professional teams, perhaps from Puerto Rico, to play on the field, but then I look at it. In sunlight it is ragged as a page ripped from a magazine. Chesty and I stand, our eyes staring out of dust-powdered faces. The fence bulges occasionally— sometimes I hear nails groaning in the night as the boards warp. The grass is coming along nicely, though. I have been primping and priming it in hopes that the phantasm will appear for Annie and Karin while I am away.

There is nothing I can tell Chesty Seidlinger that he will truly understand. I shrug off his questions and grin like a kid caught smoking behind the barn. Chesty penguins off toward his pickup truck, his back stiff with disapproval.

"I'm going to plant some hollyhocks," says Annie as we are walking across the field one day, then claims she wants to put them right against the outfield fence, in the final six inches between the green boards and the warning track. I have told her about—in fact, we have been to—Wrigley Field in Chicago, and she has seen the fielders virtually disappear in greenery as they spread-eagle themselves against the living outfield wall.

"But why hollyhocks?" I complain. I can visualize the gangly plants with plate-sized flowers the color of faded raspberries.

"It will give the park that little touch of beauty it's been lacking," and she wrinkles her nose at me, putting her arm around my waist, holding tightly to my belt.

And as it often is with Annie, I am not positive whether she is kidding me or not. I wonder what brawlers like Swede Risberg and Chick Gandil would think of hollyhocks.

"I read about it in a magazine just last night," says Annie, keeping her face averted from me. *"Better Homes and Gardens* had an article called 'Ten Ways to Beautify Your Baseball Park for Less Than $100.'"* And she dances away from me, her laughter like music, and we are joined by Karin, who dances and laughs too, not knowing or caring what is funny.

"I had you going for a minute there, Champ," cheers Annie as I chase them across the pitcher's mound and into left field where we tumble like puppies on the angel-soft grass.

Ready to leave now, I hug Annie and Karin one last time. "Tell your family I've gone to a funeral in Florida—a relative of mine was stung to death by a swarm of non-Christian bees. It's something they'd understand."

"You're terrible," says Annie, mischief crackling like static electricity in her eyes. Annie and Karin are wearing buttercup-colored blouses, and Karin's pigtails are tied with yellow wool. Annie's jeans fit like a rubber glove. She kisses me sweetly, her petal-soft tongue counting my teeth. I lean out the car window for Karin to reach up and grab me just behind each ear and hug and kiss me. She smells fresh as melting snow.

"Take care," says Annie. "Do whatever it is you have to do."

I know I should stay in Iowa, should be working a second job in hopes of fending off creditors. But my compulsion is stronger than my guilt. As I ease my battered Datsun out onto I-80, heading slowly toward Chicago, I try to measure the pain of exile, but my ruler is blank, my calipers rubber, my thermometer a grass stem. I feel like a detective. I feel like a criminal. I feel like an explorer. I feel like a fool. But most of all I feel like a baseball scout for a miserly second-division team, reluctantly traveling away to woo an extravagantly priced free agent.

Chicago: from the Indian *Shee-caw-go*—the place of the skunk. The Cubs were on a road trip. All I saw of Wrigley Field were the foliage-covered walls as I drove by on the expressway. But as I did, I thought of Eddie Scissons—the oldest living Chicago Cub. And of his stories about playing for the world-champion Cubs in the era of Tinker-to-Evers-to-Chance, the most illustrious double-play combination baseball has ever known.

Was Eddie still spinning his yarns in the afternoons at the Bishop Cridge Friendship Center on Gilbert Street in Iowa City?

"It was in the late innings of the fourth or fifth game of the World Series," Eddie told me once, sitting across a round maple table in the recreation room at the center. "They weren't as fussy as they are nowadays about who played where. I was a relief pitcher, but it was late in the game and our manager had used a lot of pinch hitters, so he was short of outfielders and he said to me, 'Kid'—that was what I was known as then, Kid Scissons, I was the youngest man on the team, barely nineteen—'Kid, you play left field.' I mean it wasn't a dumb or desperate move, I was pretty handy with a glove and I was no slouch at the plate either, if I do say so myself." Eddie's face, pink as strawberries, glowed across the table at me.

"Three Finger Brown was pitching and we were ahead, but only by a run, and they had the field crawling with base runners because of an infield hit, a walk, and a sacrifice that got booted. Then Eddie Collins, I think it was—oh, sure it was, I couldn't forget that—slammed one, and as I went back the ball was no bigger than an aspirin and traveling fast as a bullet. I could hear the whack of the bat ringing in my ears and the crowd sounds rising that would drown it out—either if it was a hit or if I caught it. I pedaled back fast as I was able, and as I leapt up against the wall, why my arm disappeared in the ivy leaves the same time as the ball. I felt as if I was hanging there. As I hit the wall backward, I thought of how my shape would be imprinted on the wall of Wrigley Field forever—funny the crazy things you think of in a split second of action. God, but I wish they'd had that there instant replay like they have on

TV now—I'd of liked to have looked at myself hanging there, white against green. I didn't even feel the ball hit my glove. The voice of the crowd kept rising, the runners had scored, the batter was rounding second when I hit the ground and rolled over. I still didn't know I had the ball until I stood up quick as you please, and there it was, white as a leghorn egg, like a big white eye in my old black glove."

My thoughts of Eddie drifted away as suddenly as they had come. In Chicago it was the White Sox who were at home, a chance for me to see left field of Comiskey Park (or, as it has been renamed, White Sox Stadium), in a new light—as the place where Shoeless Joe Jackson performed.

Chicago, as always, is cold, grimy, impersonal. I rent a room at a decaying hotel with fly-specked fluorescent lights in a shabby lobby full of gaunt black men slouching in ratty, knife-scarred leather chairs.

There is intermittent rain, cold drops that pelt down at odd angles, stinging like tiny slaps.

I leave my car in a locked, guarded lot, and decide to walk to the stadium. The rain has let up although the clouds are still low and angry.

It is unwise for a white person to walk through South Chicago, but I do anyway. The Projects are chill, sand-colored apartments, twelve to fifteen stories high, looking like giant bricks stabbed into the ground. I am totally out of place. I glow like a piece of phosphorous on a pitch-black night. Pedestrians' heads turn after me. I feel the stolid stares of drivers as large cars zipper past. A beer can rolls ominously down the gutter, its source of locomotion invisible. The skeletal remains of automobiles litter the parking lots behind the apartments.

A man in a tight leather coat passes me. I look at the ground. I can hear the leather creak as he turns to stare, hear the cough that is really a laugh. I think of the gun burrowed like a rat in a box of rags in the trunk of my car. Gangly young men in white T-shirts and running shoes loiter in the doorways of the apartments I pass.

Two young women are approaching me; one has an Afro, the other's hair is corn-rowed as tight as if she is wearing a ridged black bathing cap. Both are wearing jeans and satin blouses, one purple, one green. They are almost past me when one turns and speaks.

"Hey, man, you better watch out. There's some boys in the doorway of that block up there; they's figuring to rob you." It is the corn-rowed girl who has been speaking. She is about eighteen and has a silver beauty mark on her right cheek that glows like a tiny moon.

I look at the slim brown hand that points toward the dark front of an apartment a block away. I imagine I can see indistinct, sinister forms lurking there.

Before I can speak, the other girl says in a kindly voice, "We don't want to see you get in any trouble. If you got any money on you, you better cross the street." She waves vaguely toward the other side of the road, where there are a number of equally unfriendly buildings.

My inclination is to turn and run or at least walk fast, but what if they are joking with me? Can I stand the sound of their laughter? I actually have very little money on me: enough for the baseball game and a taxi back to my squalid hotel. My money, what there is of it, is carefully stashed in the driver's door panel of my Datsun. But I do have credit cards. I picture young black men in felt fedoras going on a lavish spending spree with my very white Iowa credit cards.

I consider crossing the road.

Why did the baseball fan cross the road? I can't think of an answer.

"Thank you," I say.

"Them boys is bad little buggers," the girl with the kindly voice says. I notice she is smoking a cigarette—the white tube very conspicuous in her ebony hand.

What if they are setting me up? I hadn't noticed where they came from. What if the boys *are* on the other side of the road, and don't want to waste their time mugging a broke white man?

"If you have any money cross the road," the girl's words ring in my ears.

I smile feebly. "If I had any money, would I be walking down here?" I try to say matter-of-factly, as I shove my hands deep into my pockets and move on, trying to inject some bravado into my walk. I may be going to get myself killed because I am afraid to back down.

"Suit yourself," one girl says.

"Don't say we didn't warn you," says the other.

After a dozen steps I hear them burst into high-pitched laughter. I wonder if it is because I have not taken their advice, or if it is because they are pleased with themselves for scaring a white man half to death.

My fists are clenched as I approach the pale hulk of a building. The front of the apartment is black and foreboding, but empty. The entire area seems only sparsely populated. It strikes me that everyone except criminals and morons is inside. I exhale and I am surprised by the sound of my own breath: I have been holding it for at least a block. My stomach feels as if I have swallowed razor blades, my fingers ache as I uncurl my fists.

Across the street is an amateurishly painted rose-and-white 1967 Pontiac; the trunk is open and two loose-jointed boys are stuffing something inside. Two more lounge on the curb-side of the car, only the thistly tops of their heads visible.

Traffic lights loom at the next intersection. I feel like a fur trader who has just run the gauntlet. I notice that it is spitting rain, very hard, and, by the wetness of my clothes, has been ever since the girls first accosted me.

At a bus stop stands a lone black woman, conspicuously pregnant.

In the ballpark it is bleak and raw. A few hundred fans huddle miserably under blankets. I purchase a box seat, but the rain forces me to retreat to a drier, less expensive seat higher up. The wind is cold and ice-pick sharp.

The White Sox pitcher is overweight and perhaps dreaming of his home in Venezuela. The rain stops and starts like a jackrabbiting car. Raindrops blow onto my scorecard, smudging the ink. I shiver and long for Annie's fierce warmth.

Socked away in my suitcase, like an apple in a brown-bagged lunch, like a grandfather's gift for a favorite grandchild, lies a baseball—but a very special baseball. I can only imagine what it will mean to a dedicated fan of the game like J. D. Salinger, to have someone turn up on his doorstep—a stranger, but with the aura of a prodigal returning—and present him with a baseball, shiny and fragrant as new, but with a signature and construction that labels it as being from the 1920s.

"This is a home-run ball hit by Shoeless Joe Jackson," I'll tell him. That should be sufficient to shift his blood into overdrive.

What I won't mention, right away, is that the ball was hit over the left-field fence of *my* stadium, clubbed by Shoeless Joe off a ghostly relief pitcher during an extra-inning game, a blue darter of a line drive that thudded into the stands a few seats from Karin and me. Karin leapt from my lap and chased it down as it ricocheted off the bleacher seats like a rabid pool ball.

When she returned with it, it had a darkish bruise on one side, from being hit by Joe's immortal bat, Black Betsy.

The disappointment of Chicago fades away as I take to I-80 again, headed for Cleveland. But my experience in Cleveland turns out to be little better, hardly the kind of adventure I would have chosen.

A meager crowd, scattered at random throughout the cavernous Cleveland ballpark on a blustery afternoon, watches as the Indians lose. Many of the fans carry radios, as if hoping the crowd noise will somehow be amplified and the game will be more interesting secondhand than in person.

After the game I go to a café near my hotel for supper. It is a plastic restaurant so archetypal of twentieth-century America that it could have been created by the motion of a cookie cutter: a counter, two rows of booths; the booths separated from the counter by a row of plastic foliage growing out of a divider full of white stones that look like they, too, were manufactured.

I am sitting at the counter eating a synthetic veal cutlet covered in a bland, tasteless gravy when the holdup man comes in.

The owner, a swarthy Greek with hair like tufts of black quack grass, is behind the counter. I am staring directly into his apron, which is a Rorschach test of grease spots. The holdup man walks the length of the counter and stops behind me and to my right. In fact, I don't even notice him until I hear the Greek give a strangled cry that sounds like *"Wan... graaaaaaaach!"*

Raising my head from my cutlet, I look directly into the

Greek's stricken face. I peer over my right shoulder. The holdup man is short and wiry and has his right hand buried in the pocket of a dirty brown windbreaker; his chinless, ferretlike face has not seen a razor for several days.

"I'm gonna blow everybody away," the holdup man says clearly, with what I take to be just a trace of a southern accent.

The Greek continues to stand directly in front of me. I can see a field of tombstones emerging from the stains on his apron. He raises his hands palm out, at ear level, and makes the sound again, a rasping gasp as though he were swallowing his false teeth.

"I'm gonna blow everybody away," the holdup man says again, louder. He is looking only at the Greek. Behind him, behind the divider full of geraniums and rubber plants with Tupperware leaves, some customers are padding rapidly toward the exit. I edge one seat to my left; the Greek moves with me, keeping me between him and the gun.

I wonder what would happen if I edged my way all the way down the fifteen or so empty stools to the door. I move one more. The Greek moves with me.

"Sit still," the holdup man says.

Unaccountably, I reach back two stools and drag my congealing cutlet after me. I consider bolting and running, but as I stare at the Greek's belly I imagine the holdup man pumping a number of bullets into my escaping back, and, simultaneously, an Iowa highway patrolman, his boots blood-colored in the glow from the porch light, informing Annie that I have been shot.

A woman emerges from the metallic-colored swinging doors at the end of the counter to my right. She looks around, tosses her head, rearranges her hair like a horse shaking away a fly. She walks toward us, stopping beside the Greek, again right in front of me, only three feet or so from the gunman.

"Put your hands down, Demos," she says to the Greek in a nasal twang. "This creep ain't gonna hurt you."

She wears a thin grayish-white uniform with two front pockets at waist level. A red cigarette pack shows clearly through the sparse material of one, a yellow order pad is in the other. Above her left breast is a white plastic name tag with the word WANDALIE impressed in black letters.

"What are *you* doing?" Wandalie says in a whiny yet contemptuous voice.

"I'm gonna blow everybody away," the man says as an answer.

"Like hell you are," says Wandalie. She is about thirty-five with steam-straightened black hair, a wide face with a very small nose, and a large mouth with spaces between her teeth.

Wandalie steps even closer to the gunman. "Frank, you haven't got a gun in there," she says, her upper lip curling into a genuine snarl, "and even if you did, you wouldn't have the guts to use it."

Under her flimsy uniform, like a twenty-dollar bill stuffed in her bra, Wandalie apparently harbors a death wish.

It becomes apparent that I am in the middle of a domestic dispute of some kind, not a holdup. The Greek lowers his right hand, keeps his left at ear level. Among the spots on his apron, I see silhouettes of Annie and Karin dressed in black. The police hate domestic disputes worse than holdups. I decide to move one stool closer to the door.

"Sit down!" Frank says to me. "I have so got a goddamned gun," he says to Wandalie.

They play "Yes I have," "No you haven't," for a few moments. As they do, they let little bits of their life loose like items of I.D. pulled from a billfold.

Frank is Wandalie's boyfriend, live-in lover, maybe even an ex-husband. Wandalie keeps baiting him. I wait for him to indeed produce a gun and splatter Wandalie and the Greek against the mirrored wall, then start looking around for witnesses.

Suddenly the Greek says, "Hey Frank, what you think of the Indians losing again today? I hear it all on the radio," and he points to an ancient brown radio with a fret-sawed design on the front.

"I was at the game," I say hopefully.

Wandalie has been seeing someone on the side. Frank doesn't know who, though I'd guess it is Demos, by the way he keeps his left hand in the air.

"Slut!" shouts Frank.

"Why should I stick around you, you can't even get it up anymore."

If he has a gun, he'll use it now. I consider fainting. Surely he wouldn't shoot an unconscious man.

There is a trick to fainting. Annie taught it to me. In her high school senior play, at West High School in Iowa City, Annie played the mother in *The Man Who Came to Dinner*. She was required to faint about five times during the play. You just cross your right leg behind your left and let yourself down onto the floor, sideways on your right side. When Karin or I tell Annie something of earthshaking importance, she still sometimes clasps her hand to her forehead and executes a faint.

"Oh, Mommy," Karin will say in exasperation, "you're not really dead."

The Greek, who has been inching his right hand closer to the counter utensils, sees his chance. He picks up off the counter one of those glass sugar containers shaped like a small white rocket, and, with deadly aim, at close range, bounces if off Frank's forehead.

Frank pulls his right hand, white and gunless, from his jacket pocket, and tests his forehead where blood is emerging in a bright semicircular brand near his temple. He turns and runs staggering from the restaurant.

"I told you he didn't have a gun," says Wandalie, standing triumphant, hands on hips.

Next time he will, I think, almost say.

"On the house," says the Greek, pointing to my sad cutlet and cold coffee, as two burly police officers, summoned, I suppose, by departing customers, rush in, guns drawn, then rush out again as the Greek points in the direction in which Frank has fled.

Outside, a woman in a black kimonolike dress, body big as an oil drum, her head a wild tumbleweed of hair, her cheeks like halves of a black grapefruit, cuddles to her flabby chest what must surely be an albino baby, its skin the blue-white color of skim milk, its head covered in a crocheted bonnet woolly as a lamb's back.

I stop at a motel near Pittsburgh.

"Only got a family unit left," says the bored old woman who sits sideways on a chair watching a microscopic black-and-white television, "but I'll give it to you at regular price."

The outside of the motel is finished in gray imitation brick. Inside are two bedrooms, a kitchen, a living room, a bath—enough room for a large family dragging along an ailing grandmother. The building is old and depressing: swaybacked linoleum floors, a brown hulk of a space heater, dead flies on all the windowsills. The place has obviously been rented out on a permanent basis over the winter months, as I discover when I look in the freezer compartment of the squat yellowish fridge and discover some frozen fish. There is a bottle of Dr. Pepper on one of the shelves, and some brown lettuce in the crisper. I move to the kitchen cupboards and find a half-package of graham crackers, an unopened box of Minute Rice, and a plastic bag half-full of potatoes growing slender feelers the cold color of ivory.

I wonder how these things came to be here. Where did the winter tenants go? Did they steal off in the dead of night, rent unpaid, carrying only essentials in brown shopping bags?

I eat the crackers and drink the Dr. Pepper in front of a fuzzy TV as full of moving shadows as a prisoner's past.

Before leaving, I check the cupboards again—I have already packed the Minute Rice and consider absconding with the potatoes.

In New York the weather is warmer, and an unusual thing happens to me at Yankee Stadium.

I stand in a long line for tickets.

"Right-field bleech-has is all we got fo-ya," I hear the ticket seller intone to those in front of me.

I plunk down my Master Charge and say, "One of your best, please."

I sign for the $7.50 ticket and am surprised when the man at the turnstiles directs me toward the lower box seats.

By some miracle, my seat is ten rows directly behind home plate. The man next to me has paid a scalper thirty dollars per ticket for him and his family. His wife is surly and disinterested, his sons too small to concentrate for long. He spends the game trekking back and forth to the concessions.

I am so close to the game that when Thurman Munson tosses his mask and charges back to the screen after a pop-up, he is nearly close enough to touch. I'm glad I got to see him. No one knows that he will be dead before the leaves turn.

I drive on to Boston even though it is out of my way. I want to have the tickets in my pocket when I travel to New Hampshire; I want to feel them in my hand, solid as passports with convictlike photos. Perhaps secret codes will be punched in them.

I park the car and walk in the sun along the sleazy street outside Fenway Park, where winos, unkempt as groundhogs, sun themselves and halfheartedly cadge quarters, supposedly for food.

"I'm a little short for a meal, Mac. Can you help me out?"

"I'm eighty cents short of the price of a ticket," says a tiny bald wino with a sunburned head. He eyes me carefully, smiling sardonically from a toothless mouth. He must know from the way I hitch my jeans that I'm not a local, or perhaps he can tell by my green and white cap with the red letters ORKIN on the peak.

I give him a dollar and say I hope he enjoys the game. He winks at me.

Again I am fortunate. Two tickets in Section 17.

"Right behind the Sox dugout," the elderly ticket seller assures me; his right eye is sightless, rolled back, and what is visible looks like a mixture of milk and cherry blossoms.

I drive as far as the intersection of highways 90 and 91. A little more than an hour of traveling upward along a vermilion line that parallels the Vermont and New Hampshire borders will bring me to Windsor, Vermont. Salinger country. My project seems more absurd all the time. What in the world am I going to say to him?

Salinger's twenty-five-year silence has bred rumors that rise like mosquitoes from a swamp and buzz angrily and irritatingly in the air. And I've collected them, as a child might collect matchbooks and stash them in an unruly clamor in a dresser drawer already full of pens, tape, marbles, paper clips, and old playing cards.

"He hasn't eaten anything but soybeans for fifteen years," I recently heard an American Literature professor say authoritatively when we were at Mark's home in the University Heights area of Iowa City, Annie and I the only non-academics present.

Tired of answering the question, "How is your corn crop coming?" I had mentioned my interest in Salinger, to let them know I read more than International Harvester repair manuals.

Mark's house is wide and spacious, with a lot of windows and much glass and chrome furniture. In fact, the living room looks a little like a furniture-store display window, and smells of new fabric, plastic, and waxed floors.

Our own sofa was plucked from the front lawn of a frat house in Iowa City, not long after we were married. It has rounded arms and is covered in a ferny green cloth soft as a plush toy. It has endured abuse. I lifted a cushion one day to find an atrophied doughnut in among the Lego, pencils, matchbooks, and Karin's lost socks. I looked at the doughnut for a while, feeling very happy, and covered it up for posterity.

"He arrives at the store every afternoon at three-thirty and he speaks the same words every single day, 'Three pounds of soybeans, please,' unless of course a long weekend is coming up, then he orders five pounds." Mark's party is bulging with tweed and intellect. As I steer Annie toward the door, she informs me brightly that she has just learned that Chaucer died of cancer of the testicles.

Mark, besides being a burgeoning business tycoon in partnership with a dishonest-looking accountant named Bluestein, is a minor celebrity in the university community. He had been written up in a number of learned journals, has had articles published, and is often invited to give lectures to government officials, farm marketing boards, and Future Farmers of America conventions. Mark's theory is that the impudent corn weevil is bent upon conquering the world.

When Annie first told me about this, she looked me straight in the eye and warned me not to snicker about it, especially in the presence of my brother-in-law, who wrestled as a light-heavyweight during one of the numerous years when Iowa won the NCAA wrestling title.

"University people treat that kind of thing very seriously," she said, exploring my forearm with her small freckled hand. She added that it was probably wise never to snicker in the presence of my brother-in-law, who holds atheists, Catholics, Democrats, and the University of Oklahoma wrestling team in equally low esteem.

"But if you want to snicker when we're alone, it's okay," said Annie, throwing herself into my arms, sitting on my lap, her denimed legs bracketed around my thighs. "Imagine, devoting your life to corn weevils." Annie buried her face in my shoulder as we laughed and rocked back and forth.

"It can't be as bad as selling life insurance," I said, and told her about selling a $5000 policy that week to a Portuguese house painter who thought he was insuring his half-ton truck.

"I'm Ray Kinsella," I'll say confidently, after I've rung his doorbell and he has answered. Then I'll just stand and wait for his incredulous reply.

At the same time I can picture myself sitting for days in his driveway, while my chin stubbles and the car interior begins to smell of orange peels and stale bread.

I have breakfast at a Motel 6 near Holyoke, Massachusetts. It has rained in the night, and the parking lot is peppered with pink petals. As I drive toward Windsor, Vermont, I remember once driving through Iowa City with Karin at my side, over streets where trees formed a dizzying arch of pink and white. Petals fell silently on the car as we drove.

"Don't run over the flowers," she said to me.

We stopped the car and Karin and I walked on the tender grass between sidewalk and street, Karin gathering the velvet droplets, pressing them to her face, scattering them over her head.

I had to go to Iowa City again that night. As I tucked Karin into bed in her room with curtains covered in kittens and ballerinas, I said, "Is there anything I can bring you?" figuring on an ice-cream bar, a Dr. Pepper, or a slice of cheese pizza, which, incredibly, she likes to eat cold for breakfast.

"Bring me the flowers, Daddy," she said. "I want some to touch when I wake up in the morning."

That night, after my meeting, I drove back to the spot we had visited by day. It was like a cathedral, the filtered light of stars and streetlights peeking through the thatch of blossoms and leaves.

From the jumble in the back seat, I took a large Styrofoam cup that had once held a cherry Coke, and, walking along the dark street rather sheepishly, scooped handfuls of petals from the overflowing gutters, wondering how I would explain myself if someone chanced to ask.

I carried them home on the seat beside me like an urn of ashes, and placed them on the night table beside Karin's bed. I watched her sleeping; she slept on her back, her right-hand palm up beside her head. She looks like Annie run through a copying machine that reduces things in size. I bent and kissed her freckled nose. I will probably never love her more than I did at that moment.

A tiny sound, like a soap bubble bursting, pops me back to reality. I stop at a rest area and try to regroup. I feel like an eighth grader bringing home a bad report card. In daylight, when I'm alone, what I am about to do seems so ludicrous. I don't have Annie to reassure me, to put her arm around my waist and her head on my shoulder and say, "Oh, love, if it makes you happy you should do it."

This land is foreign to me. The hills are blanketed with trees and foliage. I am used to being able to see for miles in any direction, and, if I'm able to find a hill, being able to count the houses on nearby quarter-sections. I grew up in Montana under the Big Sky, where the landscape outruns the vision. Here, I am surrounded. Perhaps I won't be able to find him. The sky is clear, with a rumble of clouds on the horizon. I walk into the woods—oak, maple, white birch, conifer, poplar, the ground clothed in green crawling vines decorated with tiny purple flowers. Acorns cover the ground like pebbles. The trees are a golden-green; spring bristles all about me. There is more rock than I imagined, although the mountains, compared to the real mountains of the West, are only green hills.

My impulse is to turn back, but I know I won't, even though it is so easy *not* to do something. Pretend you're selling life insurance, I tell myself as I wheel the car out onto the highway.

As I near Windsor, anxiety crawls along my arms like ants. I am really quite shy. Why didn't The Voice pick a real sales-man for this job? I hated to contact people when I was selling life insurance; only my empty bank account, my love for Annie, and knowing that at the time it was the only way I could stay in Iowa, made me pick up the phone and don my optimistic and charming voice as I lured another potential commission check to lunch.

I press on. Make two trips back and forth through the town of Windsor, Vermont. At the edge of town, golden writing on a black sign reads WINDSOR, BIRTHPLACE OF VERMONT, 1777. As I cruise the main street, I see the Old South Church with four whitewashed Greco-Roman columns at its front; I pass the drugstore where I've read Salinger buys his newspapers; American flags everywhere; I pass the home of the Benevolent and Protective Order of Elks, their hall white as a Klan convention. And a covered bridge—I drive over it twice, windows down, enthralled by the rumble like stampeding horses, the earthy smell of this place permanently protected from the sun.

Finally I force myself out of the car, walk stiffly into the post office, and make the first of my inquiries.

In reply to my hesitant question, a tired clerk with a pale face and silver spectacles reels off a list of directions I don't have time to assimilate before he has gone back to counting stamps. I lack the nerve to tell him I don't quite understand, that his accent is thick as porridge to my midwestern ears.

I have to make three more stops to ask directions. One lady raises her eyebrows and says she doesn't know where he lives, indicating by her tone that if she did, which she probably does, she wouldn't tell me anyway.

An old man in a store that smells of oiled floorboards and coffee rolls his eyes as he would at a grandson who has just asked an embarrassing question about sex, and asks, "Why do you want to know?"

"I'm a friend of his, from the city," I stutter.

"If you was much of a friend, he'd of give you the directions hisself," the old man says, and goes back to his newspaper.

Eventually, a gas-station attendant, upon hearing my request, walks from my window to the front of the car, notes my Iowa license plates, and walks back grinning laconically.

"Lots of si-reens an kafuffle up around his place one evening about a month ago." He shakes his head solemnly.

"I just want to take a look," I say.

He gives me directions for the nine-mile drive. I give him a dollar for his trouble.

"Be careful."

"I will," I promise.

* * *

The road along the New Hampshire border is mainly dirt, but beyond the Private Property sign the surface is graveled. The new May leaves of the white birches and poplars dust the roof of my elderly Datsun. The leaves, delicately veined as a baby's hands, are not full grown but are already gathering a film of dust. As I approach, I catch a brief glimpse of some brown siding and the sun glinting off window glass. I park next to the curving driveway that spirals up a steep hill. I explore gingerly, trying to walk without crunching gravel, ready to leap into the underbrush like a shy animal. A two-car garage is built into the side of the hill, like a bear's den at a zoo. One side of the garage stands open and empty. I look up through the lacy leaves, and the sky seems very high.

What I remember most vividly about the landscape is that on the way into Windsor, from a high point on the road, I could look out over the very area where I now sit. Everywhere was a smooth, liquid green, with no indication of habitation, no sign of houses or towns. Yet here I am, near a very real house, on a road with other houses on it that are all camouflaged by leaves.

I walk back to the car, get in, roll down the window, and wait. The sweetness of honeysuckle fills my senses.

A jeep grinds up the road behind me, swings sharply into the driveway, sending up a spray of potato-colored dust. As if by afterthought, the jeep brakes, spewing up more dust, and stops, with only the rear end visible, protruding from the ferns and low-hanging branches that swaddle the driveway. I wait, tense as if my neck were tipped back, my mouth agape, and I was preparing for the dentist's needle.

A tall, graying man appears from the driver's side of the jeep. He walks confidently, even a little arrogantly, toward my car.

Panic falls over me like a net. It is as if my bills are due while my corn sways in a dark rain. Is it Salinger? The only photographs I have seen are over twenty-five years old. The one in *Mademoiselle* shows a very ordinary young man with downcast eyes. The other...

"What do you want?" the man says, frowning. His hair is gray and white, the color of street slush, and is combed straight back. There are tension lines, like two ruts, between his brows. If it is him, he looks older than I imagined he would.

"Are you J. D. Salinger?"

"What can I do for you?"

"I—I want to talk to you." What a banal, hopeless thing to say! I have promised myself, for close to 1500 miles, that I will say something brilliant, witty, charming. Entice him into my car like I was sugar and he an ant.

"I suppose you're a writer," he says, and smiles, not unkindly, through snowy dentures.

"I—no."

"Not a reporter," he says, taking a step backward, as if the Datsun and I were fire or boiling water.

"No."

"Then what is it you want?"

He is wearing faded blue jeans, a khaki work shirt, and a spruce-green down vest like duck hunters wear.

"I want you to come with me," I stutter, and let my trench coat-covered left hand peek above the car's window ledge.

It is wrong. All wrong. Completely wrong. I feel like a rookie runner caught off first base by a wily pitcher, hung up in that vast area between first and second, fluttering back and forth like a wounded bird who knows he's doomed.

What must he think? Is he used to dealing with crazies? I should have brought Annie. She could smile at him, bouncy as a red squirrel, and say, "My honey here has come to take you to a baseball game, because he thinks you need to go," and he would believe her.

Salinger frowns, and the stress lines between his brows deepen. His forehead is furrowed. There are long age lines from cheek to chin, making him resemble a tired but friendly hound.

"Are you kidnapping me?"

"Oh, please, that's such an awful word. I'm sorry. I planned things so differently. I wanted to convince you to come with me. I never wanted to have to do this . . ."

"Then you *are*."

"I just want to take you for a drive. I have tickets for a baseball game. A *baseball* game," I say again. Even though I emphasize the last line, it has no visible impact on him.

"And if I don't?" His eyes look quickly to the jeep submerged in forest.

What can I possibly say? I am inarticulate as a teenager at the end of a first date, standing in the glare of the porch light, a father hulking behind the curtains.

"I'm Ray Kinsella," I say, trying a new tack. My right hand is rigid under my trench coat; my left, fingers spread, makes a musical motion, as if playing a single note on the tinny car door with my middle finger—a note that I hope will strike a response with Salinger.

He remains silent and looks around, and I know he is trying to decide whether or not to run. If he does, it is all over.

"I thought you might want to meet one of your own characters," I say. Salinger continues to frown, looks blank. I notice that he has large ears.

"Who?"

"Ray Kinsella," I repeat. "I was a character in one of your stories. 'A Young Girl in 1941 with No Waist At All.'"

"So?" He shrugs. "It was just a story. Not even a very good one. Where did you dig it up?"

"In a back issue of *Mademoiselle* at the University of Iowa Library."

"Well, Ray Kinsella, I suppose you're under psychiatric treatment."

"You really did write about me," I protest. "The boy in the story *is* Ray Kinsella."

"What does it matter? I don't understand." He looks around, wishing, I'm sure, that someone or something would come by and distract me.

"There aren't many of us around—Kinsellas, that is. There are only nine in the Manhattan telephone directory," I babble. "I stopped and looked on my way here. In 1946 or '7, whenever you wrote the story, there were probably less."

"Yes, there probably were. Still, it's just a name. I don't see . . ."

"It's *my* name. You used my brother's name in *The Catcher in the Rye:* Richard Kinsella—he was the boy who gave rambling speeches, and everybody yelled 'digression' at him."

"I remember that, but I don't understand why it is important.

Why should I be thrilled to meet someone with a name I once used in a story? I write fiction."

"But surely you knew someone by that name."

"What if I did?" Salinger stops, squints his left eye slightly. It is as if he realizes that arguing with me is like trying to dissuade an overzealous missionary. He eyes me carefully, scratches behind his right ear.

"Perhaps we could talk about it," he says, and I sense that in his desperation he has called up words that are hidden unknowingly inside him like scissors lost in a sewing basket. I picture him, alone these many years, watching endless reruns of *Emergency One, Barnaby Jones, Policewoman, Cannon, Marcus Welby,* and *The Eleventh Hour,* in which the good doctor, officer, detective, or paramedic cautiously approaches the disturbed person and says, not patronizingly but with a calm air of authority, "Perhaps we could talk about it?"

"I've come to take you to a baseball game," I say doggedly.

"Why?"

In my anxiety, I see a grotesque cartoon of a pale, lumpish blob of a person with a flashing light bulb over his head. It is as if I am trying to pile gifts in front of Salinger, in hopes of distracting him from my real purpose.

I conjure up my last trick. "I've brought you a baseball," I chirp, and reach my left arm over my right and open the glove compartment. The ball rests in the safe darkness behind the maps, sunglasses, and a couple of paperback books. I pull the whole mass onto the floor, duck my head, and eventually pop up with the ball.

I hand it out the window to him. He reaches for it, then pulls his hand back like an adult does when a child tries to hand him a sticky, drool-covered toy.

"It's yours," I say. "I've carried it all the way from Iowa. I'm from Iowa, you know."

"No. I didn't know," says Salinger. He steps back and sideways and checks my license plate, just in case I don't know where I'm from. I am still offering the ball in my extended hand.

"Please," I say. "It was hit by Shoeless Joe Jackson. A home-run ball."

"It must be valuable," says Salinger, eyeing the ball with

its red and blue stitching; the ball looks as if it has been aged by several coats of varnish.

"It's yours," I say again. "A gift. No strings attached— from one baseball fan to another."

Salinger frowns, narrowing his dark eyes. Then he reaches out and takes the ball, using just his finger tips, handling it gingerly, as if it might explode.

"What's all this about baseball?" he says, and my stomach drops as if I'm in a balky elevator. What if he *isn't* a baseball fan? The fates are known to play tricks on innocents. But I've come this far, I can't even think of the possibility.

"Fenway Park," I say. "I have tickets for tonight's game. Good ones. I want you to come with me."

"Are you seeing a psychiatrist?" he asks again.

"I suppose I will be if this doesn't go well," I say, making a rather pitiful attempt at a smile. Salinger plods on, ignoring my attempt at humor.

"What makes you think I *want* to go to a baseball game, *need* to go to a baseball game?"

"It's a long story," I say.

"Perhaps you should bore me with it." There is a hard edge to his voice, but his eyes seem to me to hold a few flecks of amusement, floating like golden needlepoints.

"I'll tell you on the way. Please," I add, like a child begging to stay up an extra hour.

There is a long silence. I can feel the wetness under my arms; the sweat trickles down my ribs. I suddenly itch in a dozen places.

Salinger appears much more composed than I would if I were being kidnapped by an armed stranger in a faded dirty Datsun with Iowa plates. He nods toward his own vehicle. "I left the motor running," he says almost apologetically. He edges back toward it. Another step or two and he'll be gone. I leap out of the car, stumbling as I do, pointing my trench coat at him. Salinger raises his hands halfway, more in a gesture of self-defense than surrender.

Establishing my footing, I try to appear very cool and trusting as he disappears into the foliage. Leaning on the rear fender of the jeep, I peer after him, the spicy ferns touching my face. He shuts off the motor, pockets the keys, and returns.

"You don't need that," he says, pointing to my coat-covered hand. "I have great respect for my life. I won't do anything to risk it."

We get in the car. I kill the motor twice, then remember to release the hand brake, and we roll slowly down the hill toward Boston and Fenway Park.

As we drive, it strikes me that I haven't searched him. As I look across at him, it appears to me that there is an ominous bulge on the left side of his vest. I picture concealed there a German Luger, resting like a cold rock in a homemade holster under the friendly goose down. Perhaps the first time I am forced to slow for a stop sign or a traffic light, he'll whip out the weapon and with military accuracy blow me away. I can feel my rib cage exploding as the bullet slams me against the driver's door.

"Now *really,*" says Salinger, "are you under psychiatric care?"

"No. Not now or ever." I try to keep my voice from breaking. "Perhaps it's just that they haven't got me yet."

"Then please," says Salinger, referring to my trench coat-covered hand. "About the only reason I got in here was because you seemed so hyper. I was afraid that if I ran, you might shoot up the whole side of the mountain, and maybe by accident get lucky. I don't for a moment believe you have a gun in there. Still, I believe in going with the odds."

I'm glad he is insisting. I find it very difficult to drive while pretending to hold a gun. The real gun is still in the trunk, sleeping like a fish at the bottom of a cool stream. In the movies, the hero, or antihero, often drives across a whole city or state with a loaded gun trained menacingly on a carful of hoodlums. I assume movie heroes don't drive cars with standard transmissions.

I toss the dun-colored coat into the back seat, revealing my hand, empty as a politician's promise.

Now, *he* will probably pull a gun on *me,* and direct me to the nearest sheriff's office.

"Do you do this often?" asks Salinger. I glance over, and there may actually be a twinkle in his eye.

"No. You're the first. And, I hope, the last," I add.

"I didn't really believe you had a gun. Still, there was always the chance. I read somewhere that it is better not to excite disturbed persons." Then he looks at me and half smiles and half frowns. I imagine him wondering why he is talking to me like this, as if we are at least acquaintances, if not friends.

"If I'd had a gun I'd probably have shot myself about five times by now. I'm not mechanically inclined." We both laugh a little reluctantly, as if the situation doesn't call for laughter. "I *do* have a gun," I add quickly, "but it's in the trunk. I know I was supposed to buy one, but I guess this isn't where I'm supposed to use it."

Salinger looks at me out of troubled eyes. "As it should be," he says. "I mean the gun...in the trunk."

I have not been paying attention to where I am driving. I virtually never pay any attention to where I am driving. When Annie and I travel together, she drives, especially in Minneapolis or Chicago—even Iowa City. If Annie has been somewhere once, she remembers where she has been and how to get there again, if necessary. Even when I'm just driving in Iowa City, I often find myself parking at the University of Iowa Library, or heading up Johnson Street toward the house I lived in ten years ago.

The road I am driving on might have been transferred from a Snakes and Ladders board. The trees are tall and leafy, the trail narrow. I pull up at a T-intersection. I have to choose between left and right. There are direction signs, but neither town means a thing to me. I will have to pull out my red-veined road atlas and try to figure out where I am. How humiliating. I must be one of the most inept kidnappers since the bumblers in "Ransom of Red Chief."

"Boston, is it?" says Salinger, noting my long hesitation.

I look hopeful. "Yes."

He nods his head to the right.

I turn gratefully. But what if it is all an act? What if he is directing me to the nearest jail?

"Is your name *really* Ray Kinsella?"

"Yes."

"And you really have a brother named Richard?"

"Yes, though I haven't seen him since he was fifteen. Since *I* was fifteen, we're identical twins."

"And you came here all the way from Iowa?"

"Drove all the way."

"And you brought me a baseball?"

"Hit by Shoeless Joe Jackson."

"Yes. He was thrown out of the game or something."

"He was."

"And we're going to Boston to see a baseball game?"

"We are. The Red Sox are playing the Twins. I'm a Twins fan—if I have to make a choice. Usually I'm just a fan of the game."

"Now what about . . . ?" but we are interrupted as the snaky highway brings us into a town called Claremont, and a mass of road construction. I'm no longer certain whether we are in New Hampshire or Vermont. Traffic comes to a standstill. A sign at the side of the road reads TURN OFF YOUR RADIO IN BLASTING ZONE, while another says, USE YOUR LIGHTS. Construction crews appear to be rearranging the very center of town. A front-end loader scoops and dumps concrete fragments from one pile to another. Not one but two policemen are directing traffic. I look at Salinger. He looks at me—a steady brown gaze giving no hint of what he plans to do. We sit for a couple of moments as a fine white dust like volcanic ash drifts in the windows. He can open the door and walk away if he chooses. I notice that he is turning the baseball in his large hands. The backs of his fingers are heavy with white hair. His eyebrows are the gray-white color of gull wings.

As I inch along, the second police officer shrills his whistle and, when I look back, waves me over.

"Could I see your license and registration, please?" he says to me.

I comply meekly.

Salinger must be tempted to turn me in. I believe there is a certain compulsion in each of us for orderliness of a sort: a desire to clip off loose fabric ends, to refold newspapers with the first page on the outside, to empty ashtrays, to turn in kidnappers.

But there is no evidence. It would be his word against mine, and, in that circumstance, it would be an advantage to be an unknown Iowa farmer instead of a mysterious writer, a known eccentric.

My mouth becomes drier as I think of the gun. It seems to

me that there are laws of some kind about transporting girls and guns across state lines for illegal or immoral purposes.

How embarrassing it would be to use my one phone call from some varnishy-smelling, leaf-encased police station to tell Annie that I have been arrested.

The police officer is young and earnest, scrubbed pink as wild roses, brought up by a mother who taught him to wash behind his ears.

He scrutinizes my license, turns it over to look for convictions, checks my face against the staring, felonlike photo lacquered with plastic. He leans in and looks over at Salinger. There is a tangy scent of fresh-cut lumber about him.

"What is your name, sir?"

Salinger keeps his face turned toward the passenger window.

"Jerry," he says quietly to the glove compartment.

"Could I see some identification, Jerry?" the young officer says politely.

They say you can tell you are getting old when police officers and cocktail waitresses start to look like teenagers. This young man looks like a nine-year-old dressed up for a play.

Salinger digs in the back pocket of his jeans, produces a wallet, and passes it over for inspection.

"Jerome David Salinger," the officer reads without emotion. "And where is it that you and Mr. Kinsella are going, Jerome?" The officer's bright eyes stare straight at Salinger without the slightest spark of recognition.

"Fenway Park," he replies, and all three of us can hear my breath escape with a rush. "The Sox are playing the Twins."

The officer takes in the back seat with a steely, well-trained eye, and, finding nothing suspicious, withdraws his head.

"Your right taillight is out, Raymond," he says to me. "I'd suggest that you get it fixed at the first opportunity."

"Thank you," I say as we pull away. Salinger remains silent. "You could have done me in back there."

"I know. It crossed my mind. But think of the publicity. I'd get more headlines than Aimee Semple McPherson. The press are just waiting for something like this—some excuse to swarm up here like locusts and eat the leaves off my trees and snap the blooms off the flowers in my window boxes. I won't have it!" His voice rises theatrically on the final words.

He is silent again. We pass a wave of willow trees with leaves as green as lime juice.

"I envy you your craziness," he says quietly. "It has been years, far too many years, since I did something absolutely crazy."

"Would you like me to bore you with that story now?"

"Yes. I think I'd like to know why you think you're here, doing this."

"Well, let me see . . ." I am embarrassed about beginning, like an author about to read his work for the first time to an audience. "I read an interview with you, one you gave long ago, where you talked about the importance of titles. So let me try a title on you. My saga would be called 'The Story of How Shoeless Joe Jackson Came to Iowa.'"

Salinger tosses his ball in the air and catches it.

"My father said he saw him years later . . ." I begin.

"J. D. Salinger has an obsessive fear of aging," one of the guests at Mark's party had said to me. "There are no mirrors in his house; no pictures of anyone past their fortieth year—parents, grandparents, wives, himself. When he is forced to leave his house, he avoids even glancing at any possible reflections of himself, no matter how vague or distorted. He is afraid that if he sees himself, he will look older than he really is.

"The reason he hasn't published anything new is that he spends all his time rewriting work done before he was forty, distrusting anything he has written since then, trying to achieve the ultimate in perfection. This, however, is impossible, because his mind has not stopped maturing and growing. So what he is eliminating from his early work is what makes it most valid and readable. He trusts no one to view what he is doing. He is living in a closed circle, without fulfillment or escape."

"How do you know that?" a woman with a body straight as a tree trunk demanded, her voice whining with excitement.

"You'll have to wait for my book," said the speaker, smiling sagely. "It's due in the spring and is called *The Existential Salinger*."

I often get caught in thunderstorms. While clouds slowly levitate from the western horizon, or even when they come rolling in, I remain too long in the fields or at the ballpark, long after the first giant drops have plopped on the green-painted boards beside me, or the corn is bent, leaning away from the wind. I have, it seems, absorbed, perhaps by osmosis, some of Annie's optimism. Only when I am wet as a bathed cat do I accept that the clouds are not going to veer to one side or the other.

My mother reads the weather forecasts in the newspaper and believes them religiously, even though they are generally less truthful than statements made by "diplomatically reliable sources." Thus she perpetually carries an umbrella, for such forecasts usually say, even in time of drought, "chance of rain, two percent." Her umbrella is about a foot long and patterned with purple pansies. He would be horrified if someone suggested that its shape is phallic.

I suppose I should pay closer attention to weather forecasts and storm warnings. My brother-in-law represents, at least symbolically, the icy-white clouds that foretell hail, the farmer's worst enemy. Mark and his friend Bluestein already own a good portion of Johnson County, Iowa, but for some reason have become inordinately interested in the past few months in buying *our* quarter-section.

Mark cornered me at his party.

"Well, Ray," he said, "I've decided to make you one more offer for the farm. Bluestein put it in the mail to you this afternoon." He waved his hand vaguely behind him, where Bluestein lurked like a funeral director at a christening.

My brother-in-law has always looked to me like the villain from a nineteenth-century melodrama. He is tall, slim, but solid, with hawkish features. His dark-red hair, in spite of being carefully styled, slips down over his forehead, requiring him to flip his head every ten seconds or so, like a bull testing the air for odors of sex. Today he wears a tight, tailored sports jacket that looks as if it has been skinned off a long-haired, cinnamon-colored monkey. He wears a green tie, thoroughly knotted. His hands are immaculate, his ring finger featuring an emerald that if sold might get me out of debt. Mark has a wine-colored mustache that turns up wickedly at each corner, apparently of its own accord. I've never seen him twirl the mustache like a genuine villain, but I'm sure he will one day.

"Tell Bluestein to save his postage," I said as we headed for the door.

Bluestein, Mark's business partner, is a squat little man with terminal five o'clock shadow and shifty eyes.

Mark, regardless of the queerness of his notions concerning the corn weevil, displays considerable business acumen. He and Bluestein own apartments and older homes all over the city, which they rent to students at exorbitant rates. They also own, or have optioned, several thousand acres of farmland that is planted and harvested by a crew of hired hands headed by a foreman who wears a black hat and looks a lot like Jack Palance. It is curious that at one time the land barons owned prairie ranches as far as the eye could see. Their authority was eventually undermined, and the farmers took over, dividing the land into checkerboards, each square crowned with a white castle of sorts. Now a new breed of land baron is buying out the farmers one by one, and I suppose corn farms like mine soon will be operated by computer. Instead of a farmhouse and family, there will be a small metallic box studded with red, green, and blue lights, which will tell a foreman which quadrant needs water and in which area the cutworms are hatching.

"You're going to have to face the facts," Mark said to me. "Your financial position is no secret. It appears to me that you either have to sell the farm now or lose it in the fall. Even if you have a bumper crop, which doesn't appear likely, you'll never be able to keep up with the mortgage payments. You can't make a living off a quarter-section anymore. The days of the small farmer are gone forever. You're an anachronism."

"Let's hear it for the anachronisms," said Annie, joining us. "It sounds like a baseball team. The St. Louis Anachronisms."

"As you know," Mark said directly to me, not even bothering to acknowledge Annie's joke, "we're offering you more than the place is worth, simply because of Annie."

"I'd never want you to pay me more than the place is worth, Mark. And by the way, I will not have you tearing down our house and replacing it with a computer."

Mark looked at me strangely.

"We'll get by," said Annie.

"Sure, you're going to discover diamonds in your corn-field," said Mark.

I have a twin brother. An identical twin. His name is Richard, and the only way anyone, including my mother, can tell us apart is that Richard has an inch-and-a-half scar on his left eyebrow. When we were about three we were bouncing on a bed, and Richard bounced himself off the headboard—four stitches' worth.

Mother had us fingerprinted, or rather, footprinted. She had our birth certificates tacked to the wall of our room. The reverse side of each featured purplish left and right footprints and statistical information about the mother and father. I'm not sure whether it's just that I've heard the story so many times, or if I can actually remember as a child screaming loudly as Mother held my ankle in an iron grip and forced my foot onto a cherry-colored stamp pad. Mother claims that until Richard's accident, she often footprinted us in the evenings after our bath, just to be sure which was which.

I've often told Annie, only half jokingly, that after I've been away, she should check me over carefully when I return, to make sure I don't have a scar on my left eyebrow.

"Oh, I'd be able to tell," Annie says, grinning her evil grin.

"Not likely," I say. "We tried once when we were about fifteen to find something different about us. Anything different. Our voices were the same, people always mistook us for one another on the telephone. Our hands were the same size, we were the same height, and our shoes were the same size."

"I get the picture," says Annie.

One night in our room we set out to see if maybe our cocks were different. We got them hard and then argued about where we should measure from—the top or the bottom. We had an old steel ruler, the color of railroad tracks, that Mother had had as a child; it was cold as hell no matter where we measured from. But it didn't matter, we were the same length from any and all angles, and if we'd measured circumference, it would have been the same, too. Every part of us is interchangeable.

The morning of our sixteenth birthday, Richard came down-stairs, flexed his muscles, and said, "I'm a man now. I'll do anything I please from now on."

"Like hell you will," my father replied.

They argued for a few minutes, and finally Richard took a poke at my father. He missed and his fist smashed through the wall, which was not wood or wallboard but heavily calcimined wallpaper. Fortunately he didn't strike a joist, or he might have broken his hand.

Richard then walked out the door of that old ranch house not far from Deer Lodge, Montana, and has not been seen or heard from since.

We are nearly to Boston when I finish the story of my baseball stadium and of Shoeless Joe Jackson and the other suspended White Sox. I also tell Salinger about the second coming of the voice.

"Ease his pain," repeats Salinger in a tone of wonder, shaking his head. "How could you possibly know that I was the one your voice was referring to?"

"It must be akin to religious conversion," I reply. "Something you have to experience to understand. But I was right the first time," I point out.

"You don't have any witnesses. What if it was all a hallucination? Religious fanatics are known to have detailed visions. You're obviously a baseball fanatic."

"Karin and Annie experience it too. When you meet Annie you'll see how reliable she is."

"When!"

"Sorry. I am . . . just taking you to one game."

"But what pain? I don't have any pain. Well, no more than anyone else."

"You haven't been to a live baseball game for over twenty-five years."

"It's not a big deal. To some people that is not pain."

"But surely to you . . ." But I stop, fearful of probing further, in case my worst fears materialize. "You'll feel better for it. Trust me."

We hit Boston at the beginning of rush-hour traffic, and of course I become lost immediately. I travel over a number of bridges and drive along the ocean, trying all the while to weave in the general direction of the Prudential Building, which I know is in the vicinity of Fenway Park and is the one landmark in Boston that I know. But the traffic sweeps my Datsun along like a cork in a swift current, past corners where I want to turn, and I am carried onto and over expressways. I eventually work the car to an exit and return to the bunched streets. Quite by accident, we end up on a main street and I can see the silvery light standards of Fenway Park.

I have to make a left turn. Pedestrians in the East behave like lemmings rushing dispassionately to their deaths—it takes a good ten minutes to make a left turn into the blinding rush of oncoming traffic, with pedestrians thronging suicidally into the intersections. As I turn the corner, I enter two rows of traffic. Cars bound together like tiny coupled trains stretch over a hill and beyond the baseball park. I picture myself being forced onto another expressway, and in an hour or so reappearing at this corner, only to be swept by again.

Then suddenly, like the parting of the Red Sea, a parking place appears one row to my right. Two or three cars ease by it, the drivers apparently having their minds on home. I turn the car in an S motion, cutting in behind a bus that spews out fumes black and substantial as octopus oil. As the bus inches forward, I slip into the parking place.

I raise my hands. "More of a miracle to find a parking place on a baseball night in downtown Boston than for a man to throw away his artificial leg and grow a new one in front of an enraptured congregation," I say to Salinger.

He sits impassive. "You are not impressed by magic," I say sadly. "Are you hungry?" I ask as I bend my neck back, letting some of the tension drain from me. "We have time to eat before the game. On me, of course. This whole evening is on me."

We walk back down a small hill toward a main road. "There used to be a Greek restaurant around here," Salinger says. Then noting my surprise, he adds, "It's been years since I've been to Boston, but the geography kind of leaves an imprint."

I stop a fat man who looks as if he should know the location of all the restaurants that have ever been in Boston, and ask if he knows of a Greek restaurant nearby.

"Right across the street," he says, pointing a monstrous arm. And it is. *Aegean Fare* is written in black script across the face of a gray building.

"You have a good memory," I tell Salinger. He is loping along beside me, taking exceptionally long strides.

"Do you always wear that hat?" he says.

"It's illegal to farm in Iowa and not wear one," I reply. "Bill 1402 passed by the legislature in Des Moines last summer stipulates that a farmer can be fined ten ears of corn or a pound of soybeans if he's stopped by the Highway Patrol and found to be bareheaded."

"Oh really?" says Salinger, smiling a little lopsidedly as we turn into Aegean Fare. The restaurant is part cafeteria, part bakery, and has a glass display case full of Greek desserts radiating enough calories to power an atomic bomb. The restaurant walls are covered in mirrors. I catch sight of my arms, tanned as burnished maple. I tug off my cap, revealing my forehead, which, in contrast, is as white as sliced chicken breast. I practically dance to our table, I am feeling so manic. I have done it. I am eating supper with J. D. Salinger; we are in Boston; we are going to see the Red Sox play baseball.

"What . . . what do you do up there on your hill?" I say as tactfully as I know how. We have kept the conversation general, although I can tell he wants to ask me questions and I babble a little, every so often, about Shoeless Joe, or Annie, or Karin, or my stadium.

He calls me Ray. Sometimes he addresses me by my whole name. "Call me Jerry," he says to me. I have been careful not to address him by any particular name. I have not yet called him Jerry. I very seldom use another person's name in conversation. I think it is because when I sold life insurance, I was deluged with sales material that screamed, "A man's name is the most important sound he ever hears," and I was taught to work a client's name into the conversation at every possible opportunity. It was as if I was armed with a little basketful of darts with Arthur, or Charles, or Amos written on them and could not sell a policy until I had stuck each and every one into my prospect's body. Now that I am free, I try to erase that loathsome period completely from my mind.

Salinger—Jerry—looks at me over his plate of moussaka. I am eating Greek salad out of a bowl large enough to wash in, the lime-white feta cheese resting heavy on the crisp lettuce and tomatoes.

"I live. I write. I watch old movies. I read. I watch the sunset. I watch the moon rise."

"That's all?"

"That's *all?* Isn't it enough? Serenity is a very elusive quality. I've been trying all my life to find it. I'm very ordinary. I've never been able to understand why people are so interested in me. Writers are very dull. It's people like you who keep me from achieving what I'm after. You feel that I must be unhappy. A neurotic, guilt-torn artist. I'm *not* unhappy. And I have no wisdom to impart to you. I have no pain for you, unless"— and he smiles mischievously—"you and your family were to be plagued with strangers lurking in your bushes, trampling your flower beds, looking in your windows, or, in your case, skulking about your baseball park, crushing your corn sprouts into the ground, and stealing your doormats. Once someone stole the valve caps off my jeep. I suppose he sold them or displays them under glass in his library. I don't deserve that!" he suddenly shouts. And at the next table, two young men in Red Sox T-shirts look up from their food to see what the commotion is about.

"I've done nothing to deserve that. I've had twenty-five years of it—strangers gawking at me like I was a two-headed baby bobbing in a specimen jar." He eyes me up and down, waiting for my reaction. The lines have been delivered with actorlike precision and projection.

The inside of Aegean Fare is very Old World—heavy, varnished tables and chairs, some of the tables covered with red-checked tablecloths. The walls are mirrored, and high on each wall are pink neon phrases written in Greek. Hoping to ease Salinger's tension, I point them out and begin speculating on what they might mean:

"No trespassing."

"Don't pinch the waitresses," says Jerry, but without enthusiasm.

"Why are you looking up here?" I suggest.

A small boy about tabletop height, who has been weaving in and out among the tables in a private game of some sort, pulls a chair out from our table, circles it a couple of times, then slides onto it, trying to coil his lithe little body around it. He has straight dark hair, delicate features, and eyes the color of Coca-Cola.

"I know something you don't know," he half sings.

"I'm sure you do," I say, smiling.

"Car wash fifty cents," says Jerry.

I look at him blankly.

"The sign."

"Oh yes."

"I had strawberry pie," the boy informs us. "The strawberries were this high." He raises his slim-fingered hand about six inches above the table.

As Salinger and I prepare to leave, the boy skips along behind us.

"Ah, so he's with you," the bullet-headed man behind the cash register says to us, and points a fat white finger at the boy who stands scuffing one shoe on the other.

"Not us," I say.

"You sure?" says the cashier. "He had pie and milk, and he's been walking around for about an hour."

"His folks must be here somewhere. He's too well dressed and fed to be abandoned," I say. I look back as we leave, and the boy is staring after me as if I'd just kicked his cat.

I wait until we are settled in our seats at the stadium—good seats directly behind the Sox on-deck circle (although the seats are much too close together and we are hunched knees close to chins, as if we were passengers in the rear seat of a foreign car)—before attempting to discuss Salinger's life with him again.

"If I'd known, I'd have bought three tickets so we could sit one seat apart and angle our legs," I say, laughing a little too loudly.

Jerry keeps his eyes mainly on his program, occasionally staring furtively around. He is still a little worried about being recognized. The incident with the police officer was not enough proof for him.

At one point on the drive down, I had suggested stopping for coffee when we gassed up.

"I don't think so," Jerry said, looking around like *he* was the criminal.

"Why?"

"Well, what if people recognize me and make a fuss?"

"I didn't recognize you, and I have a special interest in you. I can almost guarantee no one else will."

"Almost."

"That's the best anyone can do," I said.

The game begins and the Red Sox are in trouble early. The last notes of the national anthem have barely faded on the wind before Mike Torrez is bombed. Ken Landreaux homers; Roy Smalley homers; Bombo Rivera triples to deep center field.

Don Zimmer, the Boston manager, trudges to the mound. The crowd erupts in a chorus of boos. Booing Don Zimmer appears to be a favorite pastime of Boston fans.

"Hey Zimmer! Whatcha doin' out? They cleanin' your cage?" screeches a man with a beer belly and a Boston baseball cap. Zimmer is round and heavy and built close to the ground; his beady eyes are buried deep in a jowly face.

"Ya joibal!" the man yells. "Whatatheydoin' with a joibal managin' a baseball team?" The man looks around for approval. He draws a few scattered smiles.

It is difficult to imagine that Zimmer was once a pretty good second baseman, that he scooted after sizzling grounders like an unattended lawn mower.

As a long-reliever warms up, I speculate on how best to draw Salinger's pain out in the open. I've got him here in the proper surroundings. I want to be a metaphorical poultice applied to his wounds, but so far it has been like trying to open a seamless tin can with only my fingernails.

"I wrote a sonnet to you once," I say, staring across at his large ear; his profile that emphasizes a fleshy nose.

"So you're a writer," he replies accusingly.

How can I be so adept at saying the wrong thing? I wonder. "No. No. It was in a college English course I attended, oh, ten years ago. I had forgotten it completely until right now. Everyone had to write a sonnet. It was horrible, really, sentimental and melodramatic, but it was a plea to you to hurry and publish more stories. The sonnet was a cheap imitation of Keats's 'On First Looking into Chapman's Homer.' Your work has been described as touching the soul of the reader. That's the way I felt. Feel. Honestly. You've touched my soul. I'm sorry if I sound like a middle-aged librarian at a book-auto-graphing session. Your writing has drawn me nearly fifteen hundred miles, allowed me to make a fool of myself, actually made me a criminal. That's what I call having influence."

"But I didn't ask you to do it," says Salinger. "I didn't ask for you to feel the way you do. You're influenced by an illusion. Writers are magicians. They write down words, and, if they're good, you believe that what they write is real, just as you believe a good magician has pulled the coins out of your ear, or made his assistant disappear. But the words on the page have no connection to the person who wrote them. Writers live other peoples' lives for them. I don't write autobiography. I'm a quiet man who wrote stories that people believe. Because they believe, they want to touch me, but I can't stand to be touched. They would have been chipping little pieces off me before I knew it, as if I were a statue, and pretty soon there wouldn't have been anything left of me. That's why I chose to drop out."

We are loaded down with orange drinks, ice-cream bars, peanuts, and hot dogs. The hot dogs at Fenway Park are the smallest in the majors, scarcely bigger than cocktail franks. "Designed for midgets," is the way Jerry describes them. I have a sense of déjà as I look at Jerry and the scene around me, for it is exactly as I envisioned it so many months ago in the October sunshine.

"Haven't you been lonely? Aren't you lonely?" I ask. "*That* was one of the reaons I did what I did . . . I've been alone." Surely I can't be wrong on all counts.

Jerry looks crossly at me, having been engrossed in the antics of a base runner striding arrogantly toward second then lunging back in a colored blur and pouncing on the base as if it were a chicken trying to escape becoming Sunday dinner.

"It was just a question . . ."

"I don't know any answers," he almost shouts, and slams his hands down on his knees.

"Look, *I'm* not trying to bleed you," I say, spreading my hands to show my innocence. "I want to renew you. I want to do something nice for you. I don't think I'm doing this for myself. I drove all the way from Iowa. I made stops along the way. I had to have the right odors about me before I could approach you.

"I consider myself happy. I'm one of the few happy men in the United States. I own a farm. I grow corn. I have a wife who not only loves me but understands me; and a daughter who has red hair and green eyes like her mother.

"I love to stand in my yard at dawn, smell the dew, and watch the sun come up. I've built a magical baseball diamond at the edge of the cornfield, and I spend my evenings there watching . . ."

"Watching?" says Salinger, as if he has been called back from another world.

"You know—baseball games. I'd like to take you there. We could sit in the bleacher I built behind left field. The hot dogs are like they were in the old days, long and plump and fried on a grill with onions, and you smear the mustard on with a Popsicle stick, and there are jars of green relish. But Boston is the best I can do right now. Unless . . ."

"It's not possible," he says, a stern set to his jaw. "You've made it up. It's too preposterous to believe. You're probably not even from Iowa."

Suddenly I am the one who is shouting. People are turning to stare at us. "Watch the game," somebody says, but the voice is far off, like a vendor two sections away extolling beer.

"Open up your senses!" I shout. "I've come fifteen hundred miles to drag you to a baseball game. Stretch the skin back from your eyes! Take in *everything!* Look at Yaz there in the on-deck circle. Look at the angle he holds his bat. There isn't another player in the majors can duplicate that stance. Look at that left-field fence, half as high as the sky. The Green Monster. Think of the men who patrol that field, the shadow of that giant behind them, dwarfing them." It is ironic, I think, that the place chosen for me to bring Salinger has no left-field bleachers, while in my own park I have *only* a left-field bleacher.

"This one idea has run like a colored thread through all my thoughts for all these months. 'Ease his pain. Ease his pain.' I have repeated it ten thousand times, in my dreams, in my fantasies, to my wife, to my daughter, to myself as I drove a tractor over my black fields. Well, I'm doing what I can. Look! Look at the yellow neon running up the foul poles. You won't see that anywhere else in the majors. Watch the players, white against green like froth on waves of ocean. Look around at the fans, count their warts just as they count ours; look at them waddle and stuff their faces and cheer with their mouths full. We're not just ordinary people, we're a congregation. Baseball is a ceremony, a ritual, as surely as sacrificing a goat beneath a full moon is a ritual. The only difference is that most of us realize that it *is* a game. Good writing is a ritual, I've been told, so many words or so many pages a day. You must know that . . ."

The people around us have pretty well dismissed us as eccentrics of some kind, perhaps drunks. Except for an occasional "Shhhh," they have turned their attention back to the game. Someone doubles, tries to stretch it. I don't watch the play at third but keep my eyes on the pitcher as he scuttles over behind third base to back up the play.

"I've thought about you and baseball," I go on. "I haven't thought about much else for months. What does he have in common with a baseball player? I ask myself. He dispenses joy, I answer. He has fans—hundreds of thousands of them. Almost every North American boy has played baseball, so we know what has been accomplished, are able to appreciate it when we see someone like Freddy Patek or Rick Burleson scoot like a motorcycle after a grounder, capture it, and make the long impossible throw to first. I know I can't duplicate their feats, and I applaud them for being able to do what they do. I'd like to meet them, shake their hands, tell them how I appreciate their ability. With you it is the same. You've captured the experience of growing up in America, the same way Freddy Patek corners a ground ball. *The Catcher in the Rye* is the definitive novel of a young man's growing pains, of growing up in pain. Growing up is a ritual—more deadly than religion, more complicated than baseball, for there seem to be no rules. Everything is experienced for the first time. But baseball can soothe even those pains, for it is stable and permanent, steady as a grandfather dozing in a wicker chair on a verandah.

"Open up your senses, Jerry. Smell the life all around you, touch it, taste it, hear it. You may not get a chance for another twenty-five years."

Salinger takes a bite of his hot dog, cups his hand to catch a fleck of green relish as it falls.

"Watch the game," he says, a half-smile on his face.

And I think of where we are, banked around this little green acreage. The year might be 1900 or 1920 or 1979, for all the field itself has changed. Here the sense of urgency that governs most lives is pushed to one side like junk mail shoved to the back of a desk. We can take time out from the game almost as if we were participants, and run toward the umpire as a play ends, holding up our hands in the recognized signal for calling time.

The game has moved along, gentle and unhurried as a brook in a pasture. The Sox are chipping away at Jerry Koosman, the veteran Twins' pitcher. They only trail by two runs.

We stare at the feather-green field in silence. But after coming so far, I am not prepared to abandon what I am doing. I decide to keep on probing. I dig into my bag of tricks, my mind as rumpled and disorganized as a duffel bag after a two-week road trip.

"Why have you never written about baseball?" I ask.

Salinger turns his head slowly and his sad eyes rest on me, a forlorn question mark bobbing corklike in their dark centers. He does not answer, so I chatter on.

"I can't remember Holden Caulfield talking about base-ball—though the story takes place in December, doesn't it? He wouldn't have any reason to . . . The World Series had been over for a couple of months. You even had him end up in California, but at the time you wrote it the Dodgers and Giants were still in New York. Oh, sorry, I didn't mean to bring up painful memories." Salinger continues to stare as though memorizing me, perhaps so that I'll appear exactly as I am in one of his stories.

"Buddy never mentions that he's a fan. Never says that Les took the family to the Polo Grounds on Sunday afternoons. Sorry, I don't mean to keep bringing that up. Seymour, as a little boy, made that statement in 'Hapworth 16, 1924.' But that's all . . . I mean, I shouldn't be asking, it's your business, but if you love baseball so much, how can you keep from writing more about it?"

"I have no idea what you're talking about," says Salinger irritably.

"Oh, but you did, you did." I am bouncing up and down on my seat. "Allie had a left-fielder's mitt with poems written all over it in green ink. How could I forget that? Holden wrote an essay about it for Stradlater. *I* had a glove with green writing on it when I was a kid. I was a lousy baseball player, if you want to know the truth. Sorry. But there has to be something significant about it being a left-fielder's glove. Don't you see that? And, oh, Holden talking about a cabin in the woods and hiding his children, and the way you live—and I have a cabin, except it's a big cookie box of a house, with an iron fence in a square shape at the very top and a lightning rod in the middle like a spike on a soldier's helmet, and I have my own baseball stadium, but I've told you that story."

"Do you always babble like this?"

"I don't know how else to convince you."

"Of what? That I'm really Holden? I've told you about that. I am a very ordinary man. I want to be treated like a very ordinary man. I just want to stay home and be left alone."

"But don't you owe your public something? I remember reading a sociological study when I was in college, all about ex-cons who do stupid things so they'll be sent back to prison because they can't make it on the outside. No matter how much they protest, they really want to be on the inside. It's the only place that they can be big shots."

"Are you saying I can't make it on the outside? That's a lousy parallel. I stay to myself because I make it *too big* on the outside."

"Too big. Too little. It looks like a logical comparison to me. Think about it." Why am I baiting him, posing these questions he must hate?

"You don't understand," Salinger says, his voice rising. "Like everyone else, you take everything at face value. It baffles me how supposedly intelligent people can be so dumb. Once and for all, *I am not Holden Caulfield!* I am an illusionist who created Holden Caulfield from my imagination."

A number of people turn their heads. One or two point. But they soon lose interest.

"Look, on the drive in here do you remember passing a square white church with a big sign that said CHURCH OF THE EVANGELICAL COVENANT? We commented on the size of the sign, remember?"

"I remember."

"I know absolutely nothing about that church. But in half a day, I could do enough research to do an article that would make the members of that church weep with pride. And everyone who read the article would assume that I was a dyed-in-the-wool, lifelong, devout member of that church. And that is as it should be.

"Writing fiction is the same, only instead of culling facts from reference books at a library and putting some life and love into them, I create everything out of my imagination." He taps his forehead.

"You're too good at it," I say. "No one will ever believe you, including me."

"You should know about imagination," he says. *"You* imagine you own a baseball field where strange and wonderful things happen. *You* imagine you heard a voice that told you to come here. Suppose you wrote all that down and people believed you and started snooping around your farm looking for the real field . . ."

"But why quit publishing altogether?" I persist. "You should be entitled to as much privacy as you desire, but why deprive all the people who love you of hearing your voice on the page?"

"Because people take me seriously. It interferes with my privacy. Can't you see that? They swarm up the mountain like monkeys or commandos, peer in my windows, slip notes under the doors, carry off anything portable as souvenirs, lay in wait like you did. I've had to call the police many times. But I have to admit, none of them has ever done anything as crazy as you did. All this, and I haven't published a book in fifteen years. What would it be like if I suddenly released a new series of stories or a novel?"

I sigh. He is making good sense.

"You're out of soda," I say. "I'll go get you some more."

"Not so fast."

I am half standing. "Why?"

"You figure on sneaking away just when I'm getting in some good licks. What we've been talking about, whether you know it or not, is sharing."

"I suppose it is."

"You're putting all this pressure on me, but how much sharing are you willing to do? Be honest. If you've got what you say you have out there in Iowa, then it shouldn't be hidden. You're making thousands of people unhappy. It's like hoarding the secret of eternal life."

"But I would be willing to share. Only, who would set the criteria? Who would come?"

"Your board of directors would work that out. Picture it. At dawn every day there would be private planes leaving New York, Washington, D.C., Los Angeles, and Miami. Cedar Rapids Airport would have to build new runways to handle the traffic. Of course it would all be very secretive, the pilots wearing dark glasses, fake mustaches, military uniforms."

"Baseball uniforms."

"Too crass. The operation would have class, panache. No one who earns less than one hundred thousand dollars a year knows what *panache* means. Frosted windows on the planes. The passengers would be herded to buses, blindfolded like political prisoners, driven to the farm by a circuitous route. The blindfolds would be taken off only after they were seated in your bleachers."

"Perhaps I'll give a short welcoming speech before the game begins," I say, trying to get into the spirit of the moment; but the whole idea is quite frightening.

"You? Oh, you won't be there. You'll be lucky to be home once every three months for a day or so. You'll be off doing the talk-show circuit, and interviews with *Playboy* and *Cosmopolitan*. And the *Los Angeles Times* will pay Jim Murray's way to your stadium, and he'll write a column about being there, and there will be two hundred thousand new people beating at the doors of travel agencies all across North America. You'll be busy setting up trust funds, someone will ghost a book for you, and you'll have to hire a bodyguard for your wife and child. The governor of Iowa will declare you to be a national resource, and your park will be open every day of the year except Christmas, just like Cooperstown. In the winter, you'll sell hot apple juice and cinnamon, and postcards, and little plaster statues of Shoeless Joe Jackson with a halo over his head. You wouldn't mind all that, would you?"

"Of course I would," I squeak. "I'd never let things get out of hand like that."

"You wouldn't have any choice. Don't you ever watch the late movies? A scientist makes a wonderful discovery, but it just grows and grows until it destroys him."

"I've never looked at it quite that way. A bodyguard? Really?"

"Now, perhaps you see why I don't publish?"

"Touché."

It is the Boston seventh. We stand for two choruses of "Take Me Out to the Ballgame." The score is tied. Just as the fans settle back in their seats, relaxed and ready for action, it happens.

There is no voice this time. It is the scoreboard. Boston has one of the most sophisticated scoreboards in the majors. It flashes pictures of the batter and the pitcher and does instant replays of action that doesn't involve controversial calls by the umpires.

It flashes a line of statistical information, leaves it on the scoreboard for, I suppose, thirty seconds. Being no stranger to the *Baseball Encyclopedia*, I recognize the information as an entry, but not an entry I would ever have considered important. The words and figures glow like rare minerals giving off a halolike whitish vapor. I look around furtively to see if anyone else is aware of what is happening.

I eye Salinger carefully, but he is involved with his orange drink. The sign speaks only to me. What I know is that I have to perform another assignment after I am finished with Salinger.

"I'm too tired. I don't want to think about it," I say.

"What?" says Jerry. He looks first at me, than at the scoreboard, then back at me.

Salinger starts to speak, but the crowd roars as Craig Kusick, the Twins' lumbering first baseman, lunges to his right for a sharply hit baseball. He goes down slow as a toppling tree, the ball snapping into his glove as little puffs of dust rise in the air all along the length of his body. He scrambles to a sitting position and prepares to throw to first, but the rookie relief pitcher is watching in awe from his position in front of the mound. He has forgotten to cover first. Then out of the corner of my eye I catch sight of Rob Wilfong, the second baseman, who has sensed the problem in that way good ballplayers have of anticipating a play. He sprints toward first, screaming like a hawk making a long dive at a rabbit, in order to alert Kusick, who throws from his sitting position, throws to an empty bag. But the ball falls into Wilfong's glove as he sprints across the picture like a breeze, touching the corner of the bag, avoiding a collision with the galloping runner; their shadows collide but their bodies miss.

The play reaffirms what I already know—that baseball is the most perfect of games, solid, true, pure and precious as diamonds. If only life were so simple. I have often thought, *If only there was a framework to life, rules to live by*. But suddenly I see, like a silver flash of lightning on the horizon, a meaning I have never grasped before.

I feel as if I've escaped from my skin, as if I left a dry shell of myself back in Iowa. My skin is so new and pink it feels raw to my touch; it's as if I've peeled off a blister that covered my whole body. Within the baselines anything can happen. Tides can reverse; oceans can open. That's why they say, "The game is never over until the last man is out." Colors can change, lives can alter, anything is possible in this gentle, flawless, loving game.

I take a pen from the pocket of my jeans, and check my various pockets for paper, without success.

"Paper," I say to Salinger.

He shakes his head.

"What kind of a writer are you?"

"I'm a writer who was kidnapped on his way home from the grocery store and taken one hundred fifty miles to a baseball game."

"Oh." I use my program to write on, and copy down the information that still glows on the scoreboard in phosphorescent wonder.

MOONLIGHT GRAHAM   Graham, Archibald — 5'10½" 170 lbs.
                         B. Nov. 9, 1879, Fayetteville, N.C.;
                         D. Aug. 25, 1965, Chisholm, Minn.

	G	AB	H	2B	3B	HR	R	RBI	BB	SB	BA	SA	G by POS
1905 NY N	1	0	0	0	0	0	0	0	0	0	–	–	OF-1

As I finish copying the information onto the available white
space on the program, the public-address announcer speaks to
me. "Go the distance," he says.

Why? Why me? I almost scream, but don't. I glance sur-
reptitiously around me, to see if anyone else is aware, but the
game moves on, the crowd drones lazily, and Jim Rice swings
his bat in the on-deck circle.

"I'll get you that drink," I say to Salinger. He has just
crushed his wax cup under his shoe. "Is there anything else
you want?" He is involved in the game, his face relaxed and
more youthful looking. If he hears me, he doesn't let on.

As I climb the steps two at a time up the narrow aisle to
the concession stands, there is a solid crack of the bat loud as
a gunshot. I turn my head and, looking over my shoulder, see
Jim Rice cross first base. I have taken perhaps three full steps
with my gaze averted. As I once more face upward, I walk
directly into a sharp steel girder that stands like a galvanized
sword in the middle of the aisle.

Although I am stunned, I try to pretend that nothing unusual
has happened, in that way people behave after they've tripped
on a curb or stepped into an unseen hollow. I hold my hand
to the left side of my forehead and climb on for three or four
more steps before I feel my stomach drop slowly and my arms
become hundred-pound weights dragging me into a sitting position.

"Are you all right?" a man says to me.

He looks as if he's staring at me from under sunlit water.

I try to answer, but my mouth won't open. I take my left
hand away from my forehead and find it dripping scarlet, warm
and sticky as honey. I wipe it on my shirt front.

By this time there are two ushers bending over me.

"We'll take you to the first-aid room," one of them says, and takes hold of my elbow. My legs are soft as butter in sunshine.

They finally manage to half-drag me to the top of the stairs.

"Is he drunk?" I hear a voice from the bottom of the bucket say.

I pull my ticket stub from my shirt pocket with a bloody hand. Taking a deep breath I say, "The man in the goosedown vest is with me. Tell him to bring my program." Then I slip down into a world soft as the lining of Salinger's jacket.

Salinger insists on driving back. He holds my arm solicitously as we make our way slowly from the park to my car. I have four stitches in my left eyebrow and my shirt looks as if it's been worn by the loser in a dandy barroom brawl.

"Who won the game?" I ask.

"I don't know. It was long over by the time you came around. For being such a baseball fan, you pick strange times to take naps. The game was tied when the usher came and got me."

"You didn't have to stay, you know."

"How the hell was I going to get back home? I can just see myself sitting all night in the bus depot with the winos and shopping-bag ladies, waiting for a bus to Windsor, Vermont."

My head throbs dully.

The headlights make two grapefruit-colored tunnels on the road, and dark shrouds of trees rush by on either side. I lean my head against the window and look up, noticing a few lamb-like clouds in a chrome-blue sky. The moon is full.

"I'm still not entirely clear why you chose me," Salinger says. "How did you interpret the cryptic message you received to mean me? Was it just because a voice told you to?"

"Yes. And I saw you and me at a baseball game—a vision."

He is silent for a mile or so.

"But why did you obey it? You don't seem like the type who always does what he's told. Just from spending this day with you, I can tell you have a healthy contempt for authority, big business, academia, religion—all the forces that control our lives. You have all the prerequisites for being a rebel, yet you hop to when an unknown voice delivers an ambiguous message."

"There were a lot of reasons. Baseball, for one. As you can tell, I love the game. And I admired you as an author and a person. I've always wanted to follow Holden's dictum in *The Catcher in the Rye* and pick up the telephone and call you . . ."

"Which is why I've had an unlisted number for twenty-five years."

"But it was the interview that decided it. Don't you remember?" I look at him, genuinely surprised. Perhaps he is not as astute as I imagined.

"Remember what? What interview?"

"I didn't see it in whatever magazine it was in originally, but the newspapers picked it up. It ran in the *Des Moines Register;* even the *Iowa City Press-Citizen* picked it up."

Salinger continues to eye me suspiciously, watching me instead of the road as we round a gentle curve. So I babble on.

"The interview was mainly about baseball. Don't you remember talking about baseball? The interviewer asked you a question about what you would have liked to be if you hadn't been a writer. 'When I was a kid,' you replied, 'I wanted more than anything else in the world to play baseball at the Polo Grounds.' Over the years I've spent an inordinate amount of time thinking about that dream of yours, and about you being locked away like a hermit on top of a hill in New Hampshire. 'I saw myself grow too old for the dream,' you went on. 'Saw the Giants moved across a continent to San Francisco, and finally they tore down the Polo Grounds in 1964!' I cried when I read that interview, if you want to know the truth. I couldn't help myself. I admit I'm overly sentimental about baseball, but it appeared that you were too. I read that passage thousands of times, smiling sadly at the thought that you must love the game as much as I do. That's why I leaped at the chance to come here and take you to a baseball game—even if I might have ended up in jail because of it. Now how can you say you don't remember?"

Salinger is now looking at me with genuine concern.

"I don't know how to tell you this. Since you claim to know so much about me, I thought you'd know. I almost never give interviews. That's not to say that people don't try. I have some persistent lunatics removed from my driveway, and they babble to the police while they're being driven away; they get two words from a grocery clerk or a gas-station attendant and then write and publish an exclusive interview. I always know about it, because a thousand or so people send me copies. Did you send me one from your Iowa City Press-whatever?"

"Yes," I mumble.

"For some reason, people out there think I'll wither away and die if I don't see every word that's written about me, no matter how bizarre. Do you know I'm supposed to have six wives and twenty-one children, and that I service my wives only for the purpose of procreation?"

"Yes," I whisper again.

"I stopped reading the reports years ago. I don't even want to imagine what they're saying about me now. But I assure you, I *never* gave an interview about baseball. Those are very touching words you quoted. The writer must have had a better-than-average imagination."

"Then you don't..." I can feel my insides slipping away as if they are on a greased slide.

"Baseball is not a passion in my life. I've attended a few games, years ago. I occasionally watch one on TV. I read the papers, glance at the standings."

"I'm really sorry," I say. Salinger tenses a little. "I've caused you a lot of trouble for nothing." He shakes his head, waves a long white-fingered hand in a conciliatory gesture. "It wasn't just the baseball game. I wanted it to be a metaphor for something else: perhaps trust, or freedom, or ritual, or faithfulness, or joy, or any of the other things that baseball can symbolize. I only wanted to make you happy..." I feel myself choking up as I say it.

"You don't know how those words affected me," I go on. "It was the line 'They tore down the Polo Grounds in 1964' that got me. Those words flew off the printed page, hovered in the air, assumed the shape of a gray bird, and landed on my shoulder. I reached up and picked off the bird and held it in my hand, tiny and pulsing, pressed it hard against my chest, and it disappeared like mist. If I were to open my shirt, and you looked closely, you could see its faint silver outline on my skin."

* * *

The rest of the trip back is thick with silence. We are both exhausted. I slump dozing, defeated, as Salinger drives with two hands on the wheel. We stop for gas and coffee. Salinger is still reluctant to enter the café, although I am the one people will look at. I reassure him and am relieved to be right. No one even glances at him. Salinger dips into his jeans and pays for the coffee.

His mountain is blue with moonlight as we arrive at the foot of the driveway. The high windows of Salinger's home glow like mirrored sunglasses in the cloudless night.

"I wish I had your passion for baseball," Salinger says. "However misdirected it may be, it is still a passion. If I had my life to live over again, I'd take more chances. I'd want more passion in my life. Less fear and more passion, more risk. Even if you fail, you've still taken a risk."

"I could come back again," I say. "It wouldn't have to be baseball. A movie. A concert. I wouldn't mind."

"No. You keep on listening to your voices, even if they're wrong. Keep on doing what it is you do. Another time here, there would be no thrill in it for you. Keep on taking risks."

He opens the driver's door and light floods the interior.

"I enjoyed the baseball game. I'll read the statistics with a little more interest from now on."

His speech sounds like a spoken bread-and-butter note. He bends down and looks closely at the car registration, which is strapped to the steering column in a tiny leather-and-plastic holder.

"Just checking," he says. "I have a naturally suspicious nature, you know. Ray Kinsella, you puzzle me very much," he adds, shaking his head.

"No one is more puzzled than I am," I say.

"Is this some kind of penance you're doing?"

"I've never thought of it that way, but perhaps it is. Oh, how I wish you could see my baseball park. I've built it all with my own hands. I'm not a carpenter. I'm not even competent when it comes to mechanical things."

I feel desperate for someone else to see my creation. My mother. I would like to show it to her. Let her see what I have brought to life. Have her to be there when my catcher gets to play with the White Sox, as I know he will. What I've brought to life is much, much more than one tiny bird.

"There is a magic about it," I say. "You have to *be* there to feel the magic."

"What is this magic you keep talking about?"

"It's the place and the time. The right place and right time. Iowa is the right place, and the time is right, too—a time when all the cosmic tumblers have clicked into place and the universe opens up for a few seconds, or hours, and shows you what *is* possible."

"And what do you see? What do you feel?"

"Your mind stops, hangs suspended like a glowing Chinese lantern, and you feel a sensation of wonder, of awe, a tingling, a shortness of breath..."

"And then?"

"And then you not only see, but hear, and smell, and taste, and touch whatever is closest to your heart's desire. Your secret dreams that grow over the years like apple seeds sown in your belly, grow up through you in leafy wonder and finally sprout through your skin, gentle and soft and wondrous, and they breathe and have a life of their own..."

"You've done this?"

"A time or two."

"Is it always the same?"

"It is and it isn't. The controlling fantasy is the same: the baseball stadium, the Chicago White Sox, Shoeless Joe Jackson. But the experiences are different. Baseball games are like snowflakes and fingerprints; no two are ever the same."

He has moved slowly away; reluctantly, it seems to me. He stops at the rear of his own vehicle and makes the motion of pitching an imaginary baseball to me, where I stand outside the passenger door of my Datsun.

I have my hand raised in a gesture of farewell when he says softly, "New York Giants, 1905, one game, one inning."

"You know!" I accuse him.

"No. What would I know?"

"About the scouting trip. Somehow you know. That's why you're hedging about saying goodbye. When did it happen? At the game? In the car? When you were walking down to the first-aid room?"

"I have no idea . . ."

"Moonlight Graham!" I say. "Chisholm, Minnesota. Did you see one line out of the Player Register of the *Baseball Encyclopedia* flashed on the scoreboard tonight?"

Salinger is shaking his head. By the marveling look on his face, I can tell that he did.

"We were the only ones who saw it. You must know that. It was in the seventh inning, just after Carlton Fisk struck out."

"It was . . ."

"Did you hear the voice, too?"

Salinger glances at me, then looks away.

"It's all right to admit it. It was my own private ballpark announcer. It's all right. He told me to find you . . ."

Salinger looks as if he might be facing a TV camera. He speaks slowly and clearly; only his eyes blinking rapidly betray his feelings.

"Highly disturbed persons often feel that they are receiving direct and personal messages from TV, radios, billboards, and road signs . . ." His voice runs down like a record player after it has been unplugged. A smile spreads over his leathery face; he advances a step toward me.

"You know!" I shout.

"Something," says Salinger quickly.

"What thing?"

"That we're going to Minnesota."

"How do you know?"

Salinger stares around at the dark, listening trees; somewhere deep in the foliage something moves—a brief swishing of leaves.

"The announcer," he says quietly. "Go the distance."

"I knew it," I crow triumphantly. "You heard him too."

"I want you to tell me everything you know about this. Tell me the story of Shoeless Joe Jackson again. I want to hear it again and listen more closely; and about how and why you came to get me."

"While we travel, I'll tell you all I know." My head seems to have stopped aching. "Do you want to get a change of clothes? Some books? Annie and I read to each other while we travel. Some paper? Your typewriter?"

"No." And it is as though I have sneezed on him, or breathed in his face, and he has caught some of my energy. "I'm afraid that if I walk up that driveway all this madness will disappear."

"Okay, let's roll," I say.

He hesitates for a few seconds. His feet stutter toward his jeep. "I'll leave a note." A pause. "No, I won't." And he moves to the Datsun.

"On the way I'll tell you a story."

"About Moonlight Graham?"

"What I know about him, and Shoeless Joe Jackson, and my father, and the kidnapping of Jerome David Salinger."

We are happy as children with bats over shoulders, gloves dangling, on their way to a sandlot. I release the brake and let the car roll down the moon-dappled hill.

III

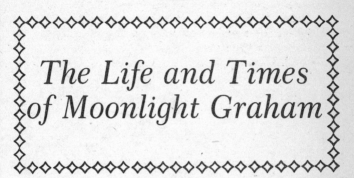

The Life and Times of Moonlight Graham

Ten miles later, at the side of the road, the dome light of my Datsun bathing us in a pale yellow glow, we huddle over the road map like spies.

"We're going to Chisholm, Minnesota," I say. "Is that agreed?"

"Something has dialed us to the same frequency," says Jerry, looking at me, his brows furrowed, shaking his head as if I have just pulled a string of Christmas-tree lights out of my mouth. Rather than me talking, as I have promised, Jerry for these past ten miles has been marveling that when he heard the ballpark announcer intone "Go the distance," he knew with incontestable certainty that he was to travel to Chisholm, Minnesota, the place where Moonlight Graham died.

"Now you know how I felt when the voice said 'Ease his pain,'" I tell him. "I knew it was you I was to contact. It was as certain as a brand burned into my arm."

"But there's more," says Jerry.

"More?"

"'Fulfill the dream.' Did you hear that?"

"No. Who said it?"

"The announcer."

"Not to me."

"No. To me."

"Oh." I actually feel a tiny twinge of jealousy, green as a worm, wiggling deep in my center.

"What does it mean?" says Jerry. "This fellow Graham is dead, isn't he?"

"He is." I drag out the program and check the information I scribbled down. "August 25, 1965, Chisholm, Minnesota." I want to go on and say, "You haven't listened *that* carefully. Shoeless Joe Jackson had been dead longer than that." But I don't say anything, for I really am a little jealous that the wonder I am a party to has been sprinkled over Salinger's gray head. Let him find out for himself. I run my hand down and touch my stomach area; the muscles are taut as cowhide stretched over a baseball.

"Then where do we start?" says Salinger, his voice so sincere that my jealousy moves several inches in the direction of guilt.

"You're the writer. I'm just a corn farmer," I say, and try to smile enigmatically like Karin's square-jawed orange cat when he stands by my chair and taps my leg with his heavy paw, tentatively, like a mother testing bath water.

"Do *you* know who Moonlight Graham is?" Jerry asks.

"Only what you know—a baseball player who was patted on the head by a dream. A man who played one inning of baseball for the New York Giants during the 1905 season. He never came to bat. He was just a substitute fielder for one inning."

"How can he be important?"

"That's what we have to find out. It's kind of exciting, isn't it?"

"But how do we find out?"

"Well, we could be in Cooperstown, at the Baseball Hall of Fame, in just a few hours. That might be a good place to start."

"But one inning..."

"They have records there on everyone who ever played in the majors, and cabinets full of minor-league records. Do we keep on driving? Or, we can find a place to stay, catch a few hours' sleep. I have a state-by-state listing of Motel 6's in the glove compartment; they're inexpensive and clean . . ."

"I'd like to keep going," says Jerry.

"I know how you feel. If I were walking, I'd be a foot off the ground. It's like just falling in love—you want the sensations to last forever. You don't want to go to sleep because you know that no matter how good you feel, in the morning it won't be as good as it is right now."

Salinger nods. "I'm very good at reading maps," he says. "Something I learned in the army." He hefts my five-year-old *Rand McNally Road Atlas,* dog-eared and covered with ice-cream stains. From under his goose-down vest he produces a square-tipped yellow marker.

"I'll act as navigator," he says. "That is, if you don't have any objections."

"Start by finding Chisholm, Minnesota," I suggest. He flaps pages, flutters indexes, lowers his face until his ample nose almost touches the map.

"Here. Way up here. Beyond Duluth, not that far from Canada. Desolate country. He must have been a logger or a miner."

"In the same general area as International Falls," I say. "The coldest part of the U.S.A. Why would a man from Fayetteville, North Carolina, go way up there and stay?"

"He might not have stayed. Maybe he just died there. Maybe a son or daughter took him up there to live his last days. He was eighty-five when he died. I bet he lived all his life in the South."

"It *is* kind of exciting, isn't it?" And we grin at each other like kids clutching shiny quarters—his inscribed "Fulfill the dream," mine engraved "Go the distance"—heading for the ice-cream store. "Point me toward Cooperstown," I say, "and as we drive, I'll get around to telling you that story I promised."

I do tell the story, and some of it I even repeat, as the adrenalin continues to flow. Salinger, though I think he is listening, seems preoccupied. He draws yellow lines on the map, and I follow them.

My eyebrow throbs. I decide to bait Jerry.

"You never talk about writing," I say. "You've never brought up the subject on your own, not even once."

"And what do you do?" counters Jerry. "I don't hear you babbling on about the joys of barn cleaning, or pouring anhydrous ammonia on your stubble, or whatever else it is you do."

"That's different. It was Annie who got me to rent the farm. It was Annie who got me to buy it. Not that I don't like it. But I don't know enough about it to talk about it all the time. I talk about baseball, though, and about my stadium. How many times have I told you about my stadium?"

"Don't ask," says Salinger. "You're worse than a kid wanting to show off a new toy."

"That's what I mean. You and I, we do something worth talking about, but I talk and you don't. I mean, *everybody* talks about what they do. Hell, have you ever had a plumber or a TV repairman at your house? They yap on and on about the jobs they've done—the sinks they've unplugged, the vertical-hold buttons they've replaced. My father owned a farm, too, but he didn't know or care much about it. He was a plastering contractor, and his every conversation was dotted with words like scratch coat, sand finish, scaffolds, hawk and trowel, cement, lime, and stone chips. Even on the farm he used to talk plastering in his sleep. 'Move those scaffolds,' or 'More mud, dammit!' he'd holler out while he was dozing on the sofa on a Sunday afternoon.

"I could talk a good game of life insurance when I was in the business. Why, I sweat endowments, and I could work Twenty-Pay-Life into any conversation, even one about baseball. I hated the job, but I still talked about it. Now if I were like you and did something I really loved..."

"Writing is different," says Jerry. "Ordinary people don't understand. Even other writers don't understand."

"But that doesn't hold up. That doesn't stop other people. Mechanics talk about widgets and glodrobs and units of compression, and get off on the looks of incomprehension they get in return."

"Writing *is* different," Salinger insists. "Other people get into occupations by accident or design; but writers are born. We have to write. I have to write. I could work at selling motels, or slopping hogs, for fifty years, but if someone asked my occupation, I'd say writer, even if I'd never sold a word. Writers *write*. Other people *talk*."

"How do you feel about your books being banned? At least *Catcher?*"

"Are they still doing that?"

"You mean you don't care?"

"I stopped caring years ago. Someone once said, 'Any publicity is good publicity,' and I guess I believe it."

"They do still ban *Catcher*, here in the United States and in Canada too. There were a couple of cases recently that made the papers. One in Michigan and one just across the border in Ontario."

"I think it's quite charming," Salinger says, his eyes twinkling. "In these days when anything goes in literature, movies, and even TV, to think there are some places so isolated, so backward, so ill-informed as to what's going on in the world that they can still get all hot and bothered about something as innocent as *Catcher*. I mean, if there was ever a crusader against sin, it was Holden Caulfield."

"It doesn't make you angry then?"

"Oh, I wasn't pleased years ago, but now it's like browsing in a cool antique store full of Mason jars, big iron stoves, and wooden churns. Maybe banning or burning my books could become an annual event in these little uptight communities, like re-creating the first flight at Kitty Hawk."

Stopping only for fuel and coffee, we navigate a series of back roads that meander along lakes shaded by evergreens, and these eventually lead us into Cooperstown in midafternoon.

At the ticket office I say, "I'm Ray Kinsella. We're doing some research on an old-time ballplayer named Archibald Graham."

The cashier is not interested in anything but our money. "The library's around back," she intones, as if she has said it a hundred times today, and she probably has. But I am still too manic to be affected by her indifference.

"This is J. D. Salinger," I say, pointing to Jerry as if he were a trophy I was delivering.

"Yeah?" says the clerk, her face coming alive. "Really?" She looks at both of us for the first time, smiling.

"It's a pleasure to meet you." She extends her hand to Jerry. "You used to work for Kennedy, right?"

"Indeed I did," says Jerry, his eyes flashing across mine, mischief rearranging the kindly lines of his face. To keep from laughing, he turns away.

"Did I say something wrong?" says the cashier.

"He was very fond of Jack," I reply.

We walk through the museum and around to the library, which has high ceilings, cold walls, and soft carpets.

It is a ghostly feeling, standing chest-deep in history here at the Baseball Hall of Fame. We tour the museum until our ankles swell. Salinger has never been here before. I have. I guide him back over the years as if he were a time traveler. We are both red-eyed and unkempt. My eyebrow is swollen and unsightly, the skin around it saw-blade blue.

Among the larger relics present is a turnstile from the Polo Grounds in New York—one of the same ones that counted the 2000 fans who watched Moonlight Graham's brief appearance that June day in 1905. It is with reverence that I touch its pocked silver surface, as if I were in a basilica reaching out tentatively to finger the face of a holy statue.

We ask to see the historian and are ushered up a long curving flight of stairs. Clifford Kachline appears and greets us warmly. He is a slight, soft man, pale as newspaper, but there is an aura of warmth about him and he puts us instantly at ease.

There are rows and rows of dun-colored filing cabinets, and Mr. Kachline digs into the *G*'s and extracts a single sheet of paper from the file of Archibald Wright Graham. The form was completed in 1960 in an old man's heavy handwriting. From it we learn that Graham was married September 29, 1915, to Alicia Madden, that he attended the University of Maryland and Johns Hopkins University, Baltimore. After the question "If you had it to do over, would you play professional baseball?" is scrawled an emphatic *yes*. His length of residence in Chisholm, Minnesota, is listed as fifty years. But most interesting of all, on the bottom line the form is signed, *Dr.* A. W. Graham.

While we study the form like archeologists gaping at a newly exhumed mummy, Kachline goes from filing cabinet to filing cabinet, interweaving cross-references as if following a trail of dropped corn kernels. He waves a piece of paper over his head as he disappears around a corner; a copier whirs; he returns and hands to me, tenderly as a nurse passing a new child to its mother, the box score of Moonlight Graham's only major-league game:

NEW YORK WON EASILY

New York, N.Y., June 29—New York
scored another easy victory
over Brooklyn to-day.
Attendance: 2,000. Time: 1:55.

BROOKLYN	AB	H	PO	A	E	NEW YORK	AB	H	PO	A	E
Dobbs, cf	4	1	0	0	0	Browne, rf	3	1	0	0	0
Hall, lf	4	0	1	0	1	Graham, rf	0	0	0	0	0
Lumley, rf	4	1	3	0	0	Donlin, cf	4	2	1	0	0
Batch, 3b	4	0	1	2	0	McGann, 1b	3	2	3	1	0
Malay, 2b	4	1	6	2	0	Strang, 1b	2	0	3	0	0
Babb, ss	0	0	3	5	0	Mertes, lf	3	0	2	0	0
Mitchell, 1b	4	1	9	0	0	Dahlen, ss	4	3	1	1	0
Ritter, c	3	0	4	4	0	Devlin, 3b	3	0	1	0	0
Eason, p	1	0	0	0	1	Gilbert, 2b	4	2	2	3	0
Doescher, p	2	0	0	0	0	Bowe'an, c	3	1	7	0	0
Bergen*	1	0	0	0	0	Clarke, c	2	1	6	0	0
						Matt'son, p	3	1	1	1	0
TOTALS	31	4	27	13	2	Elliott, p	2	0	0	0	0
						TOTALS	36	13	27	6	0

Score: INNING	1	2	3	4	5	6	7	8	9		
Brooklyn	0	0	0	0	0	1	0	0	0	–	1
New York	0	2	6	0	0	3	0	0	x	–	11

And there are so many strange and wonderful bits of information—things no one but baseball fanatics would care about, like Lena Blackburne's Mud. It is a special mud trucked all the way from New England, from Lena Blackburne's farm, and used to rub up new baseballs before they are put into play. And the fact that the Louisville Slugger bat is named for an 1880s Louisville baseball star named Pete Browning. And that bats, which were originally made from hickory, are now made from mountain ash.

There is even a poem in the Hall of Fame, in honor of the legendary Chicago Cubs' double-play combination of Joe Tinker, Johnny Evers, and Frank Chance:

> These are the saddest of possible words
> Tinker to Evers to Chance
> Trio of bearcubs and fleeter than birds
> Tinker to Evers to Chance
> Making a Giant hit into a double
> Words that are weighty with nothing but trouble
> Tinker to Evers to Chance.

We find our way to I-90 and begin the long haul across Ohio, Indiana, and Illinois. We promise each other sleep, but it is as though we are driven. Each time we approach an exit, we decide we can make it one more. Salinger puts the passenger seat back and dozes fitfully for a few moments, sweat forming on his brow, a large white hand continually brushing imaginary objects from his face. We change drivers. My ankles are swollen. I prop my stockinged feet on the dash and try to sleep, but as soon as I relax, my feet slide with a thud against the steering column and into Salinger's lap.

We push on and on until the adrenalin finally seeps out of us like sawdust oozing from a stuffed toy.

Salinger is no longer shy about being recognized. He uses a credit card at a mom-and-pop motel within sight of the Indiana Turnpike, the self-styled Mainstreet of America.

"I'm J. D. Salinger," he says to the clerk. She is about sixty-five with hair white as spun sugar, piled up in a beehive hairdo that has been out of style for twenty years.

She looks at him steadily. She has orange eyes like a mother hen.

"Not the guy who used to write or something?"

"The same."

"Oh." She is busy making out the credit-card slip. The silence lengthens.

"How soon they forget," I say in a stage whisper.

"I thought you was dead, maybe," she says, pushing the slip at Salinger for a signature.

Our plan is to sleep until we are rested, but for me it is as if I have small bells attached to my body. In five hours we are both awake, wide-eyed as kids on Christmas morning.

I phone Annie and waken her—can scarcely contain my joy.

"I'm with J. D. Salinger," I sing. "We're going to Minnesota, way up past Duluth."

"To hunt?" says Annie.

"Sort of," I reply.

"See, it wasn't so hard, was it?" says Annie. "I bet he was just waiting for you to come and take him to that baseball game."

"I love you," I say.

"Me too," she replies, making a kissing sound into the phone.

"I'll be just a few days more."

"I know you'll be back as soon as you can, love. Oh, Mark's been around again. He insists we should sell."

"We can't."

"I know."

"Hug Karin for me."

"Don't take any wooden baseballs."

I keep dreaming of Eddie Scissons, the oldest living Chicago Cub. I can't imagine why, unless it has to do with his secret, which only I seem to know. Last night in the cool darkness of that old, linoleum-floored motel that smelled of mildew and rose-flavored room freshener, Eddie Scissons slid into my dreams as gently as if he were stealing second base in slow motion.

It has been five years since I met him. A chance meeting that resulted in our buying his farm. I have encountered little ghosts of Eddie Scissons these past five years: a hubcap in the grass that must have belonged to a vehicle of his, a can of Zambuck Ointment found on a shelf high above a door in the machine shed—ointment Eddie must have rubbed on aching joints when he came in from the fields.

I still drop in on him occasionally at the Bishop Cridge Friendship Center on Gilbert Street in Iowa City, where he spends his afternoons, and we talk baseball, or rather Eddie talks and I listen. Cridge was the Episcopal Bishop of Iowa at one time. He opened his large home as a center for senior citizens long before they were called senior citizens. Thaddeus Cridge occupied the upstairs of the house until his death. The story goes that after he died, they carted out over 2000 pounds of pornographic magazines and books, as well as a number of albums full of compromising photographs of Cridge and neighborhood children. After the furor died down, however, no one had the energy to change the name of the center, and it still stands.

Eddie's presence bothers me, for he has no place in my dreams, my fantasies, or my life. He's a Chicago Cub, and I collect White Sox. Yet his story has perched like a crow in the back of my brain ever since I first heard it. I have visited Eddie less often in the years since I first heard my voice; I guess I'm afraid I'll share the story with him, and I fear that telling him will somehow destroy the magic. I kept the magic sealed inside for a long time, as if I were airtight, like a radio tube or a Mason jar. It was with relief that I shared it with Jerry, and shared and shared. Somehow I keep retelling my tale, as if it is a song I'm humming under my breath. Still, Eddie is often the last thing I think of at night, his hair white as whipped cream, his back straight, his cheeks the luscious pink of ripening strawberries. Across the table from me, he often resembles some wise old doctor, or senator, or scholar, plucked from a yellowed photograph.

But as I cuddle down on my stomach, prepared to dream, my left hand lonely, missing the touch of Annie's thigh, Eddie Scissons's words peck at the warm honey of my sleep. Why, I wonder, of all the people in Iowa City, Iowa, did he decide to stop me on the street?

Why, after he had asked the time and I had responded, did he add, his blue eyes glistening in the March sunlight, "I used to play for the Chicago Cubs, you know?"

"No, I didn't know," I said, but I was thrilled at the idea of talking with an ex-major-leaguer.

"I'm not in bad shape for eighty-seven," he said, his wide-set eyes looking me up and down as if daring me to contradict him. He carried a white cane, and his mittened hand only partially covered the brass serpent's head that served as a handle.

What I had first seen was a tall old man in a full-length overcoat the color of dirty snow, standing on a street corner, his feet planted on the curb as if he were standing solidly on second base eyeing the outfield after a standup double. His cane was pointed straight ahead, waist high, as one might hold a fencing foil or a baseball bat. It was an earachy day, and an evil little wind chewed along the icy sidewalks.

Suddenly, with a fluid motion more agile than I had expected, he turned toward me, his cane stopping just short of the middle button of my parka. He asked the time in a pleasant, resonant voice that was younger than he. As I looked at his bird-bright eyes, I remember thinking, even before he spoke of baseball, "Wide-set, great peripheral vision."

Then he mentioned his age and the Chicago Cubs. The traffic light in his direction turned to "Walk," but he made no move to leave.

"Where are you from?" he asked.

"Montana," I replied. "I was born there, but I live here now."

"I used to play ball in Montana. Do you know Bozeman?" His face, pink as a child's, was slowly and cautiously forming a smile.

"I'm from Deer Lodge," I said. "My mother lives in Great Falls."

"I played in Helena, too, and against Great Falls and Butte. Tough teams from those mining towns—you filed your spikes before you went out on the field."

"When did you play for the Cubs?" I asked, the wheels of my brain turning, trying to get traction. When did Tinker-to-Evers-to-Chance play? Would he have known them? I stared down at his cane bobbing an inch from my navel as if looking for a place to plug in. If he was eighty-seven as he said, then he must surely be the oldest living Chicago Cub. The very idea of finding this living piece of history excited me, and I was about to say, "My dad played semipro ball," when he answered my questions both asked and unasked by saying, "Oh, that was a long time ago. I played on the same team as Three Finger Brown and Tinker-to-Evers-to-Chance. You ever heard of them?"

Indeed I had, for my father had extolled their virtues just as a pitchman might sing the praises of a patent medicine or an unusual sideshow.

But Eddie Scissons didn't stop for me to say I had.

"Oh, I wasn't a regular or anything," he went on, smiling, showing he still had most of his own teeth. One old foot in its overshoe was pawing rhythmically at the sidewalk ice as he spoke. "Just sat in the bullpen and spit tobacco juice at the horseflies that used to buzz around us—take a bite out of you like a small dog, then buzzards would. Once in a while I'd get to play in the late innings of the second game of a double-header, after all the other players were used up." He chuckled briefly, wagging the cane up and down dangerously close to my body.

"I was a relief pitcher before there were relief pitchers, if you follow me. Starters almost always pitched the whole game in those days—thought it was a sign of weakness if they didn't. Ball wasn't made out of India rubber like now. I was fifty years ahead of my time, yes sirree." He chuckled again, a friendly grandfatherly sound. He was wearing a brown farmer's cap with the earflaps pulled down. The laces, which were supposed to be tied under his chin, hung loose, vibrating in the wind.

"What's your name?" I asked, putting a hand over one of my ears to ease the bite of the wind. I tried to remember the names of some ancient Chicago Cub pitchers, but the only one I could recall was George Washington (Zip) Zabel, who ended his three-year Cub career with a 14-14 record.

"Eddie Scissons," he replied, then abruptly changed the subject. "I spend my days, since the wife passed away, over at the Friendship Center. They feed me lunch and I play cards, and sometimes bingo. I'm gonna catch the bus home, that's why I asked you the time. I used to farm out east of town, until my daughters insisted we had to move to town; my wife died the very next year. Did you know the life expectancy of a retired farmer is only two years? Say, you wouldn't want to rent a farm, would you?"

Late that night I posed the question to Annie, and a week later, with a sense of relief, like waking from a nightmare, I quit my job selling life insurance and we moved into the big white biscuit box that had once housed the oldest living Chicago Cub.

I racked my brain, but the name Eddie Scissons meant nothing to me. My father would have remembered him. When he lived in Chicago after the First World War, he sometimes traveled across town on a Sunday afternoon and sat sweating in his shirt sleeves, watching the Cubs perform in Wrigley Field.

It is fortunate that Jerry has a sense of humor, for he has had more than his share of difficulties. At first he was paranoid about being recognized and having people demand autographs. But after traveling these past few days, he would like to find someone who recognizes him.

"I'm J. D. Salinger," he says to a middle-aged, suede-faced gas jockey near Cleveland.

"The writer," I prompt.

"Oh yeah, for real, eh? I'm a great fan of yours." He reaches out and pumps Jerry's hand, using both of his oil-soaked paws to enclose Salinger's long, pale one.

"Yes, sir, you are some writer. Did you really go right into the prison there and watch them hang Perry Smith and that friend of his?"

Salinger shrinks back.

"You've mistaken my friend for Truman Capote," I say. The attendant's eyes are dark and deep-set and not quick to comprehend. "Truman Capote wrote *In Cold Blood*, the book about Perry Smith."

"That so? Well, what did you say your name was? I recognized you as one of them fellows who wrote."

"I'm just someone who used to be a writer," says Jerry, in his best theatrical tone, as he climbs back into the car, wiping the grease from his hands onto the thighs of his jeans.

* * *

"Way up there," is the way people in Minneapolis and St. Paul refer to the Iron Range. I have a close friend from college who comes from Duluth, the industrial center nearest to Chisholm. Even he says "up there" when talking about the Iron Range.

North of Duluth the landscape grows harsher, the trees shorter and more gnarled, the grass tougher and wirier. We pass Virginia, Minnesota, where all about the land is scarred. From above, the earth there would look as if it were criss-crossed with sutures. Above the town, the mines sit like sand-colored bunkers in the cliffs. From a distance they are stern and silent, like Greek ruins.

As we pass the town of Buhl and near Chisholm, the land reminds me of a pasture rooted and rerooted by giant hogs. It has been split and gutted; greenery has grown back, but at weird and unnatural angles.

Then as we swing down into the town, the highway divides, and we cross a beautiful and tranquil lake, so smooth and shiny it might be a scene painted on a glass plate. A sign reads WELCOME TO CHISHOLM, and underneath that states that calendar parking is in effect, taking several lines of fine print to establish which side of the street one may park on, and how often. It rather spoils the welcome, and makes it clear that even in this wild and breathtaking land, bureaucracy is alive and well.

There is a charming old hotel with a dark, beery tavern on the ground floor, but they are reluctant to rent us a room; assure us we would not be comfortable there. So we settle at the Ron-Son Motel, one of two in Chisholm: clean, comfortable, cable TV, air conditioner, complete, too, with a religious tract on the nightstand, signed in pen by "Your Maid, Ron-Son Motel."

Above the town a barrel-shaped water tower stands like a gopher raised on its hind legs. In black print on the silver walls is written, HOME OF THE MINNESOTA MINING MUSEUM.

Jerry attracts service-station attendants. Soon after we arrive in Chisholm, with Salinger driving, we stop for gas at a small station. The gas jockey checks the oil, water, battery, fan belt, and tire pressure, washes all the windows inside and out, cleans off the license plates, and apologizes for not having a vacuum cleaner to do the inside of the car. He is slim and dark with neatly trimmed hair and a quizzical smile. He has heavy black eyebrows that look as if they might have been blackened for a theatrical performance. One ear, the right, sticks out as though he is cupping it forward to hear an important whisper. His face is smooth as a child's, though he could be anywhere from sixteen to thirty. He assumes Jerry to be the car's owner, and talks about the car with him.

Jerry mouths the usual inanities about it being a good car, getting forty miles per gallon and still having its original brakes at 105,000 miles. The boy wrings Jerry's hand, thanks him profusely for his business, refuses a tip, and sprints off to service a van with a red and black rodeo scene glazed on its silver sides.

The station owner lumbers by, carrying an extra hundred pounds, above his belt and wearing a dirty sky-blue shirt with a faded ARCO crest on it.

"First day on the job," he apologizes, nodding after the running boy. "Just appeared on my doorstep yesterday, like he knew I needed help. Didn't know the first thing about cars, but he's sure learned fast. He's a go-getter, but he'll get over it soon. Everyone does."

In the quiet of the motel room, subdued by the thought of actually being there—the realization that we have to venture out and contact real people, ask intelligent questions—we sit silently on opposite sides of the bed, like Rodin's statue seen in a mirror. Neither of us wants to start a job that could be like digging with a pick into a wall of rock. What are we suffering from? Postfantasy depression?

The *Chisholm Free Press* is located in a small storefront that I suspect may have been a confectionery or a dry-goods store, in a previous incarnation. There are several desks close together and immersed in a foliage of paper. The room smells of mucilage, ink, and varnish. The publisher, Veda Ponikvar, is a handsome woman with a sweet, innocent smile and a habit of pausing a second or two to assimilate each question, replaying the words in her mind before answering—a politician's trick. On the wall of the tiny office are framed photographs of Veda with Jimmy Carter, and with Vice President Mondale. A separate photograph of Mondale is inscribed, "To my best friend, Veda." A large photograph of George Wallace, and a certificate of some kind from the state of Alabama, take up part of another wall. Veda, we learn later, is a highly respected Democrat, has worked in Washington, and has traveled the world as part of State Department delegations to international trade conferences and state funerals.

She smiles slowly as she emerges from a back room where the actual printing is done; her glasses are on a fine chain around her neck, and she puts them on before asking if she can help us.

"I'm Ray Kinsella," I say, "and this is Jerry Salinger. We're trying to gather some information on an old-time baseball player named Moonlight Graham."

She lets the statement hang in the air until the last echo of my voice has died away. Not certain that she understands, I am about to speak again.

"Doctor Graham?" she says.

"Yes. Yes. Did you know him? Do you remember him?"

Without a word, she turns, and from the top of the bluish filing cabinet, from under the drooping leaves of an African violet, she picks up a tiny 2″ x 3″ framed photograph and places it softly in my cupped hands.

It is a chest-up shot of a handsome young man in a baseball uniform. There is no insignia on the cap, but the large letters *N* and *Y* dominate the chest. Jerry looks at the picture. We stare at each other. The young man is dark and earnest looking, staring at the camera as though it owed him money.

"Well, we certainly seem to have started in the right place," I stutter. The photograph, warm in my hand, leaves me short of breath. I can feel my heart beating exuberantly, and I look down, expecting it to be fluttering the material of my double-pocketed khaki shirt.

Veda Ponikvar is a woman of few words, but she produces from her files the newspaper story about Moonlight Graham's death, and also an editorial from the same paper. Salinger and I read them at the counter, mouths hanging open as if we expect to be fed. We read one each, then exchange them.

The editorial is entitled "His Was a Life of Greatness." I take a sheet of paper from the pocket of my shirt and copy a few sentences:

And as the community grew, Doc became an integral part of the population. There were good years and lean ones. There were times when children could not afford eye glasses or milk, or clothing because of the economic upheavals, strikes and depressions.

Yet no child was ever denied these essentials, because in the background, there was a benevolent, understanding Doctor Graham. Without a word, without any fanfare or publicity, the glasses or the milk, or the ticket to the ballgame, found their way into the child's pocket.

There were many simple, humble things that made Doc happy, but his eyes beamed brightest, whenever he read or heard of a student from Chisholm who did well . . . who reached the apex of perfection in his chosen endeavor.

He remembered everyone by name and in his travels, took signal pride in telling about a town called Chisholm and its cradle of people of many tongues and creeds.

For the old and young of this little mining town who knew Doctor Graham . . . his era was historic. There will never be another quite like it.

Salinger is considerate enough not to see the tear that oozes out onto my cheek and sits like a dewdrop for a few seconds before sliding into one of my sideburns.

I am satisfied with my notes, but Salinger asks for, and receives, photocopies of the obituary and the editorial. Along with these, Veda Ponikvar gives us the names of a few people who knew Doc Graham well. As we leave, Salinger clutches the newspaper articles sternly like Bibles. At the motel we read and reread them. I am as tense and anxious as if I were waiting for a 3–2 pitch. The magic energy that has brought us here seems to seep from us like sweat, now that we have something concrete to begin with. We are calmed by the high-country chill of the air. We are drained and ready to sleep.

I close my eyes seeing Annie's red hair, the color of passion, but a persistent Eddie Scissons again elbows his way into my dreams.

"Do you believe in a hereafter?" he asks.

"Seems to me that's getting into religion," I say softly. "I try never to discuss religion or politics—I don't have enough friends that I can afford to."

"I'm a very religious man," says Eddie, spreading his large hands on the maple tabletop at the Friendship Center. My dream is an exact videotape replay of a conversation we have had.

"When I go, I'll have them bring my body down here to the Friendship Center, and my baseball boys will come down and look at me laying there, and they'll say, 'Yep, that's Eddie, and he's dead as Billy-be-damned, so you can put the lid down on the coffin now and drive in the nails,' and they'll carry me over to the graveyard where I got a plot not far from my Ellen, and not very far from the Black Angel."

"The baseball boys?" I say. And I think of Eddie's plot being near the Black Angel, a twelve-foot bronze monument of a dark angel with wings spread in a protective gesture. She has stood for over half a century above the grave of a much-loved son of a Czech immigrant woman. The angel has become part of Iowa City folkways, and one of the many rumors about it is that if you kiss a virgin girl beneath the shadow of the angel's wings at midnight, the statue will turn white.

"The baseball boys," Eddie repeats. "Kept in touch with my teammates over the years, I have. They're all gone now, but their sons are around. We exchange cards at Christmas." And he smiles and shakes his head up and down as if stirring memories up from darkness. "I've asked some of them, one of Heinie Zimmerman's boys; and Wildfire Schulte, why one of his grandsons was here to see me not three years ago, lives in Chicago and has a season ticket to the Cubs, took me there for a three-game series against St. Louis and I slept in his guest room, a very successful boy he is; and King Cole, he come from out around Toledo, Iowa, his son's gonna be one of my pallbearers. They all are. They're my baseball boys, and they like to hear about the old days and about their daddies and their granddaddies." Eddie's eyes move far away, and he stares over my head, far beyond the window that overlooks Gilbert Street, perhaps at a varnished coffin being wheeled out onto the diamond at Wrigley Field. Perhaps he sees the flag at half-mast, and the players, hats in hands, standing solemnly at attention as a bugler plays taps in feeble memory of the oldest Chicago Cub.

In the morning, while Jerry goes for a haircut and to buy a clean shirt, I head for the Chisholm Public Library, where I immerse myself in yellowed issues of the *Chisholm Tribune-Herald*, picking my way through the town's long-dead past, feeling as if I have just entered an attic untouched for three-quarters of a century.

Almost immediately, I uncover a baseball-sized nugget.

POPULAR DOCTOR CUPID'S VICTIM

Miss Alicia Madden and A. W. Graham Take Solemn Vows. Wed at Rochester.

The popular Dr. A. W. Graham left Chisholm on Monday, ostensibly to attend a clinic at the Medical and Surgical Center at Rochester, but from a clipping taken from the *Rochester Daily Bulletin*, which follows, the clinic is entirely the doctor's own. He is still enjoying it, having left immediately for a honeymoon trip to the far eastern states. The boys are waiting for his return.

"Amid the most charming autumnal decorations, fifty guests assembled at Silver Creek Farm to witness the nuptials which united Miss A. V. Madden and Dr. A. W. Graham of Chisholm. The ceremony took place at the parsonage of St. John's Church, the officiating priest being Rev. Fr. Murphy."

The remainder of the clipping lists the guests and brides-maids, and discusses the attire of the bridal party. What is interesting is that none of Doc's relatives were present.

I meet Jerry and suggest we start the long process of interviewing people. I imagine we will work together. Jerry has purchased a stenographer's notebook, and I assume he will studiously make notes of conversations while I lurk in the background.

"I work alone," says Jerry, holding the closed notebook against his chest.

"You sound like a detective in a 1947 B movie," I say, trying not to appear offended.

"I have my own assignment to complete, remember. I'm the only one who knows how to do it."

Jerry walks away, his shoulders slightly stooped, and I am left alone in the middle of Lake Street, the main street of Chisholm, Minnesota.

People are friendly and eager to talk about Doc Graham, but a pattern soon develops. "Oh, I don't know much about him," they say, "but you should talk to so-and-so." I conscientiously write down the name of so-and-so. This scenario is repeated several times until the names of the first people I talked to start reappearing at the top of the list. After I discover this, I press each person for a memory of Doc.

"Do you remember anything special, or funny, or wonderful, or awful?" I ask again and again. And much to my surprise, I come to life more with each interview, become happy as a boy selling magazine subscriptions to long-suffering neighbors.

At the motel we compare notes on what we have found, but Jerry is careful not to let me see what he has written in the notebook. I read Jerry the most interesting quotes I have gathered:

"He never missed a baseball or football game. My daughter was a pretty hefty girl. Doc took a look at her sitting in her slip on the wooden chair in his office and he said, 'Too bad she's a girl. She'd make a great tackle for the football team.' Doc was the kind of man who could get away with saying something like that—why if anybody else had said that, we'd have both been really offended."

"We all went to a tournament in Minneapolis once. Doc found out some of us didn't have a place to stay, so he sneaked us into his room until there were eleven or twelve of us. When he realized there were so many of us he just shook his head and walked off and got himself another room."

"Doc didn't drink or smoke, but he used to chew up paper and spit it out wherever he went. If you were around Doc very long, you learned to duck. Doc was at a convention in Chicago and I guess they gave out sample cigarette packages. He didn't approve of my smoking, but he sent me the sample anyway. Just addressed it to my name with 'NORD SIDE OF TOWN' for an address."

"What are you guys doin' here anyway? It's just like you got shovels and are diggin' Doc Graham up."

"Alicia Madden was teaching school here when she met Doc. When I was a little girl, she was my teacher. We just held our breath when she walked into the room, she was so beautiful. We used to call her Miss Flower. I don't know if she knew that or not."

"Doc used to play for the New York Giants. Oh, for several years, I think. He never talked about it. I never heard of him being called Moonlight."

That night I sleep more peacefully; my only dream is of Shoeless Joe Jackson, and the phantom White Sox standing silently in left field staring down at something, sadly.

By the time I get to the nearby Country Kitchen Restaurant for breakfast, I find Salinger surrounded. Like the Pied Piper, he has accumulated a flock of followers. Several tables have been pushed together, and he sits at the head drinking coffee and making notes. As I squeeze in beside him, I can feel the room get quiet. Salinger gulps the last of his coffee, excuses himself. Those around the table are mostly men past retirement age. I have not been introduced, but the men obviously know I am connected with Salinger, and after a long, uneasy silence, they begin talking to me.

"Everybody's talking about you two," says Louis, a stalky, balding man with a broad face and bent nose. "Mario and Frank," and he waves his hand to indicate two others at the table, "came over to my place last night, and we told Doc Graham stories until after midnight. I bet it was the same all over town. I have some stories to tell you. I even wrote some of them down." He drags from the pocket of his plaid shirt a lined paper ripped from a coiled-ring scribbler, the left edge ragged.

"Memory's a funny thing," he goes on. "It's like all those memories we have of Doc Graham had gone to sleep and sunk way down inside us." He pats his ample tummy. "But once you started asking about him and started us talking about him, why they swum right up to the surface again. It's almost like you brought Doc back to life.

"This morning while I was walking down here, I looked south from Lake Street, down Third toward the school, and I thought I seen him, his white hair bobbing along, his black overcoat open, like it always was even if it was fifty below zero, and him carrying an umbrella, like he always did. He claimed he carried it out of habit, for something to hang on to and 'to beat away all my lady admirers,' and he used to laugh about that. Only the umbrella he was carrying must have belonged to his wife, because it was all pale blue and silky and had little flowers growing out of it. She always wore blue—I bet you didn't know that. My wife was a student of hers. Anyway, you see what you've gone and done. I'm seeing Doc Graham walking down the street like he was, oh, thirty years ago. And him wearing his overcoat in June. The memory sure does you strange sometimes."

"He's been dead about twenty years. You should write about the living. To heck with the dead," says a gruff voice from the end of the table. But he is quickly shouted down, and everyone present passes me one or more bits of information about Doc Graham.

"Alicia did like blue. Doc used to buy hats for her—most always blue ones with lots of flowers on them. I think the stores used to order in blue hats because they knew Doc would buy them. When they tore down the old school after Doc retired, why they found a half-dozen hatboxes in his closet with brand-new hats in them. I wonder if anybody ever told Alicia. It would tickle her to know—if she's still alive."

The man who said crossly that I should write about the living is now pacing up and down behind me, racking his brains, stopping frequently to put his hand on my shoulder.

"Let me tell you a story," he says finally, tapping his glasses frames. "Doc gave me my first pair of glasses, but that's not the story. Doc had as many pockets in his suit as a magician. Why, he'd reach in, and out would come an orange or a peanut or some candy, or there'd be a silver flash and he'd pop a dime into the hand of each child he'd meet. Doc had money in every pocket, and not just silver. He gave away more free glasses than any man in Minnesota. Can you imagine a doctor giving away eyeglasses today?"

"I thought of him like he was Joe DiMaggio," says a quiet man who declines to elaborate.

"He wrote by moving his paper up and down under the pen. And he used to chew up his prescription slips, so he was always looking for scraps of paper, and sometimes his patients used to have to dig into their pockets for a piece of paper so Doc could write a prescription."

"I went with him to make a housecall up at one of the camps," says a woman who has not spoken before. "The husband was sick and they had no heat—no stove. When we got back to Chisholm, Doc went to the hardware store and bought a stove for them and paid to have it delivered. And I bet that wasn't the only time he did something like that."

"He could show you every spot where there had ever been a hitching post in Chisholm. He had that kind of mind."

"And that man had an arm on him," says another. "'Feel my muscles,' he used to say to us boys. Never put on an extra pound in his life, and used to brag that he never let another doctor examine him. One day over at the ballpark, he wandered down from the stands after a game. 'Let me see that ball,' he said to us, and one of us tossed him the ball. He studied it for a minute, looked at it so long I thought he'd forgotten what he was doing with it, and then he walked over behind home plate, cranked up his arm in a kind of comical way, reared back, and fired that ball over the left-field fence, and it was still *rising* when it disappeared. He just smiled at us and nodded, and then he wandered off, shuffling along, looking kind of lost the way he always did. But what an arm. There ain't many *young* men could have done that—three hundred thirty-five feet it was, and him at least fifty at the time. A hell of an arm."

"Doc came here in 1909 just after most of the town burnt up. He just grew with the town. Chisholm's a mining town, always has been, always will be. Whole area is called the Iron Range. Town used to have ten thousand people, but we're down to four thousand now. All the underground mines are closed, just strip mining left. Needed a lot of men to dig in the old days, there was mining camps like sores all over the hills. But the mines were good to the town. Better than most big industries. They paid for the doctors to come here, and brought in the first teachers and built the schools. It wasn't all take; they put back into the community. Even in the thirties there was a market for iron ore, so we hardly felt the depression up here."

Back at the newspaper office, Veda Ponikvar hands me the small wallet-sized photo of Moonlight Graham in his New York Giant uniform. She passes it to me as a bishop might hand a religious object to a peasant—formally, hoping against hope that no harm will come to it. I hold it in both hands as if I am receiving the sacrament. I'm tempted to offer to leave my watch or wallet or belt as security—something tangible to prove that I intend to get it back to her safely. I carry it off to Chisholm's only photo studio and order reprints, pay for them to be mailed to Iowa, and extract a solemn promise from the photographer to return the photo to Veda as soon as he is finished with it.

On the way to the motel I buy a newspaper, a *Chicago Tribune*, thick as a folded bath towel. On an inside page, above a two-column story the shape of a paperback book, is the headline: J. D. SALINGER MISSING. In summary, the story states only that a relative in California notified police after receiving no answer to repeated telephone calls. The piece concludes by saying that there are no known clues and that the police, for the moment, state that they do not suspect foul play.

I show the paper to Jerry.

He goes immediately to the phone and places a call to his son in California.

I decide to leave him alone, and head across to the Country Kitchen Restaurant for coffee and an apple dumpling. The apple dumplings may be addictive. I picture myself, years in the future, toothless, in rags, begging quarters in front of a Country Kitchen. "Spare change, sir? I only need thirty-five cents more for an apple dumpling. Sixty cents and I can have cinnamon ice cream with it. God bless you, sir."

"My son says they're camped in *his* driveway. Way out there. Can you imagine it?" exploded Jerry when I return to the room. "They're probably breaking up my jeep and selling the pieces for souvenirs." He laughs a little wildly and shakes his head.

"My son's going to issue a bulletin. He'll say he's had a call from me and that I'm in a monastery in Peru eating goat cheese and contemplating the meaning of life. That's what they expect. I told him to say that I'm thinking of changing my name to Dusty Chisholm because I'm planning to write a western novel. But he says that's too silly. He has a level head, my son."

"You must be getting lots of material out of this trip," I say to Salinger late that evening as we linger over apple dumplings at the restaurant. I am on my second one. "I get abusive if I eat more than one," says Jerry. "You wouldn't want to have to bail me out, would you?" We smile. Then his expression changes.

"Material? Like what?" As he looks at me, the tension lines between his eyebrows deepen, and I realize that I have ventured over that mystical line into a writer's domain, a place where I do not belong.

I can think of nothing to do with the stories I've gathered about Doc, except to tell them to Salinger, who, to my consternation, makes no notes. "Doc's life. Couldn't you write a wonderful story about Doc? I mean, sixty years the small-town doctor—pillar of the community . . ."

"Friend to those who have no friend; enemy to those who make him an enemy," says Salinger, in a good imitation of a radio announcer.

"That's cruel."

"But accurate. Nobody cares anymore. Half the communities in North America have a Doc Graham. We've come up here and spaded up people's memories of Doc, but what we've uncovered is all good: no paramours, no drunken binges, no opium habit . . ."

"No illegitimate children."

"No crazy wife locked in the attic."

"No shady financial dealings."

"No evicting orphans, or midnight abortions." Jerry stops and shakes his head wearily. "It's a sad time when the world won't listen to stories about good men. It's one of the reasons I don't publish anymore."

"Oh, but you should. You should. Look. I want to show

you something." I dig frantically through the compartments of my wallet. Past shining Master Charge and oil-company credit cards, past a picture of Karin, her baby face smiling from inside a white bonnet; past various pictures of Annie, her red hair shimmering: Annie in pigtails standing beside her father's 1950 Ford; Annie as a cheerleader for West High in Iowa City; Annie pregnant, looking as if she is hugging a watermelon; Annie all in denim smiling at me in that way she has. From inside one of the plastic photo holders, I produce a ratty clipping and thrust it at Salinger:

> You do something in your stories that few writers do well—especially today—and that is to make the reader *love* your characters. They exude a warm glow. They are so real, so vulnerable, so good, that they remind me of that side of human nature which makes living and loving and striving after dreams worth the effort. I, for one, came away with a delicious smile on my face and a soft little tear in my eye—and I felt pretty damn good about being alive for the rest of the day. Thank you.

"Have you ever seen that before?" I ask.

"No."

"It's an excerpt from a fan letter to you. I cut it out of the *Saturday Evening Post* in 1957, and I've carried it with me ever since. How can you not publish, when people love you so?"

But Salinger only smiles sadly and continues to shake his head.

What are we doing here? I keep asking myself. Dispatched blind, like a taxi given only the number of a house, we root in the memories of the people of Chisholm just like the gargantuan machines that open and upend the earth outside of town. We are dredging up the past and laying it out in the sunshine to dry.

The house on our farm in Iowa is nearly a hundred years old, and several times when Annie and I have dug in the back yard, guessing at where the garbage piles must have been, we have come up with wonderful pieces of glass, old dishes, crockery, and, above all, bottles—blues, greens, rubies, small tri-angular bottles, dimpled long-necked bottles the color of ice, round milk bottles with the name of the dairy permanently imprinted on them. There was once a bottle manufacturer in Iowa City, and many of the bottles we unearth are unique and invaluable. Annie has filled the back windows of the sun porch with them, after washing and polishing them, and they sit in rows like soldiers from different armies, the evening sun flash-ing off their surfaces.

Here in Chisholm, we take the memories we unearth and carry them back to the motel, recording them, storing them, until we feel the presences moving, the voices whispering, grow-ing in momentum like a breeze turning into a wind.

"What's going to happen?" says Jerry. He brushes his hand across the seat of a chair before he sits down.

"Something," I say, for that is all I know. We are mixing a cocktail of memories, and history, and love, and imagination. Now we must wait and see what effect it will have on us.

"He always carried an umbrella and was always losing them," says a voice that filters into my dreams. "Businesses around town would just lean his umbrella somewhere near the door. If anybody asked, they'd just say, 'Oh, that's Doc's um-brella.'"

And I dream, too, of Annie. Behind our house a hundred yards or so is a collapsed building, its unpainted wood aged to the softness of owl feathers. Annie loves old buildings. It was perhaps a granary or a henhouse once, but stood abandoned for years, until, as if nature had given it a gentle karate chop, the roof collapsed in the middle, sinking slowly downward like an old camel attempting to kneel. It rots with dignity into the earth. A window is now at ground level, and the strangle grass, bent by evening breezes, peers inside.

Late one evening, I looked out and saw Annie standing in the knee-high grass, her hands in the back pockets of her jeans, staring dreamily at the building.

I joined her and slipped an arm around her waist as I did so.

"Oh, love," she said, turning and laying her head on my chest. "One day I want to travel around the country, in no hurry, no hurry at all; I want to stop and explore old buildings, walk through them and listen to my footsteps—funny old houses with porch pillars and turrets..."

On our honeymoon, in New England, we passed an elegant old home painted an olive green with white trim and shutters, and a turret, like a medieval castle, obviously unused.

"Maybe we could rent the turret," I said to Annie.

"I'll bet the lady who owns it has her hair in a tight bun and hasn't smiled since 1933. I can just hear you. 'Excuse me, Ma'am, we'd like to rent your turret.' 'Why young man, I'm shocked, I'm not that kind of girl.'"

Annie and the turret fade away and I am wide awake, my senses tense as if I'm hiding from soldiers. I ease out of bed and dress quietly.

I feel a little like a werewolf as I slip out the motel door, leaving Salinger asleep, his head gray on the white pillow, dividing it evenly. The night air, sweet with the smells of summer, has a high-country chill to it. The sky is cloudless and might be a lake reflecting stars and a golden sickle of moon.

I walk from the motel down the highway and into town, down Third Street as far as the school, back up to Lake Street, over to Second, and down past the Graham Apartments, a massive natural-stone building where Doc and Alicia lived in one unit and rented two others. The apartments are built on the site of the old Rood Hospital, where Doc first practiced medicine in Chisholm, where he was doctoring when he met and married the young school teacher, Alicia Madden. I walk across to Third, look at the school again, then return to Lake Street, completing my circle. I walk slowly, staring at the silhouettes of the trees and houses dark against the pure sky, knowing that much of this cannot have changed since Doc last saw it. He has been gone only fourteen years. I scuff along the boulevard of the sleeping street like a boy reluctant to reach school. The toes of my shoes are damp with dew.

Then, as I approach the Graham Apartments for the third time, a door closes softly and a figure moves smartly down the steps of the southernmost entrance and turns in the direction of the town—toward me. There is no doubt in my mind that it is Doc Graham—I've seen a picture of him at eighty, in the 1959 Chisholm High School yearbook, which is dedicated to him. "Because most of all you are our friend today, as you have been the friend of our parents and grandparents before us . . . His mind is a storehouse of Blue Streak campaigns and memories of his own baseball career. Our school doctor, whose studies have won him national renown . . ."

He is about seventy-five, I decide in the split second I have for decision making. He is stooped a little, but his body is still lithe, an athlete's body. He is wearing a black suit, the white shirt underneath open at the collar. His eyebrows are thick, and each could be the feather of a white bird. There is a fringe of neatly trimmed white hair, like a halo, around his head. He walks briskly, as if he has a destination in mind; he holds an umbrella, gently as he might a fencing foil, and swishes it vigorously with each step. It is as if he has stepped out of an issue of *The Ranger,* the Chisholm High School yearbook.

"Doc?" I say, as he draws abreast of me. "Doc Graham?"

He stops and raises his head to look at me. His eyes are bright and reflect the stars overhead. He is already smiling, narrowing his eyes, trying to see me clearly, trying to decide who I might be: whether or not he delivered me, and whose son or nephew I am.

"Moonlight Graham?" I whisper.

"Well now, you must be a fan of the game to know about that," he says.

"I'm Ray Kinsella," I say. And I suppose that wouldn't be a bad epitaph for me: "He was a fan of the game."

"You're not from around here," he says, measuring me carefully.

"No. From Iowa."

"I've been there. Took the train down to Iowa City once—to the medical center. They have fine equipment there. And once to Council Bluffs, the Blue Streaks were in a tournament."

"Baseball?"

"No. Basketball. Baseball's not that big here. Season's too short. Football's the game around here. But you learn to adapt. Any game becomes important when you know and love the players."

"I'm from near Iowa City. I farm a little and I own a baseball field," I say as I swing into step beside him. We head north toward Lake Street.

"Who are you again?" Doc says, eyeing me shrewdly.

"Ray Kinsella. I'm interested in baseball. I want to ask you some questions."

"Then it wasn't an accident that you were waiting on the street for me?"

"I'd been out walking. I had a feeling that you might appear..."

"Appear? That's a funny word to use. How could you know I wouldn't be able to sleep tonight? 'You're flopping around like a fish,' Alicia said to me, and she was real happy when I got up and got dressed. 'Going to go for a walk,' I said to her, but she'd already turned over and gone back to sleep.

"I had this feeling, in there when I woke up—a pulling, like there was a magnet somewhere drawing me slowly toward it. Are you a magnet, Ray Kinsella?"

"I don't know. Perhaps we were just meant to talk for a while." We turn the corner and head east on Lake Street; the newspaper office is across the way, and I think of Veda Ponikvar's portrait of Moonlight Graham, which until today slept in the shadows on top of the filing cabinet. Or did it? As we walk, I note subtle differences in the buildings and sidewalks. Some of the newer houses on Second Street appear to have been replaced by older ones. There are business signs along Lake Street that weren't there yesterday. Can it be that I am the one who has crossed some magical line between fantasy and reality? That it is Doc who is on solid turf and I who have stepped into the past as effortlessly as chasing a butterfly across a meadow?

I glance up at the water tower that watches over the town like a benevolent alien. It shines in the moonglow like a giant thimble, but there is no writing on it, while yesterday it advertised the Minnesota Museum of Mining.

"You must have had to go back a ways to dig up that name," says Doc. "I haven't been called Moonlight Graham for nearly fifty years. It was one of the things I left behind when I came to Chisholm. Kind of like putting my toys away in a box in a closet. I can count on the fingers of one hand the number of people I've talked to about my playing days. It was somebody else who dug up that I'd played for the Giants. I never mentioned it to anybody. Did a big story on me in the newspaper. It was kind of embarrassing; I mean, if you're a fan, then you know the truth about how much I played."

"I know," I say. I want to tell him about the line of statistics on the scoreboard at Fenway; I want to tell about it being his listing in the *Baseball Encyclopedia*, but I'm not sure I can. The *Baseball Encyclopedia* wasn't published until 1969.

I want to ask what year it is. But how can I do that without giving myself away? But maybe I can manage it. "That was quite a World Series last fall!" I say, and wait, hoping I will be able to pick up on his reply.

"You can say that again," says Doc. "I don't know when I've ever been prouder of the Giants. How about that Willie Mays? Did you see that catch? I went back to the movie theater three times to watch it on the newsreel . . ." He chatters on about Dusty Rhodes and his incredible pinch hitting, and Sal Maglie's pitching. It is the 1954 World Series he is talking about. I have been dropped, soft as a falling leaf, into a starry June night in the summer of 1955, Doc's seventy-fifth year.

"And how did you get a name like Moonlight Graham?" I ask, for some reason picturing him running wolflike across plains of scrub brush and stands of silver willow, the sky the color of deep blue velvet peppered with stars, the moon a white wheel, spinning like a spaceship.

"Why don't we walk down to the school?" says Doc, stopping abruptly, as if an invisible wall has appeared in front of him. "We can sit in my office and talk."

"I have no objection," I say.

We turn around and walk west in the direction we have just come from, past Second Street, and turn south on Third.

The school is not at all as it was yesterday. The new brick building of which Chisholm's residents are justifiably proud is only a glint in some architect's eye. Doc fumbles out a key, and the ghostly odors of an old schoolhouse wrap themselves around us—chalk, erasers, varnish, running shoes—so real they seem to float in the air, and I am prepared to duck my head or hold my hand high, as I might when walking through a room filled with cobwebs, where at any instant a bat might hurtle by.

We walk up the hollow stairs, and Doc opens a varnished door that has an opaque glass inset. He seats himself behind a desk about as neat as the bottom of a wastebasket, motions me to the black-leather sofa a few feet away. He takes a sheet of paper from his desk, expertly rips an inch or so off the corner with his teeth, and begins chewing.

"Healthier than tobacco," he says, winking a bright eye at me.

I glance around the walls of Doc's office until I find a calendar. It is indeed 1955.

"Well now, about my nickname." He lets fly with a spitball that hits the back of the sofa a few feet from me and hangs where it strikes, like a white fly.

"I went out to the ballpark one night, late at night like this. Long before there were night games. I don't even remember what town it was in. We were on the road, had been for a week or so. It wasn't when I was with the Giants; it was the minor leagues, maybe Manchester in the old New England League. It was a night like this, when I couldn't sleep. They put us two to a room in those days, two to a bed, and every time Ernie Squim, my roommate, turned over, that old brass bed sagged and squawked as if someone had stepped on a cat's tail. Ernie could fall asleep as he was pulling up the covers. Stocky devil he was, a catcher with legs like railroad ties and buttocks like one-hundred-pound hams. Well, it was humid and so dark I felt like one of the corpses we kept floating in big glass vats up at Hopkins, where I was studying. I was just suffocating, and Ernie was laying there in just his white shorts, the rest of him covered in long brown hair. The only thing I ever knew could wake Ernie up was if I got out of bed. I'd go down the hall to the john and he'd be wide awake when I came back, his tiny brown eyes glistening in the dark. He wouldn't say a word, just roll over and be asleep before I even laid down again.

"Well, I got out of bed and the closest clothes handy was my baseball uniform, hanging right where I took it off after our game. I pulled it on, the bed moaning and Ernie jigging around, tossing his mask and running after foul pop-ups in his dreams.

"I eased out the door and down the hall with its faded plum-colored carpet, and on down the stairs. The tall clock in the lobby was varnished, had Roman numerals and advertised cigars on its glass front. It said three A.M., and I guess even the night clerk had gone to sleep, for there was no one around the desk. The front door was locked and I had to turn a latch to open it, and then leave it open after me.

"The air was cooler outside and smelled kind of silvery, like a lawn that's just been watered. I walked across the street, the gravel clicking under my feet; the wooden sidewalk sounded hollow and I was standing under a streetlight, one of those kind that look like a bulb screwed into a black sombrero. I paced up and down under the light for a while. I was tired, but the thought of that room kept me outside. There was a moon, and a sky full of stars. There were clouds stumbling across the sky, too, moving fast, considering there was hardly any wind down where I was. While I was standing there with my neck bent back, a dark cloud galloped across the moon.

"And then I heard Ernie Squim's voice: 'Graham, what the heck you doing standing out there in the moonlight?'

"I looked up, but I couldn't see him. I knew he'd be bent over with his nose up against the metal-smelling screen on our window, and I also knew that when I woke up in the morning and looked at Ernie, he'd have a black smear on the end of his chunky nose.

"'The moon's under a cloud,' I called back, but quietly. I'd get a five-dollar fine if the manager found me outside the hotel this late.

"'Don't tell me I don't know moonlight when I see it,' Ernie boomed.

"'Go back to bed,' I said.

"'And you got your uniform on,' he insisted. 'What are you doing playing out there in the moonlight?'

"Just to keep him quiet I said, 'I'm going for a walk.'

"'Who the hell's that out there?' said a voice from another window.

"'It's Graham,' shouted Ernie Squim.

"Somebody else banged their window down like a gunshot.

"I started walking away, my spikes making chewing sounds on the wooden sidewalk.

"'What's all the yelling about?' said somebody else. It sounded like Luke Watson, the shortstop.

"'Archie Graham's going out to the ballpark to play in the goll-danged moonlight,' another voice said.

"As I walked away, the cloud slowly uncovered the moon, like a magician peeling his silk handkerchief off an orange.

"The voices and laughter from the hotel faded away. Well, I thought, if I have the name, I may as well have the game, and I turned the corner of the silent street and headed for the baseball field."

"And forever after?"

"Moonlight Graham, they called me. You know, I've been a lucky, lucky man. I've always done the things I've enjoyed most—doctoring and playing baseball."

Chisholm, Minnesota, was founded by a man named Archie Chisholm, a Scot who came from Ontario, Canada. Longyear Lake, the picturesque body of water divided by the highway at the town's outskirts, was named for a pioneer of that name, and not by or for an Indian. And Ed Wheelecor, a former mayor of Chisholm and a close friend of Doc Graham's, whom I interviewed, came to northern Minnesota in 1916 because he was delivering his sister to Buhl, Minnesota, five miles south of Chisholm—delivering her all the way from England to become the bride of a Methodist preacher. "I never had any intention of staying in America," said Ed. "I was going to go right back to England after the wedding. It's funny the tricks life plays on you."

It is indeed. I wonder if there are soft-spoken voices who deliver assignments to all of us at various times, and if my problem is one of hearing too acutely. It is nice to think that I have company—that others dance to the muted music I hear. And I wonder what brought Archibald Wright Graham, M.D., to Chisholm, Minnesota, in 1909. A young man with a degree from an outstanding medical school, with a wealthy family in the South: What trick of fate brought him to a frontier mining community?

Doc turns on a square white hotplate, and when the coils

burn a tomato color he sets a badly chipped bluish enamel coffeepot on the burner and cooks a pot of coffee. It arrives black and scalding. I do little more than blow on mine—I like much cream in my coffee. Doc, all the time chattering to me, downs his coffee in two long swallows. As I watch him, I remember a voice from the previous day: "He must have had an iron gullet. He poured coffee down the way you empty a water glass into a sink. And always black."

Then I ask about why he came to Chisholm.

"I've always had friends at the medical centers in Rochester, and I was there one summer and not feeling so good—just a cough that wouldn't quit, and I couldn't seem to get a suntan. 'Why don't you go up to the Range?' somebody said to me. 'The air is pure, and they have the best water on earth.' I thought, why not? So I took the train. 'Just give me a ticket for as far north as the train goes,' I told the clerk, and I landed right here in Chisholm.

"It was 1909, the year after the big fire here, and the town was rebuilding; the whole area smelled of new, sawed lumber. And I guess I got better." He stops to laugh a gentle, ironic laugh. "I've been here for forty-six years. I got on at Dr. Rood's hospital, and the air was clear and dry, and the cool weather keeps you on your toes. I never could handle the humidity down home. And then I met Alicia. She was from Rochester. I could have gone there lots of times to work at the clinic, but by then I'd settled into the school job and I knew everybody in the community and everybody knew me . . . Did I tell you I'm supposed to be a great cousin, or something, to this Billy Graham fellow who preaches on the TV and in Yankee Stadium?" Doc Graham lets go with a spitball that whaps against the black sofa like a ball hitting a catcher's mitt. "Did you know his grandfather was named Crook Graham?" He laughs again. "Some young fellow from the university in Minneapolis came up here once, and he had it all mapped out. Claimed my daddy was a second cousin of Crook Graham. Now I don't know what relation that would make me to this evangelist, or why anyone would care. I've always been too busy for that sort of thing, though Alicia's a good Catholic and my family wasn't very happy when I married her. That fellow from the university wanted to know what I thought of my famous tenth

cousin or whatever. 'You must be awful desperate for testi-
monials, to come to a shirttail relative like me,' I told him. I
don't think he liked that very well. He was tall and pale and
wore a black suit and tried to act solemn. Didn't look to me
like he found religion very joyful—that's the one word I figure
should be associated with it . . ."

"Talk to me about baseball," I say. "About what it means
to you. About dreams and reality. You must have wanted to
be another King Kelly, Nap Lajoie, John McGraw, or Wee
Willie Keeler. What was it like to see your dreams flutter
away?"

"That's a tall order, young fellow. Maybe you should try
asking me a straight question?"

"Well, it's not so much what I want to ask as what I want
to get a feel for. If someone asks, you can say, 'I played for
the New York Giants.' Willie Mays or Christy Mathewson
could say the same words, but they'd have a very different
meaning. What was it like to brush against fame like a stranger
hurrying past in a crowd?"

"I didn't think much of it at the time. Hardly anybody
recognizes the most significant moments of their life at the time
they happen. I figured there'd be plenty more days. I always
told myself I was going to crack the line-up. But looking back,
I can see that I knew. I knew, even as I trotted out to right
field that afternoon in 1905, that I was a minor leaguer in a
major-league park—that I was one step too slow on the bases,
and a split second too slow with the bat. But you don't admit
something like that to yourself when you're young and full of
hope."

"Some men wouldn't have been able to cope," I say. "You've
met veterans who sit in bars for the rest of their lives and half-
brag, half-whine about what they did in the war . . ."

"Which was usually nothing," says Doc, letting fly with
another spitball. "Heroes don't need to talk about what they
did."

"Like you?"

"Well, I maybe have the state of mind, but I never had the
game. Even in the minors, I wasn't much of a hero. I never
talk about my past unless I'm asked, and then the less the
better. I don't have my office full of pictures of me in my

uniform, and I've never been back on an old-timer's day to get photographed with the real stars. That kind of stuff rubs me the wrong way. It was kind of like going someplace you know you'll never visit again, like seeing the Mona Lisa, or touching a fist-sized diamond, or ordering a one-hundred-dollar meal in a restaurant."

"Why did you stay?" I ask, spreading my hands to show I mean the school, the town, the state. "You could have gone anywhere."

Doc looks puzzled.

"My partner checked the town records," I go on. "You don't even make five hundred dollars a month."

"I got a little practice after hours . . ."

"But you could have been wealthy, lived in a big city . . ."

"This is my favorite place in the whole world," Doc says quietly. "I don't think I have to tell you what that means. You look like the kind of fellow who has a favorite place. Once the land touches you, the wind never blows so cold again. You feel for the land like it was your child. When that happens to you, you can't be bought."

"I know," I say, and I think of the soft breath of Iowa on my face.

We simply sit and look at each other, like old friends at a reunion, happy with each other's presence. I sip the inky coffee, which puckers my mouth. Doc downs another thick cupful.

"They have one of the turnstiles from the Polo Grounds at the Hall of Fame in Cooperstown," I say, and then I look at Doc Graham and feel like making the motion of covering my lips with my fingers, to show I've said something I shouldn't have. In the time and space Moonlight and I now inhabit, the Polo Grounds still sit in New York, the floodlights cooling after a night game. I decide to try and cover my tracks.

"From the early days, it is. They put in new equipment a few years ago and donated the old one. It's lovely—operated by a foot pedal and scarred worse than a streetfighter's face. When you think of the thousands, perhaps millions, of people who walked through that gate—living and dead, famous and unknown; the first smells of the concessions reaching their nostrils—it sort of leaves you in awe . . ." I smile at Doc, who sits quietly, chewing, perhaps wondering why I am babbling so.

I've splashed down here in the fifties, landing softly as if the earth were foam rubber. I must keep my tongue from betraying me. It is another year before Don Larsen will pitch his perfect game in the World Series. "Keep it safe. Keep it safe," a little voice inside me says. I try.

"Tell me about playing for the Giants. What was it like walking out on the field for the first time?"

"I remember the situation clearly, but the other, what I felt, I'm not so sure about." And he pauses, staring over my head to where an eye chart hangs on the wall. "It was the end of the eighth inning, and we were way ahead. I was sitting on the bench, half dozing. I'd been up with the Giants for most of a month, but I'd never seen any action. John McGraw just pointed a bony finger at me and said, 'Right field.' I jumped up like I was sitting on a spring, grabbed my glove, and trotted out, hoping I wouldn't trip or do anything to attract attention to me. Afterward, the other players told me the announcer boomed out, 'Graham now playing right field,' but I didn't hear it.

"I'd practiced in the outfield all the time I'd been with the Giants, but it was a different matter to play it. It seemed like a mile to the infield; the batter looked like a midget, his bat a toothpick. I tried to take deep breaths and calm down, wondering what I'd do if the ball was hit my way, hoping it wouldn't be, and at the same time hoping it would. The fans had no effect on me. I never even knew they were there. In the minors, why sometimes I'd visit with the fans, and on the road they'd needle me, usually with good humor. But that day, if the fans made any noise I didn't hear it."

As if anticipating my next question, he goes on.

"I tried to make myself extra alert, watch the bat, the pitcher's motion, so I could get a good jump on the ball. But I felt so isolated. I kept telling myself, this is it. You've hit the top. The major leagues. You can say for the rest of your life, 'I played for the New York Giants.'"

"And did you ever get to make a play?"

"No. The ball was never hit out of the infield. A pop-up to the left side, a soft grounder to short, and a come-backer, and it was all over. I bet I wasn't out in right field more than five minutes. And that was fifty years ago." Doc smiles and laughs again. "I didn't know my memory was that good. I guess it made more of an impression on me than I like to admit. It was the top of my profession. I likely could have made it somewhere else. The Giants won the pennant by nine games over Pittsburgh that year. Christy Mathewson won thirty-one games. It was a hard line-up to crack." He is silent. We stare at each other for a long time.

"What makes that half-inning so interesting that you walk around outside my house at night, fifty years later?" he asks. "Seems to me maybe it was your footsteps woke me up."

"I think I came here because your time was so short. I wanted to know how it affected your life. But I can see you've done well. It would have killed some men to get so close. They'd never do anything else but talk about how close they were."

"If I'd only got to be a doctor for five minutes, now *that* would have been a tragedy. You have to keep things in perspective. I mean, I love the game, but it's only that, a game."

"Still, if you could do anything you wanted to do—if you could take time and turn it in your hands like rubbing up a new baseball; if you could stop somewhere in time, and in the silence and mystery and calm of that situation you could have a baseball wish . . ." I stop to let the question register.

Doc smiles wryly, takes a new piece of paper, holds it between his lips, flicks it forward with his tongue.

"And are you the kind of man who could give me that wish?"

"I don't know. I'm just asking questions."

"You don't know much, Ray Kinsella," he says, but with a twinkle in his eye. "You don't know much; you pull an old man out of bed and sift through his life . . ."

"The wish," I say softly, and take a long sip of my coffee, which is bitter and cold and almost makes me cough.

Doc leans his left elbow on the desk and rubs his forehead thoughtfully with a palm, as if it were an eraser that could erase the years and age lines and take him back to 1905 and the Polo Grounds in New York.

And as I look at him, I think of a certain twilight back in Iowa, when Karin and I walked across our field with Shoeless

Joe Jackson hours before a game was due to be played. The sounds of the other players practicing faded away.

"This is the kind of place where anything can happen, isn't it?" Joe said to me that night.

"I know it is," I replied. The fading sun was a rich orange; the shadows of the tall light standards reached across the field like long black arms. Yards away, the mysterious green and gold corn rustled like delicate guests in conversation. Beside me, Karin stood barefoot, her dainty feet barely repressing the thick plush of the grass.

"It is that kind of a place," said Joe. "It is." And he sat down on the tender grass of the outfield, untied his shoes and pulled them off, peeled off his socks and stuffed them in his shoes, then flung the shoes one at a time against the left-field wall, *thwack! thwack!* where they fell to the warning track like shot birds.

Then he stood up and walked a few steps, and the look on his face would have inspired soldiers and poets and pinch hitters to perform as never before. He stepped around slowly, letting the cool tickle enter his soles and run up his legs. Then he began to dance, at first as if his ears alone heard the music of an Irish jig. Then, high-stepping with a wild exuberance and fervor, part dance, part chase, he took Karin by the hands and whirled her, screeching with delight, until her body was parallel with his waist and her strawberry-blond hair was splayed out, fan-shaped, like a splash of sunshine.

"If I had a wish," says Doc Graham, another spitball thumping onto the sofa beside me, "mind you, I said *if*—it would be to hold a bat in a major-league game. I was a pretty fair hitter in the minors—.335 one year—and I wasn't bad in practice with the Giants. But I never got to bat. I'd have liked the chance to stare down a pitcher. Stare him down, and then wink just as he goes into the wind-up; make him wonder if I know something he doesn't, if he should change the pitch in mid-delivery. Yes, that's what I wish for, Ray Kinsella: the chance to squint my eyes when the sky is so blue it hurts to look at it, and to feel the tingle that runs up your arms when you connect dead-on. The chance to run the bases, stretch a double to a triple, and flop face-first into third base, wrapping my arm around the bag. That's what I wish, Ray Kinsella, whoever you are. Is there enough magic floating around out in the night for you to make it come true?"

"Is it time?" I ask Jerry the next morning as he shaves in front of the motel mirror, carefully scanning the silver mustache that quivers like milk on his upper lip.

"I think we've done what we came to do."

"Which was?"

"To see if one inning can change the world."

"And did it?"

"You know as much as I do," he says. At first I only smile. But I cannot contain myself. I tell him of my postmidnight rendezvous, and of all I learned from Doc Graham. Salinger is more silent than usual. I am not unhappy as I notice him thrust his notebook deep into our suitcase. Now he knows how I felt when he told me he had heard a voice I had not.

We pack the car, check out of the motel, and, moving like a tatting shuttle, drive up and down the shady, shadowy, leaf-friendly streets of Chisholm one last time.

"You *are* coming back to Iowa with me," I say, attempting not to sound overanxious about it, thinking that, if necessary, I might even apologize for stumbling into a part of the dream that should surely be his.

"I couldn't quit now," says Salinger, smiling slowly. "You've told me about your ballpark one too many times. I've got to see it. See if you've been telling me the truth."

"Not everybody can see it," I say. "You might not . . ."

"I'll give it a try," he says, in a tone that indicates the subject is closed.

Somewhere in Chisholm, at that moment, a boy, a bat on his right shoulder, cap pulled down over his eyes, his glove hung on the end of the bat, walks off in search of summer. The boy is crossing toward a park. As we turn onto the highway near Longyear Lake, he appears, arm raised in a hitchhiker's stance, thumb out, with a grin as warm as July, as American as johnnycake, on his face.

I brake the car. Jerry opens his door, steps out, pushes the seat forward so the young man can get into the back seat. He tosses his duffel bag in ahead of him; a pair of baseball cleats are knotted around the neck of the bag.

The stranger wears a baseball uniform—a standard white-striped uniform without insignia. His hair is the shiny black of a well-curried horse and shimmers in the sunshine, a few freckles decorate his nose, and his eyes are as blue as any of Minnesota's 10,000 lakes.

"Thank you," he says as he settles in. "You're the first car by. I didn't expect to get a lift so soon." His voice is soft as the skin of a ripe peach.

"How far are you going?" I ask.

"How far are *you* going?" he says in reply, flashing a disarming smile.

"Iowa," I say. "We're going home." The words choke in my throat, and I feel as if I may never breathe again. I look at Jerry, and his eyes are wide, and I know that he knows what I know. He simply makes the now-familiar gesture of shaking his head in wonder.

"Then I'll ride along for a ways," the stranger says. "I'm a ballplayer." He pats the front of his uniform a number of times, like a rookie third-base coach too conscientious about giving signals. "I'm looking for a place to play, and I heard rumors about the Midwest. They say every town out there has a team, and that they'll find you a job for the daytime so you can play ball at night and on weekends. Thought I'd give it a try," he says, and smiles again.

"We know a little about baseball," says Jerry. "I'm J. D. Salinger, and this is Ray Kinsella. Ray's quite a character."

"I'm Archie Graham," the boy replies.

IV

The Oldest Living Chicago Cub

I look at Archie and I wonder how he feels—what kind of crisscrossing the dimensions of time have done to land him here, to stand him on a curving highway by a lake outside Chisholm, Minnesota, at the very moment we come driving by. Or could this all be in my imagination? Is Archie Graham really just a kid looking for a place to play baseball in the Midwest?

"Archie Graham, is it?" says Jerry. We look at each other with secretive expressions. Expressions of childhood. "We know something he doesn't know" expressions.

"Yes sir," says the boy.

"Haven't we seen you before?" asks Jerry.

"No sir, I think not."

"You from around here?" Jerry persists.

There is a long, long pause. Looking through the rearview mirror, I try to frame the expression on his face.

"My family hails from North Carolina," he says finally. His lips curve in an enigmatic line, as if he has chosen his words carefully.

I shake my head ever so slightly at Jerry, as an indication

that he should stop asking questions. And he changes the subject to the weather and current baseball standings, which I have to help him out with.

I realize, talking with Archie Graham as the miles roll by, that there are gaps in his life, like boards pulled off an outfield fence by anxious fans. And I come to believe he has been created by the strength of my dreams, by the depth of my belief in what has been happening. The young Archie Graham is like a doll Jerry and I have conjured up to satisfy our desire that fantasy turn into truth.

"We *are* heading for Iowa, but slowly," I say. "We're stopping in Minneapolis for a Twins game, and then home. Do you want to come with us?"

But before he can answer, Jerry says, "You must be a fan of the game." I stare at him as the words hang in the air like skywriting. Jerry's face remains impassive. I glance back at Archie, who has his slim hands clasped together and is staring at the back of Jerry's head. He seems unperturbed. Is Jerry playing cat and mouse with me? Does he somehow know what I know?

"Wherever you're going is fine," says Archie. "I'm not in a rush, and I've got money to pay my own way."

We drive on to Minneapolis. We are all relaxed at the game, cheering the Twins to an easy win, chanting, "Bombo! Bombo! Bombo!" each time the Twins' right fielder Bombo Rivera is announced. He is a good young player, but not great. It is his name that intoxicates the crowd.

"Nicknames appear to be a thing of the past," I say to Jerry. "Look around the leagues, they're full of Daves and Als and Dons and Barrys."

"There's a simple explanation," says Jerry. "Baseball has become a business for the players as well as the owners. Guys who make a million dollars a year don't even want to be called by their first names. They want to be called Sir. It wouldn't surprise me if one of these years some free agent with a .280 batting average gets a clause in his contract specifying that he has to be announced as Mr. Bigstar every time he comes to bat. It was all right for a boy who earned five thousand dollars playing baseball and was an apprentice plumber in the off-season to be called Snuffy, or Peewee, or Slats, but if you spend all your nonplaying time administrating your fifteen dry-cleaning franchises, your apartment complexes, or your bank, you don't want to be known as No-Neck to your comptroller."

"What do you think?" I say to Archie.

"I don't know," he says. "You guys are a lot older than me."

"Do you have a nickname?" asks Jerry. A leading question if I ever heard one.

"Not yet," says Moonlight Graham. "You have to do something strange, or have an unusual off-season occupation. Nicknames are funny, they just land on you, like waking up one morning with a tattoo. You don't know how you got it, but you know it's gonna be with you forever."

"Would you like one?" asks Jerry.

"You a supplier?" says the kid. He's ripped off the corner of one of the baseball programs and is busy chewing it into a spitball.

"I make suggestions," says Salinger. "There's no obligation. Let's see. How about Lefty?"

"I throw right," says the kid.

"Babe," suggests Salinger.

"Been used," says the hitchhiker.

"I have an idea," I say. I am sprawled on one of the beds in the Concho Shell Motel in Bloomington, not far from the baseball stadium; Archie sits in a chair facing the television, which picks up only one shadowy channel; Salinger is pacing the room. "Let's go to the ballpark."

They look at me without comment.

"Have either of you spent any time in an empty ballpark? There's something both eerie and holy about it."

"How would we get in?" says the kid.

"Leave that to us old people," I say.

Salinger already has the door open and is switching off the lights.

"A ballpark at night is more like a church than a church," I say, as I stop the Datsun on the gravel of the parking lot and turn off the motor and lights. Gravels rearrange themselves under the weight of the car, making sounds like snapping fingers. Our breathing becomes very loud. We might be parked on a country road, the only sound that of a faraway car hissing along a freeway. Above, an airplane blinks as it drifts toward the nearby Minneapolis International Airport. Stealthily, we open the doors and step out. I look straight up at the ink-blue sky. Its edges are bathed golden by the city lights, but, with my neck bent back, neckbones cracking in protest, I can see the stars bubbling, unspoiled. We stand silent. Salinger, too, stares at the sky.

"I haven't done this for years," he whispers, massaging the back of his neck. "And I live in the country."

"You have to make time, even for something as universal as staring at the stars." The moon hangs over the ballpark like a softly glowing peach.

"Full moon," I say, smiling wryly. "Perhaps that's why we're doing what we're doing. They claim that a lot of strangeness goes on during the nights of full moon." The moon turns Salinger's glasses to silver. I cannot see his eyes.

Cops, taxi drivers, and cocktail waitresses will tell you about the full moon: a time when the most docile little wino runs amuck, tossing off twice his weight in blue uniforms; when college students scream through cities, writing on walls; when sedate businessmen drink until they vomit on linen tablecloths; when wives shoot husbands and husbands shoot wives; when little old ladies report lost cats and strange men under their beds. From dark doorways, priests hiss at hookers when the moon is full. And housewives have fearsome attacks of manic energy and shred their underclothes in the blender.

The stadium is totally dark. The silver light poles, like tall, polished trees, stand out against the dark, their tops festooned with hundreds of identical eyes. Behind us, Archie Graham picks up and lays down his cleats, softly, in order to make as little noise as possible. When the moonlight illuminates his face, I can see that it is covered with question marks.

The small door marked "Passes" is located fifty yards to the right-field side of the main entrance. When I walked by it earlier in the evening, I noted that it was held closed by a Yale lock. I know what to do with Yale locks. I have seen enough police and private-eye shows to know that one kick, properly placed, will do the trick. I wave Jerry off and take a short run at the door. What a fool I will feel like if it doesn't work! The flat of my foot hits hard right on the shiny outer portion of the lock, and the door gives with a tearing sound and a dull thud like a muffled gunshot. The kid winces as if I have hit him.

"Are you two guys all right?" he asks, looking frantically around.

There is a second bang as the door swings back against the inner wall. I reach out and silence it, and Salinger and I slip inside, scarcely more than shadows along the dark green wall.

An empty ballpark at night must be like the inside of a pyramid. We are like archeologists exploring new territory. We climb the steps and stare out over the field from behind home plate. Peanut shells crunch underfoot, and last night's waxy cups and hot-dog wrappers brush against our ankles.

"We should have a radio," I say.

Salinger looks at me quizzically.

"They're probably still playing on the West Coast. The darkness here is so smooth and soft and silent it would be like having a feather comforter around our knees. We could huddle down, tune in the game—very softly, so as not to disturb the ghosts of this park—and sit and listen. And once in a while, we could turn up the volume when the ball is whacked sharply and the crowd roars. Or better still, we could sneak in here while the Twins are on a road trip, and listen to the games, pretending they were home games and that the players and crowds were *here*. We could bring our own drinks and peanuts . . ."

"You could be accused of being possessed," says Salinger. "Is there a baseball devil?"

"Anything taken too seriously becomes a devil. Do I take baseball too seriously?" But I don't want to hear his answer, or anyone's answer. What could be done to exorcise me? Would the ghost of Kenesaw Mountain Landis, white-maned, actually named for a mountain, appear with crossed baseball bats, and stand over me as I lay pinioned to the pitcher's mound? Would he swat away baseballs that circled about my head like bumblebees? I raise my arms over the moon-silvered park like an Aztec priest.

Once, as a child in Montana, I went with my father to a baseball game. I remember the soft-drink cups beaded with condensation, and a vendor in an orange hat tossing peanuts up into the stands like a pitcher making a move to first, and us passing quarters from hand to hand down to the vendor, and my father cheering for the pitcher. I forget what teams were playing, but the pitcher's name was Tony, and he was stocky, short-haired, and looked like a taciturn cowboy with a square, dimpled chin and gimlet eyes.

"Pour it on 'em, Tony," my father cheered. I took up the refrain, and soon others did too, our voices carrying in the thin Montana air. Half the crowd wore cowboy hats, I recall, and the parking lot was full of pickup trucks.

"Pour it on 'em, Tony," we roared, and he tipped his cap to us as he walked off the field after pitching out of a jam. He won the game, and for years I looked for his name on some big-league roster, but he disappeared, absorbed into the heart of America. One of the multitude who was not chosen.

And I think of that ballpark, abandoned the last time I saw it, the fences collapsed, lying at eerie angles, the stands dark and weathered, occasionally visited on cool summer nights by voices from the past.

For some reason, I recall the question at the bottom of the form sent by the Baseball Hall of Fame to everyone who has ever played organized baseball: "If you had it to do over again, would you play professional baseball?"

The historian at Cooperstown, Clifford S. Kachline, said he couldn't recall even one ex-player answering *no* to the question. I wonder if any other profession can say the same?

Annie and I were in Cooperstown once. We looked at Shoeless Joe Jackson's shoes reposing under glass. "How come a guy named Shoeless Joe had shoes?" Annie wanted to know. That was years before I built my ballpark. I explained that though Joe's shoes were there, he was not, and might never be.

Archie Graham, Salinger, and I tiptoe down the hollow concrete tunnels to the locker rooms. The lockers look cold as coffins; silver locks with faces like clocks dangle from each door. The room smells of sweat and chlorine. We find the door labeled "Equipment," and I do my kicking number again. Our eyes are treated to rack upon rack of white-ash bats glowing like opaque jewels in the darkness. We are exhilarated by the daring of our deeds: We feel excited, but evil, like Perry Smith and Richard Hickock on a gold-mooned Kansas night, exploring the dark recesses of the Clutter farmhouse room by room. The equipment room smells of leather and varnished wood. We motion for Archie to hold out his arms, and load him up with bats until he looks as if he is carrying an armful of firewood. I, too, gather an armful of bats. Salinger stuffs his pockets with balls, holds his left arm like a broken wing, fills the crook, runs balls down to his wrist and grips two in his palm. Our silent accomplice follows us, his eyes large. He is afraid to be with us, but afraid to run.

We make our way along the cold, reverberating corridors and emerge from the home-team dugout on the first-base side.

Scarcely looking around, I trudge out to the mound like a manager removing his fourth relief pitcher in an inning. The dew has fallen; the toes of my shoes are flecked with water. Salinger stops in the coaches' box.

From out here on the field, the space seems vast. I feel as I did as a child standing on a bald Montana hill watching the Northern Lights play hide-and-seek in the infinite night sky. A momentary spray of mist across the moon makes it dull as a pewter bowl. It is as if our venture were preplanned. I straighten my shoulders, take a deep breath, walk to the edge of the outfield grass, and place bats at what seem to me to be strategic locations. Some I toss toward the right-field wall, watching them bounce at crazy angles before settling in place, white as piano keys. I take Archie's bats from his arms and scatter them randomly about right field, like tossing the I Ching.

Salinger takes a ball and rolls it over the dew-silvered grass. In the moonlight it leaves a long black trail behind it. The moon is suddenly chrome-bright.

I take a ball and roll it toward a distant bat. It hisses softly and sends up a fine spray of dew. There is a muffled bump as it hits the bat and caroms off a few feet. It is as though we are engaged in a pagan ceremony.

Archie Graham tosses a ball high in the air; it looks like a snowball as it rises, and becomes a pearl as it crosses the face of the moon. It then drops onto the green-black grass and rolls away. I try to toss a ball skyward, but my throw is a rainbow arc that doesn't even rise high enough to be glazed by the moon.

"Bad arm," I whisper to Jerry.

"No arm," he replies.

And I remember how in high school I was kept on the team because I could hit, but was stationed in right field, the place where a fielder who cannot judge fly balls and throws like a girl is apt to do the least damage. Whenever a left-handed batter came up, I traded places with the left fielder. If a hit came my way, the shortstop would be nearly to me by the time I fielded it, and I would underhand the ball to him so he could throw to the infield. But I batted nearly .500 and struck out no more than once or twice. If only there had been designated hitters then.

"Ever been on a big-league field before?" I ask Jerry, but don't wait for an answer. "Oh, but you must have dreamed of the Polo Grounds just like I dreamed of Comiskey Park, of playing for the White Sox."

"I've told you about that," hisses Jerry. "Wherever you got that story, it's wrong. I've always been a writer." We are interrupted by a tapping sound, like a judge rapping a gavel, and turn toward home plate. Archie Graham stands there. He pops a bat twice more on home plate, then tosses a ball in the air and swings. The crack of the bat sounds like a paper bag exploding, yet the sound is cold and lonely, too, like a hunter firing on an endless tundra. I hear the ball traveling overhead, whistling softly, and then there is another pop as it hits the center-field fence. I am able to follow it for an instant as it bounces back and rolls among the equipment we have strewn. Archie waves to us and holds up another ball.

For the first time, I worry about the noise we are making. My heart flutters against my shirt. What if we are discovered? I feel the sharp form of the screwdriver in my pocket, the one I brought along to tighten the locks I kicked loose. What if we are arrested? I can picture a court clerk reading out the charges: breaking and entering, willful damage, possession of burglar tools—to wit, an amber-handled screwdriver.

The bat cracks and a ball soars up, glints across the moon's eye, and disappears over the right-field wall.

"Can you do it without the bat?" I say in a stage whisper.

The young man smiles, a wide, pumpkin-happy grin, as if I've just complimented him on his sexual prowess. He cranks up his arm, rears back, and throws, and the ball, taking an even more perfect path than it took off the bat, travels in a white arc, seeming to leave behind a line like a streak of forgotten rainbow as it drops over the fence, silent as a star falling into a distant ocean.

The boy continues to grin.

"You have quite an arm," I say.

Jerry whistles softly.

I picture the ball bouncing crazily across the asphalt-and-gravel parking lot. I imagine some swing-shift worker taking a short cut across the quiet parking lot, perhaps kneeling down before the white revelation that has rolled to a stop at his feet.

Salinger has placed two bats in an inverted V on the right-field grass. He now stands just behind second base, and, like a lawn bowler, rolls baseballs toward the distant ash-whiteness. The balls hum across the grass and ricochet unceremoniously to one side as they strike a cleat mark or depression in the grass.

Watching this, I remember something Eddie Scissons once told me. "When I was in the minors there were gopher holes in the outfields of some of the parks we played in," he said. "The home team knew where they were, and how to step around them, and they'd laugh fit to kill when a visitor would sprain an ankle or take a fall. I remember once I decided to fix a guy who played right field for Idaho Falls. Before the game, from before noon until suppertime, I carried pails of water and dumped them all in a little depression in the outfield grass. It was August, and the rest of the field was baked dry. By game time that plot, about three foot square, was like quicksand.

"Second play of the game, one of our men singled to right, and the fielder charged the ball." Here Eddie stopped to chuckle heartily. "His feet disappeared right up to the ankles, and he pitched on his face just as the ball rolled by and to the wall. Our player got an inside-the-park home run."

For an hour or more Salinger, Graham, and I play like children in a forbidden room.

"Can you hear the roar of the crowd?" I say. "Stretch out your ears and listen. Smell the onions frying, smell the roasted peanuts." Salinger and our young friend are kneeling on the outfield grass perhaps twenty yards apart, rolling baseballs toward each other, trying to make them collide. The balls send up a fine spray, and when they do bump, they skitter sideways like shying horses, leaving strange hieroglyphic signatures on the turf. In the dewy morning, the baseball field under the moonglow looks as though someone has set out silver bowls of water at strategic locations. The only sound is that of a plane dozing overhead, its lights blinking hypnotically.

As I look around the empty park, almost Greek in its starkness, I feel an awesome inarticulate love for this very stadium and the game it represents. I am reminded of the story about the baseball fans of Milwaukee, and what they did on a warm fall afternoon, the day after it was announced that Milwaukee was to have a major-league team the next season. According to the story, 10,000 people went to County Stadium that afternoon and sat in the seats and smiled out at the empty playing field—sat in silence, in awe, in wonder, in anticipation, in joy—just knowing that soon the field would come alive with the chatter of infielders, bright as bird chirps.

Now, in the predawn grayness of the Twins' stadium, the loudspeaker booms out over the silent field we have invaded. The words reverberate from the outfield walls and vibrate the cold metallic chairs in the boxes along each baseline.

I look at Salinger and Moonlight Graham. They do not raise their heads, but continue with their boy's game.

I glance at Jerry, who is driving my battered, salmon-colored Datsun. He looks my way, and his craggy features break into a slight smile.

"We just crossed the Iowa border," he says. "Do you know, I've never been to Iowa?"

"I suspected."

Our young hitchhiker is scrunched into the back seat, his right knee a rigid lump in my back, his duffel bag upright beside him like a dun-colored torso.

"When we get to Iowa City, we'll take the Old Capitol exit," I say. "Before we go home, I have to stop in town."

"Groceries?" says Jerry.

"A relief pitcher," I reply. Groceries? I recall the story I heard about Jerry craving soybeans. "Do you really eat a lot of soybeans?" I ask.

"Relief pitcher? Soybeans?" He laughs pleasantly. "Never

tasted the things that I know of, though I've read they're supposed to be good for you."

"I'm glad."

"That I've never tasted soybeans?"

"Yes."

Jerry shrugs. "That doesn't sound as unusual to me as it would have a week ago. I guess I'm getting used to you," he says, then abruptly switches to a new subject. "Your wife isn't a vegetarian, is she? The thought just crossed my mind that I hate eggplant casseroles, and dishes with a lot of noodles covered in stuff that looks like powdered horse dung."

"We're meat and potato people," I say.

"Somebody say something about food?" asks the hitchhiker from the back seat. His voice is a little high, but softened by his whispery Carolina drawl. "Anytime you want to stop, I'm ready to eat again."

The deeper we penetrate Iowa, the greener it gets. It has been summer for all my odyssey, but a lean, scanty summer of thin trees and cropped yellow grass. Here, near the heart of the nation, everything is lush: The corn is waist high, the trees fat-leaved, the grass tall, and the earth soft.

I wheel off the interstate at Exit 244.

In the over-air-conditioned motel in Minneapolis during the few hours between our trip to the ballpark and our rising, I had dreamed of Eddie Scissons. As we rolled toward Iowa City, I decided on a definite plan of action. Today Eddie haunts my waking hours like a dropped pop-up. I can see him sitting across the polished maple table from me at the Friendship Center: back straight, huge hands spread out on the table in front of him, face pink as rose petals.

"Know what I'm gonna do?" Eddie said.

"No," I said, although I'm always tempted to answer a question like that with a yes.

"Goin' to be buried in a Chicago Cubs uniform." He smiled and nodded his head up and down, waiting for my reaction.

And as I thought about the statement, I pictured Eddie laid out across a circular table, stiff as a board, head and feet extended over the edges, dressed in a soft, new-smelling uniform with a grinning bear-cub insignia, his large feet encased in shiny, uncrumpled spikes, his head covered by a Cubs' cap.

"Spikes and cap, too?" I said. I felt it better to take Eddie's statement in stride, for I didn't think he was trying to shock me, only to share something he knew no one else understood.

"By golly, I hadn't thought of cleats. I got the cap." He tapped his mane of yellowish-white hair. "Just up and wrote to the Cubs one day and asked how much for a size 44 uniform and cap, and they sent back the price and I ordered one, and I got it put away with lots of mothballs, in a cedar chest my wife used to keep linen in. But I never thought of cleats. Now I'd look right foolish, I'm afraid, all laid out fit to start a new season, but with patent-leather shoes on, or brogues, or even slippers. Nope, nothin' will do but cleats, and I thank you for reminding me."

"Didn't you tell them who you were?" I asked. "They should *give* a uniform to their oldest living player."

"Well now, I never thought of that either. Why I reckon they don't know who I am anymore. I played in 1908, '09, and '10. Why it's nearly seventy years since the last time I stepped out on the grass at Wrigley Field. I was just a kid. Did I tell you I was called Kid Scissons?"

I nodded, to show that he has told me.

"It was Three Finger Brown give me the nickname. You know what his full name was? Mordecai Peter Centennial Brown. Now it was no wonder he didn't mind being called Three Finger, or sometimes Miner, for that's what he was, and how he lost part of his pitchin' hand and got his nickname.

"He was the first man ever to pitch four straight shutouts. Did you know that?" I nodded negatively, even though I did know. "And I was there. Didn't get to play. A fellow who's pitchin' shutout ball don't need no relief pitcher. That was in the summer of 1908, my first summer in the big leagues. He pitched the last one on July Fourth, and they set up firecrackers and rockets after the game, and had a rack of sparklers that spelled out BROWN in big, burning blue-silver letters—pretty fancy for that long ago."

"I wish I could have seen it."

"Yes sir, I'm gonna have to get me a pair of size-twelve baseball shoes to go with my uniform. I bet if I dug down in some of the boxes I got at home, I could find a pair of spikes from my playing days, but they'd be all gray and petrified like me, and wouldn't be classy enough to wear with a new uniform. They all think I'm crazy, you know, but I'm not."

"I know," I said.

"The Cubs have been my whole life. I've followed them for eighty years—since I was seven and an uncle of mine came from Chicago to visit our farm in Nebraska, clutching a fistful of Chicago sports pages, a copy of the *St. Louis Sporting News*, and a gift for describing the beauty and mystery of baseball. I'd listen to him for hours, both of us sitting on the front step of the house, and Ma would have to call me twice for meals and ten times for bed. And he brought me a baseball, a bat, and a glove. He showed me how to hit and how to throw, and he painted a target on the side of the barn with whitewash. 'Laziest man in creation,' was how my father described my uncle. 'Stuffed full of dreams,' he said he was, and I guess he was right.

"After he was gone, I retold his stories to my dog, so I wouldn't forget them. And after the ball was worn out, I practiced with rocks, and frozen horse turds in the winter, and I made my own baseballs out of cowhide stuffed with hay and mud. Uncle Clyde even told me how to do that; said to always put a frog in the middle of the ball, to give it a true bounce. And I did." Eddie grinned like a kid.

"The Cubs have been my whole life," he repeated. "I kicked around in the minors for a few years, but once you been to the top, it's hard to settle for less. I worked for years in Chicago, so I could be close to them—hardly missed a game, season after season. Then I got offered a school-principal job out here in Iowa, and I had a family and times were tough. But I still had the summers: used to go up for homestands. It's just the last year or two that I've got too old and tired to make the trip. Only regret I have is that I never had a son of my own to teach to love the game. Have three daughters. Used to take them to the games, but they didn't catch the fever. They're all Bible thumpers, and been treating me like I was senile ever since they were old enough to think for themselves."

I felt a genuine pang of guilt for not having shared my magical windfall with Eddie. I can't think of anyone who would have enjoyed it more.

* * *

"This is home," I say as the car glides down Dubuque Street into Iowa City, past City Park, and along the Iowa River, green and peaceful as Chinese silk, where it snakes between grassy banks with university buildings on either side. Salinger and Moonlight Graham are busy as rubbernecking tourists as we drive toward the center of town.

Iowa City: immortalized by Meredith Willson as River City in *The Music Man*. Shady streets, very old white frame houses, porch swings, lilacs, one-pump gas stations, and good neighbors. But the wagons have been gathered into a circle, and the pioneers are being picked off one by one by fast-food franchises that spring up everywhere like evil mushrooms, by concrete-and-glass buildings, muffler shops, and Howard Johnson motels. Each of these destroys a little more history. Iowa City is a town of grandfathers fighting a losing battle against time.

"We have a drugstore with a soda fountain," I say. "It's dark and cool and you can smell malt in the air like a musky perfume. And they have cold lemon-Cokes in sweating glasses, a lime drink called a Green River, and just the best chocolate malts in America. It's called Pearson's—right out of a Norman Rockwell painting. I'll take you there tomorrow."

I think about the message I received at Metropolitan Stadium in Bloomington, while we cavorted like mythical creatures on the damp grass. It was even less precise than previous ones. What I saw was Eddie Scissons seated across a table from me, the brass serpent-head of his cane hidden under his large hands. With the ambiguousness of a true oracle, the voice spoke of sharing and betrayal in a way that I knew meant Eddie Scissons.

I ease the car across town and park in the lot next to the Bishop Cridge Friendship Center, located in a renovated Victorian house. Tall honeysuckle, each stock measled with scarlet berries, clothes the front of the building, thickening the air.

As I open the door into the common room, I see Eddie Scissons, the oldest living Chicago Cub, sitting in a square green easy chair. His back is to me, but the mane of white hair easily identifies him.

"Kid Scissons," I say, stepping around his chair in order to face him. I stick out my hand.

He half stands, but his creaking joints won't let him make it all the way. "Been expecting you," he says. "At least I think

I have," he goes on, a puzzled expression drifting across his face. "I dreamed about you last night and I said to myself, I bet Ray's gonna come see me today."

He settles back into the chair, but instead of looking at me he looks at the floor. "Whatever you want to say to me, get on with it," he says to the faded carpet that was once the color of a green apple.

"It's nothing bad," I say. "You must be remembering your dream. I want you to come out to the farm with me. I have something to show you—something I should have shown you a long time ago." I find myself pacing back and forth. He looks up at me, his eyes the faded blue of dried bachelor's buttons. He stares over his hands, which are cupped over the serpent-head cane.

"Did you just come in from the farm?" he says finally.

"I've been away," I reply, "for a couple of weeks. I have people I want you to meet. Have you heard of J. D. Salinger, the writer? And a baseball player—he played in the majors—no, that's not right, quite. Anyway, I want you to meet him."

Eddie fidgets in the chair. His head is down. He mumbles something about someone named Judy, who I assume is a supervisor at the center.

"Come on," I insist. "You don't have to check with anybody here, and you live alone." I reach down and take his arm and help him to stand. We move a step or two toward the door.

"You're not gonna hurt me, are you?" says Eddie.

"Eddie! For heaven's sake, it's me, Ray Kinsella. I'm taking you out to your old farm." And I wonder how much Eddie's mind has deteriorated since I last saw him.

Once Eddie has walked a few steps, it becomes easier for him to move, and we make it down the front steps and over to the car without incident, Eddie all the time looking around as if he expects to be attacked from ambush.

Salinger moves into the back seat beside Moonlight Graham and his dolorous duffel bag, and with much difficulty, like storing an open folding chair, we get Eddie into the passenger seat.

I burble like a meadowlark at everything I see. I am happier than I have been since I left Iowa. A quick drive through town, a stop at First National Bank to see if we are still solvent, a stop at New Pioneer Co-Op for groceries, and then we head east to the farm. I can feel Annie's warmth pulling me, smell the sweetness of her, pure as spring rain, her tongue tart as raspberry. Annie is an Iowa girl, raised on a farm. I've only seen pictures of her father, a man I'm almost glad I never met. Not that we wouldn't have liked each other, it's just that I'm uncomfortable with most men, especially "men's men" who know all about gears, rifles, and how to splice rope. They always make me feel like the new kid on the block, tolerated but not accepted, and they always act as though they have a common secret that I will never be party to.

A picture of Annie's father still sits on the darkly severe mantel in my mother-in-law's home—a freckle-faced man with home-cut hair and a sunburned neck. He stares frankly at the world, with Annie's green eyes. When Annie was nine, he found his way into the whirling gears of a John Deere harvester.

Annie's mother relishes telling the story of how it took the other members of the threshing crew over four hours to recover all the parts of him from the clanking machine. I think I would have liked him, and, more important, that he would have liked me. He went to church just to keep peace in the family, Annie has told me, and he chewed snuff and was known to drop in at Donnelly's Bar in Iowa City for an occasional beer. Annie must have inherited her loving nature from him, and she says she remembers him once attending a baseball game when he was in Kansas City for a Great Plains Corn Growers convention.

The kind of people I absolutely cannot tolerate are those, like Annie's mother, who never let you forget they are religious. It seems to me that a truly religious person would let his life be example enough, would not let his religion interfere with being a human being, and would not be so insecure as to have to fawn publicly before his gods. My mother-in-law can and does work the Lord into every conversation, whether it concerns coffee prices, Karin's cat, or the weather. The understatement of the year would be to say we do not like each other.

When I appeared at her door to apply for the room she had advertised for rent in the *Daily Iowan*, the first question she asked me was, "Are you a Christian?" For the remainder of the interview, she was cold and distant, the sharp light from a circular tri-light glittering off the rims of her glasses. Housing was very scarce. I left my phone number, but held out little hope. But it was early October, her Christian roomer had been cut by the football team and had left for Georgia, after kicking a hole in his door and writing misspelled four-letter words on the wall with a crayon. I was living in a basement room where waterdrops the size of thumbtacks condensed on the walls, where the bedsheets were always cold and wet, and where large black waterbugs clacked across the linoleum all night every night. It turned out that she needed the money even if it came from a non-Christian wallet, and I needed a dry place to sleep.

As we drive toward the farm, I think of Annie and me walking, with our arms around each other's waists, toward the ballfield, in the evenings when the clouds are a dozen shades of pink, rose, and chocolate, looking as though they have been stirred in a blender.

Annie is a spectator, not a fan. Like a reader who reads a whole book without caring who wrote it, she watches, enjoys, forgets, and doesn't read the box scores and standings in the morning paper.

I have had good reason not to tell Eddie Scissons about the baseball field I've built. These past few green and gold summers, I have kept it a secret. We have Eddie out to the farm for dinner every couple of months, and I drop in at the Friendship Center to listen to him talk about baseball. But when he comes to the farm, I park at the side of the house, where my enterprise is not visible, and Eddie's arthritis keeps him from exploring the farm himself. When Annie suggests that Eddie would enjoy seeing the field, I choose not to answer her.

"A guy from First National phoned me yesterday," Eddie said to me during my last visit to the Friendship Center before I set out for New Hampshire.

"Oh," I said.

"Says you're spending four thousand dollars for a new mini-tractor. Wanted to know if you were keeping your mortgage payments up-to-date."

"Oh," I said again.

"I said you were. What bankers don't know doesn't hurt them. But what do you need with one of them little tractors?"

There was no way that I could explain to Eddie, at least so

he would understand. I bought the new tractor, an International Cub Cadet, so I could mow the outfield grass. It was taking me a full day to mow the ballpark with my rattletrap gas mower that had to be refueled every few circuits of the field, and stalled over and over if the grass was wet or more than an inch long. But Eddie knew enough about corn farming to know that there was no reason for me to own such a machine. And the mortgage payments were indeed in arrears, and the situation would get worse before it got better. I rationalized that it was not as if Eddie needed the money, and I fidgeted and gave evasive answers until he stopped asking, but I knew he was angry with me.

We drive east toward Annie, my farm, my miracle; and I have no idea what is going to happen when we get there. I might as well be the Wizard of Oz, Oscar Zoroaster Phadrig Isaac Norman Henkle Emmanuel Ambrose Diggs, heading for a Kansas farm in company of a scarecrow, a tin man, and a cowardly lion, with one eye cocked lest the wicked witch come swooping by, riding a broom and clutching a screaming black cat to her bosom.

I feel just a touch of depression, as if a hand were passed in front of my eyes, as I turn the Datsun into the long driveway and, with a rumble, cross the metal cattle guard that keeps livestock from escaping to the roadway. Everything seems smaller than I remember it. The house is neither so stately as I have described it to Jerry and Moonlight, nor as grand as I remember it. A granary lists awkwardly, weathered gray as dust. The ballpark looks ragged and forlorn.

But as I ease the car to a stop, a few of Annie's white Wyandotte hens strolling out of the way, staring at the car with bland orange eyes, Karin bolts from the back door, a blur of white blouse and pink pedal pushers. She flings herself into my arms as I step from the car, and hugs my neck in unrestrained joy, smelling sweet as red clover.

"Daddy, Daddy. It's *really* you. I can tell," she shouts.

An unusual greeting, it seems to me.

"I have a surprise. I have a surprise," she shouts, kissing me madly on one cheek and then the other. She pulls back to look at me, and her eyes widen as she spots the scar at my left eyebrow, pale pink as a worm.

"It *is* really you, isn't it?" Her green eyes are troubled.

"Of course. You're silly." I hug her to me, kissing her soft cheeks while she wiggles like a cat being dressed in doll's clothes.

Salinger has squeezed out from behind the driver's seat, walked around the car, and is slowly easing Eddie out of the passenger side, while one of Moonlight's long, dark arms pushes on Eddie's back.

I walk around the car, still holding Karin.

"This is Jerry Salinger," I say. "You remember Mr. Scissons, and the fellow in the back is Archie Graham."

Salinger makes polite noises. Karin scarcely glances at any of them.

"I have a surprise," she says again, and wriggles from my grasp. I realize I have forgotten to bring her anything as a gift, except a jar of black olives from the Co-Op that she'll eat later all by herself. But she hasn't noticed.

She climbs the three faded steps to the back door, turns, and faces us from the top one, spreads her arms as if she were a ringmaster about to begin an introduction, squares her chin, and begins talking in a twangy, singsong voice quite unlike her own: "The world's strangest babies are here. You've talked about them, wondered about them, now you owe it to yourself to see them. Once you've seen them, you'll agree this is a show the whole family should see. Mothers bring your daughters. Fathers bring your sons."

Annie appears behind Karin, smiling through the screen. She stares down where Karin continues her spiel, and flexes her hands in a gesture of helplessness. I want to touch Annie, but we have to wait. The others stand uncomfortably in the yard, assuming that I know what is going on. They must think I've forgotten to mention that Karin is an aspiring Shirley Temple, Tatum O'Neil, or whoever.

"You've read about them, heard about them, now come in and see them. Look at all the pictures—read all the signs, buy a ticket, and come on in. You owe it to yourself to see these strange babies. The world's strangest babies are here. See the famous Siamese twins. The gorilla baby. The baby born to a twelve-year-old mother. Mothers bring your daughters. Fathers bring your sons. Buy a ticket and come on in."

Karin stops and smiles, proud as a cat with a dead bird in its teeth.

I'm not certain what to do.

Jerry applauds politely, a bewildered look on his face. Eddie leans on his cane. Moonlight is extracting his duffel bag from the back of the car.

"Your brother's here," Annie says, bouncing down the steps. She gets to within a few feet of me, and then *she* sees the scar. "Richard, what are you doing—no—you're not . . ."

"It's me," I peep. "I walked into a pillar at Fenway Park in Boston. Jerry will vouch for me."

"Of course," says Annie, but she still hasn't touched me.

Richard, after all these years. He must have something to do with Karin's recitation.

"Karin was born at two thirty-one P.M. on a Saturday afternoon," I say rapidly. "Her second name is Irene. On our first real date, you and I went to the Iowa Theater on Dubuque Street, to see a Walt Disney movie. I spilled Coke on the floor under our seats, and our shoes stuck to the sidewalk as we walked back up Johnson Street toward your mother's home."

"Oh, Ray, I knew it was you," says Annie, and she fits her mouth inside mine for a few seconds. Instead of crushing her to me as I have fantasized, I barely touch her shoulders with my fingertips, as I let the thrill of her surge through me like an electric shock.

"This is Annie," I say. "Annie, I'd like you to meet J. D. Salinger."

Annie steps forward, wiping away some red-pepper curls with a hand that has recently been immersed in flour. The curls retreat, leaving a white half-moon sketched on her freckled forehead. She smiles, wipes the floury hand on the thigh of her jeans, shakes hands.

"Jerry," says Salinger. "People who know me call me Jerry."

"Where did Richard come from? How did he find us? What's he been doing all these years?" I ask questions, but they don't seem to get answered.

There is much confusion as we help Eddie into the house and I introduce Moonlight Graham. They must think it strange that I haven't seen my brother in over twenty years; that I have hardly mentioned having an identical twin; that my wife almost didn't know me. But Salinger only grins good-naturedly, and I imagine him salting the scene away for use in a future novel.

"What about the baseball team?" Moonlight interjects during a brief lull.

"Later," I say, and he goes back to his coffee.

Eddie sits, hands on cane, looking unhappy.

"You should have seen Karin," says Annie, laughing brightly. "She ran right into Richard's arms when he got out of the taxi in the yard. Then she turned her head away and said 'You smell funny, Daddy.' It took her a few days to get over that: Every time Richard would walk into a room, she'd start to say Daddy."

"And you?" I ask.

"The first words he said to me were, 'I'm not Ray. I have a scar.' And he took off his cap so I could see it. It *was* a shock, though, I have to admit."

I follow her into the kitchen when she goes for more coffee. She steps into my arms, her face against my chest, her belly solidly and warmly against mine. I kiss across her cheeks and find her lips.

When our eyes meet, I nod my head toward the upstairs and our bedroom.

"Hey, Champ, we got company," Annie says, cuddling close, letting me know she wants my love as much as I want hers.

"They can amuse themselves for an hour," I plead.

"It was you who came home with an entourage. You've got to entertain them. Some of your fantasies will just have to wait." She slips away, leaving me with my arms still in front of me in the shape of a circle.

Instead, I take my guests on a tour of the baseball field. But as we near it, I feel as if an exam has been laid in front of me and I have no idea how to answer a single question. The fence is there. The baseball field is there. But it is much smaller than I remember, and there is no magic about it this late afternoon, no concave grandstand full of thousands of fans who hum like the wind, no vendors, no banks of floodlights, no players. It looks pitiful.

Dandelions brighten the outfield like egg yolks.

I can see the disappointment creeping across Salinger's face slow as a crawling insect. He must be thinking that I have conned him, that I'm just a crazy corn farmer who has hallucinations. Eddie Scissons creaks along with us, leaning on his cane.

"Do teams really play here?" asks Moonlight Graham, and I consider the difference between what he sees and what I know is there, hidden like wondrously painted Easter eggs waiting for someone who believes to part the grass and find them.

"Yes," I say, but without conviction. The gap is too gigantic for me to try and explain it away with mere words.

The field under the sizzling sun and the high, breathless sky is sweet as a perfume factory. The grass needs cutting and raking. It is heavy and damp and cool; and all across the outfield, dense grass cowlicks glisten frog-green.

"What the hell is this?" says Eddie.

"It's a baseball field," I reply truthfully.

"Why?" he says and looks at me with his wide-set eyes, blue as a field of flax.

A valid question, and one I won't be able to answer until the magic unfolds.

"Eddie, Eddie, you'll love it here. The White Sox play here. Shoeless Joe Jackson, Chick Gandil, Swede Risberg, Buck Weaver..." I jabber on for ten minutes, extolling the virtues of my field and describing its marvels in a litany not dissimilar to Karin's monologue on the back steps. I feel as if I have had a bucket of water dumped over my head and am somehow accountable for every drop. I try to cover too much ground. While I'm talking, I remember the story of how Shoeless Joe, after he had been paid off, tried to return the money and, failing that, tried to take it to White Sox owner Charles Comiskey. He got only as far as an accountant, who slammed down a shutter, ending the conversation and leaving Joe alone in a darkened hallway. I think about how the sound of that slamming shutter must have haunted Joe for the rest of his life.

And I think of Richard. Where is he? "Gone to Iowa City," Annie told me. "He'll be home later. He works as a barker for the carnival that's passing through town." I still don't know how he found us.

"Mark's been around with more offers to buy the farm," Annie said. "Getting really pushy, as if I could sell it to him by myself, even if I wanted to. And Eddie Scissons has been phoning you every day for a week. Did he tell you why?"

"Have you been phoning me?" I say to Eddie as he sits staring out across the playerless diamond, perhaps dreaming of his days with the Chicago Cubs.

"No," he says, "I haven't." His voice is low and far away.

"It just needs a little work," I say, spreading my arms to take in the whole ballpark, trying to sound enthusiastic. Three flat, expressionless faces return my gaze.

"I'll hook up the tractor and mow the outfield," I say. "It will make a lot of difference."

After a very long pause Jerry says, "Do you need some help?" and Moonlight nods, even though I can see the skepticism floating in his eyes like tadpoles.

"*This* is what you bought the tractor for?" says Eddie in a scratchy voice.

"It's more than just this," I say. "You'll see. I thought you'd understand. You played for the Cubs. Baseball's been your whole life . . ."

"Now I don't feel so bad about what I done," says Eddie.

"What?" I say.

"You don't know already, eh? Well, you will soon enough."

I am afraid to ask for details. I have enough to worry about. I drag out my ancient gas-powered mower that burps blue smoke, and set Moonlight to mowing the infield grass. I give Salinger clippers and put him to work trimming the shaggy edges along the foul lines. I seat Eddie on an overturned bucket near first base, where he can glower at each of us in turn.

There is a flurry of activity as I carry cool, mothball-smelling blankets from the linen closet and make up beds for Moonlight and Kid Scissons in a room we seldom use. The furniture is sparse: a plastic-covered mattress, a single bureau with an amber-tinted mirror, one straight-backed chair.

"It's not fancy," I say.

"I've stayed in worse hotels," says Kid Scissons. "In the minors, there was lots of times bugs."

"I'd sleep in a strawstack for a chance to play ball," says Moonlight Graham.

Late in the night, while my guests sleep, while my magic field sleeps, while Annie sleeps with one freckled arm tossed over my pillow, while trees sigh and the night breathes softly, I pad downstairs and sit at the kitchen table, my elbows resting on the slick, patterned oilcloth that covers it. The spicy scent of oilcloth means cleanness to me, for the table in my mother's kitchen was always covered with it, and when it was washed, after every meal, it glowed in the lamplight and I would sniff its clean new-cloth odor.

I sit and watch two lemon-lines of moonlight that knife across the floor like laser beams. From where I sit, I can stare out the screen door; the moon looks as if it is covered with graph paper. I walk to the door, inhale the perfume of the Iowa night. Earlier, it has rained. A few nickel-sized drops plopped in the dust. I press my nose against the screen. Rain-green corn and spun-metal scents assail my senses.

"Just like a kid," Annie always says when she sees me this way. Sometimes she kisses the dark pattern off my nose when I turn away, and sometimes she flees in mock horror, shouting, "No. No. No one with a checkered nose will kiss these lips!"

I have just come from making love to Annie. No. Making love *with* Annie: her arms around my neck, her mouth peach sweet, tiny freckled breasts pressed against my chest. Our bodies, slick with sweat, move together when we make love, slipping as if soaped. Annie's curls are damp on her forehead, and all the time she sings to me, love songs in tongues, bird sounds, bird songs thrilling and brilliant as morning. And when I look at her face in the silky darkness, I marvel that I can love her so much, marvel that our love puts other things in perspective. I wish I had some kind of fame to dedicate to her: that I was an auto racer, a bullfighter, an author, even a politician—I see myself making my acceptance speech, thanking party faithful, then calling Annie forward to share the applause, the adoration.

But I am likely to have nothing to share with her in the near future. Eventually I turn on the light and drag out the bank books, the ledgers, and the sheaf of bills that puff up around the paper-spike. Annie is incurably optimistic. It was her idea to rent the farm, and, when we broke even at that, her idea to buy it.

"A farmer can't make a living on one hundred sixty acres anymore," everyone has said to us, especially Annie's relatives. Eddie Scissons was willing to carry the mortgage, and the bank trusted him, but land here costs over $2000 an acre. A combine is worth $70,000, and the amount of equipment Eddie had on the farm was staggering. I look at the payments that will be due in the fall, and I have a sinking feeling within me, as if an elevator has dropped five floors. Mark is right, too many things have accumulated. Even if I let Eddie's mortgage payments fall further in arrears, there still won't be enough money.

I think of the tractor sitting out in the machine shed—the one that has nothing to do with the corn crop. The International Cub Cadet 127 for which I paid $3950 in order to be able to mow my baseball field.

"Things will work out," Annie said when I came home with it in the back of our pickup truck.

Karin sat on my knee as, like a mechanical bee, we hummed around the outfield on the new tractor with a mower blade attached. Annie joined us and drove the tractor in tight circles on the center-field grass. "I'll make a target circle for you, and you can hire a skydiver, and people will come from all over to see the show."

"What show? We're the only ones who see it," I reminded her.

I recall raking the infield after supper, tweaking out an occasional weed that had infiltrated while I was away. The earth of the infield, for the most part, had that abandoned look that dirt quickly acquires when it is not tended—like a car windshield splattered with raindrops that have dried like black lace. My footprints, my players' footprints, had been erased by gentle wind and spring rain. From my hands and knees, the ground had a moonscape aura—tiny grains of dirt looked like mountains, an ant like something prehistoric. The earth around the bases was fine as brown flour when I finished.

Out in the night, the metal cattle guard twangs as a car crosses it. A taxi pulls into the yard, its roof light glowing green as an electric lime. Then Richard stands dark in the kitchen doorway. I look up from the table. It is as if I am staring into a full-length mirror.

We don't leap into each other's arms, backslapping and recalling old joys. We shake hands cautiously, as if there is a referee holding his hand out like a knife between us. "We loved each other as brothers should, no more and no less," I said to Annie once, and she looked at me uncomprehendingly. Except for occasional bursts of camaraderie, which came like thunderstorms, we were never close. Mother didn't dress us alike or try to enhance what nature had already done. Twins can never escape from each other, I read in a book once. We are like the Gemini astrological sign. I make coffee and we sit across the table from each other, staring.

How do we know which of us is which? What if it was I who punched the fist through the wall in our farmhouse near Deer Lodge, Montana? What if it has been me who has swished like a tumbleweed across the face of America for twenty years, traveling like a long-distance mover with no home base, going from New Orleans to Amarillo, Kansas City to Chicago, Cleveland to Baltimore, and back again, over and over? What if Annie and Karin are his family, and I am rootless as a pulled weed?

"So tell me, where have you been? What have you done?"

"Have you got a year?" says Richard, and laughs—my laugh.

"Where did you go when you left? When did you find out that Dad was dead? Why didn't you at least write to Mother?" The questions pour out of me. I try not to make them sound incriminating, but fail.

"I knew what was going to happen before I ever picked the fight with Dad. Hell, I've got feathers in my shoes. You were weighed down with lead, just like them. I've always thought of myself as kind of a bird, flying from one thing to another. Birds never go back to the nest once they've flown away."

"You didn't answer any of my questions."

"I've been with the carnival for ten years now. You learn how not to answer questions."

"Why did you come back now?"

"There's a little homing device in all of us. I admit I've been pulled a few times. A year or so ago, I started looking for Kinsellas in every phone book in every town we passed through. I found a Raymond down in McClean, Texas, and I phoned him. He was black, and he didn't know where he got his name.

"Then a week ago I came to Iowa City. They changed the schedule, we don't usually stop here. Have too much equipment for the single block they give us to set up; I've always gone straight on to Cedar Rapids. I looked in the Iowa City phone book and there you were. I phoned and asked the lady who answered if you came from Deer Lodge, Montana, and she didn't have to answer. I could tell by the long pause that you did, and that she thought she was talking to you and that you were playing some kind of game with her." He stops and smiles.

"That lady of yours is something else, and Karin—I'd chop off an arm, bit by bit, for a child like Karin." He smiles again. "I look around here and I see that it's not so bad to be lead-footed. I've always thought it would be like having one foot nailed to the earth and turning in tight circles ever after, but now I'm not so sure. You must be happy. With a wife and child like that, you must be happy."

"I am. But you haven't seen anything. You haven't met the others. You haven't seen the field."

"What's going on here anyway? Annie just says something about you building a baseball diamond, but Karin says there are games on it. I walked around it one night and it was eerie, like I could hear leaves rustling where there weren't any trees."

"We're cleaning it up," I say. "You can help, after breakfast, if you want to." Richard isn't the only one who can avoid answering questions.

"Have you ever been married?" I ask, but the question is heavy as a paperweight, and the silence that follows it awkward. I have moved in too close too fast.

"I have a lady," Richard finally says. "She works in the change booth at the carnival. She's called Gypsy, and only the head office in Florida knows her whole name. She ran away from somewhere when she was thirteen, says she's a Gypsy. Been telling it to people for so long she believes it herself. She's like me, got feathers for feet. We're convenient for each other, but we can, either of us, fly away whenever we want." He pauses.

"Some guy told me once that her family owns a motel in Kellogg, Idaho, and that they've offered a ten-thousand-dollar reward for information about her. Says the reward's been unclaimed for over ten years. I think about it whenever I'm broke."

At breakfast, Salinger fries the bacon, Eddie tends the coffee. "Haven't you got any eggshells?" Eddie wants to know. "Real coffee has eggshells in it. That was the way Ellen did it. Every morning of our married life, she brewed up a pot of coffee— one of them gray enamel jobs the pot was, not like this thing." He nods contemptuously at the glass-and-plastic wonder that premeasures water and coffee and even makes the brew strong or weak according to the push of a button. I am cooking the eggs, grease spitting onto the backs of my hands, for I have the burner turned too high.

"All I've got are these," I say, pointing to the glistening white shells I've split open on the edge of the pan.

"Have to be dry," says Eddie derisively. "You save 'em. Let 'em dry in the warming oven. And they have to be brown, only eggs from brown hens are any good in coffee. You dry 'em and crumble 'em and toss a handful in with the grounds, and you watch 'em boil, and roll around in the pot."

"Joe DiMaggio sold this coffee maker on television," I say, as if trying to give it some legitimacy.

Moonlight Graham is tending the toaster, while Karin, in a cardinal-colored dressing gown, standing on a chair, butters the toast and stacks it on plates. Someone speaks to me, but I barely hear, for I am thinking of the story of Marilyn Monroe returning from a trip to entertain the troops in Korea—returning to an unhappy Joe DiMaggio, who had not wanted her to go.

"There were thousands and thousands of soldiers everywhere I went," Marilyn said. "You never heard such cheering . . ."

"Yes, I have," replied the Yankee Clipper sadly.

The phone rings. Annie answers it on the upstairs extension and yells down that it is for me. "Take over the eggs," I say to Richard, who has been drawn downstairs by the bacon and coffee smells.

"Ray," Mark says in his professional voice, "it's good to

have you back. We have some business to discuss. Have you thought any more about our last offer?"

"I told you what you could do with it before I left. Why should I change my mind?"

"Oh, no reason," says Mark, as if he knows something I don't know.

"The place is not for sale."

"We'll up the ante twenty-five thousand dollars," says Mark.

"No."

"I'm afraid you're going to have to come up with some cash rather quickly then."

I feel as if I've reached for my wallet and found the pocket empty.

"How so?"

"I guess you haven't seen Mr. Scissons since you got back?"

"I have. He's right here, sitting at my table."

"Oh, really?" says Mark. I look sharply at Eddie. He becomes intent on watching the coffee dribble into the squat receptacle beneath the machine. "I guess he doesn't have the nerve to tell you," Mark goes on. "We've optioned your mortgage. At the end of sixty days, we own it. So unless you bring it up to date and keep it up to date, we have the legal right to foreclose. If you read your contract, you'll find that the full amount of the mortgage becomes due if you fall even one day behind in your payments. We wouldn't foreclose, of course, unless you left us with no choice. So I suggest you think hard about the offer we've made you." I can see Mark twirling his mustache as he says this, with Bluestein in the background rubbing his hands together and cackling. I proceed to tell Mark, spitting the profanities out like bullets, that I am uninterested in his offer, now or ever.

As I hang up the phone, I turn to Eddie Scissons. "Why?" I bellow.

"They made me," whispers Eddie, sitting down on one of the maple chairs that surround the oval table.

"How could they make you? You don't need the money."

"They know things," Eddie says helplessly. His hand shakes violently as he tries to raise his coffee cup to his lips.

I have about as much chance of cracking the New York Yankee starting line-up as I have of bringing the mortgage payments up to date. My impulse is to march Eddie to the car, drive him back to his apartment, or to the Friendship Center, and never see him again. But I know that for some reason I need him here, that he is part of the cosmic jigsaw puzzle that has so altered my life.

"Whew," says Annie, bounding down the stairs, making motions of knocking water out of her ears. "You haven't cussed like that since you stuck your tongue on the wire fence two winters ago."

I grab a slice of toast and a handful of bacon strips as I head for the door.

"I thought you knew what I done," says Eddie in a voice that for the first time sounds his age, "and that you brought me out here to hurt me." He looks beaten. What can Mark and Bluestein have used to blackmail him? It can only be something I already know; or is there more to Eddie Scissons's past than even I have guessed?

"I'll be working on the field," I say. "Anyone who wants to can help when they're finished with breakfast."

That afternoon, while the others are working on the field with varying degrees of enthusiasm, Annie and I drive to Iowa City. A check of Johnson County land-title records shows why my brother-in-law is so anxious to acquire my land. A perusal of county maps shows why my little farm is so important. On the county map, the land is divided up neatly as a checkerboard, and when I take one of Karin's yellow crayons and color in the quarter-sections owned by Bluemark Properties, Inc., it looks like a giant crossword puzzle with only a few black squares. My farm is one of the black squares. I note the names of the owners of the other privately owned land and phone them. "Yes, the farm's been sold recently," they all tell me. What Bluemark Properties, Inc., has acquired is 64 quarter-sections, or 16 sections, or 10,240 acres of prime corn-growing land. That is, they have all but one portion—my farm, which sits on the little map like a blue-black plum in a field of golden peaches.

For the last couple of years, Mark has been extolling the virtues of what he calls Computer Farming. And I can imagine what he said as he and Bluestein started buying up the farms.

"I can tell you for a fact, we won't have any trouble with this one," he would have said to the boardroom full of shadowy men in three-piece suits. "This one is owned by my sister and brother-in-law. He's a little weird—so deep in debt he'll be happy to sell."

I can visualize what they want to do. You don't need fences around corn. Farmhands will roll the barbed wire up on giant wooden spools, the staples crying like shot animals as they are wrenched from the wood. Then the posts will be pulled and stacked, to be sold in areas where farming is less sophisticated. The houses and outbuildings will all be torn down—bulldozed and hauled away, making the plains as flat and silent and lifeless as they were 150 years ago. The farm will be run from one concrete bunker the size of an electrical-transformer station. One man will sit in bluish light in front of a television screen that every fifteen minutes provides updated information about market prices, weather forecasts, legislative happenings, planting, spray and harvest advisories, USDA news, and dozens of other topics—data fed into the computer on a continuing basis. When he wants information, the Computer Farmer simply dials a special telephone number and punches the proper code on what is called a Green Thumb Box. Mark has told me about it again and again, his beady eyes blazing like those of a zealous evangelist. At a command from the single pale figure, posed vulturelike over the computer screen, battalions of combines can be unleashed to gobble up the crops and spew them into trucks to be wheeled to market—all neat and clean and sterile and heartless.

"But you owe the land something," I complained weakly to Mark. "It's not just a product. Not plastic and foam and bright paint imported from Taiwan or Korea, meant to be used once and discarded." But my words went unheeded, and I can see the ghostly accountants, technicians, and bankers lurking behind Mark, counting money and reinvesting profits.

"You have to be touched by the land," I cried. "Once you've been touched by the land, the wind never blows so cold again, because your love files the edges off it. And when the land suffers from flood or drought or endless winter, you feel for *it* more than for yourself, and you do what you can to ease its pain." Mark stared at me, uncomprehending, seeing only the money breeding incestuously, diversifying, multiplying; whereas I saw the silent tides of corn, lonely and alien in their own vast land.

But this morning on the phone, Mark's voice had risen in an anxious whine, and there was controlled desperation in his sales pitch—the same desperation I sometimes felt when I had failed to sell a life-insurance policy for over a month and could picture creditors marching in front of my apartment, carrying picket signs, chanting. As I check the maps again, I realize that I have been backed into a position of power, like a weak team aided by a spate of errors made by the champions.

Syndicates like all business transactions to go smoothly: A project is either complete or it is not. They will be irate, hopefully even vengeful or violent, if Mark and Bluestein cannot deliver on their promises. If I can hold my land, remain free, it could begin a chain reaction that, like opening a row of cages in a zoo, would free half of Johnson County, Iowa, from this computer-farming syndicate. Mark, Bluestein, and their associates have a sinister master plan for the whole area, and our little quarter-section is like a fly back-stroking in their crab bisque.

I have Annie phone her mother. Violetene, as she was named by her Alabama-born mother, is a great source of information. She sits in her parlor among her religious pictures and African violets, rocks, reads her Bible, and absorbs whatever is said around her, like a velvet dress collecting lint. She often does not understand what she hears, unless it is gossip of the most malicious kind, or a story of terminal illness—*catheter* is one of her favorite words—but she can recall whole conversations from years in the past, particularly if she was in some way slighted. She has always insisted that I call her Violetene, I suppose out of fear that I might call her Mother.

Annie asks about Mark's plans for our farm. "Mother, he spent all day Sunday with you, surely he must have talked about it. Of course Ray is here, and of course I'll tell him whatever you tell me."

She has to remind her mother several times that she will go to hell if she lies, before she reluctantly lets go of what she knows. It turns out that Mark himself is having serious financial problems; he and Bluestein have overextended themselves.

Possession of our farm is holding up an agreement to lease all their Iowa landholdings to a Texas conglomerate.

My charges are restless when we return.

"I don't think I believe you really have games out there," says Moonlight.

Salinger eyes me skeptically, but remains silent. Eddie still carps about the $4000 I spent on the tractor. Then, in the next breath, he apologizes for selling the mortgage.

"Give me some time," I say to Moonlight. "Just pretend you're on holiday for a few days. Give it ten days. If you don't at least get to see a game in ten days' time, I'll personally drive you anywhere in Iowa, so you can try out for a..."—I stop with the word *real* hanging like a corn kernel on the tip of my tongue. When I look at Salinger he has a half-smile on his face—"another team," I finish the sentence. "But look, I've bought pork chops for supper." I thump down a brown parcel on the tabletop.

As usual, it is Karin who alerts us. Two days have passed. We are sitting at the oilcloth-covered table in the kitchen, playing hearts. Eddie suggested it, and the rest of us complied. Richard and Moonlight are competitive, wailing loudly when fate is unkind to them, for hearts is a game relying heavily on luck. Eddie, too, is competitive, hating to lose, but he hides his feelings, only the occasional cross glance betraying him. I let luck take its course: I follow suit, never count cards or try to surmise who holds which cards. Salinger doesn't care whether he wins or loses, but I have the feeling that he is memorizing gestures, such as Richard's furious expression of indignation when the queen of spades is dropped on his doorstep.

Karin comes pounding down the stairs. "Daddy, the lights are on," she says. I go to the back door, from which I can see the sky awash with yellow. From above, the stadium must look like a volcanic crater boiling lazily, waiting for something to happen.

We march single file toward the stadium. Karin leads the way, high-stepping like a majorette, followed by Moonlight, Richard, Eddie tapping along with his serpent-head cane, Salinger, and then me, with Annie holding tightly to my hand and looking breathless—as strange a parade as anyone would care to see assembled: my child shining like a jewel; Moonlight Graham adrift on the sea of time; my brother who might be me or I him; Eddie limping along, his hair frosty beneath the floodlight sun; Jerry, a world-famous author, walking among us without pretension. I wonder what each will experience: who will see the wonders of the night, and who will see only an empty field eerily illuminated by a single battery of floodlights, where moths crash into the bright bulbs like determined kamikaze pilots.

The stars seem to float like flowers in a bowl only yards above our heads as this motley procession winds along behind the third-base stands. As we climb the bleacher in left field, I can see that Jerry is smiling, and I wonder how much of it is his own joy and how much is for me. He must be incredibly happy to know that I am not a fraud. Moonlight holds a long hand out in front of him, palm up, like a baby reaching to explore a bug.

"It wasn't like this today," he says, his eyes feasting on all he sees: the White Sox taking batting practice, players throwing along the first- and third-base sides. Eddie Cicotte is warming up in the corner just below us, his fast ball whapping into the catcher's mitt, sending up a small explosion of dust each time it hits.

Then it is my turn to be brushed with wonder. Annie clutches my arm as I gasp involuntarily. "The catcher," I croak. We all look at the white-uniformed young man crouching crablike in the White Sox bullpen. But only Annie and I, and perhaps Salinger, if he remembers any of my stories, realize the significance of his being a solid, tangible person and not a shade that might have been outlined and cut from fog, using a baseball bat as a knife.

"Is it him?" whispers Annie.

"I'm not sure," I reply, my voice constricted. "I never knew him when he was a young man."

I've seen a sepia portrait of him in his World War I uniform. He is handsome and square-jawed, and the photo is touched up so much as to make him seem unreal. The tiny photo in its ivory frame still slumbers on my mother's dresser in her high-rise in Montana.

As Joe moves into left field, Karin and I lean down to talk to him.

"Is it him?" I say, and I can tell by the look in Joe's eyes that it is.

"Wait until the line-up is announced," he says, almost keeping a straight face. My chest feels as if it is full of buzzing bees. Then Joe looks at Moonlight, who is sitting, neck bent forward, craning as if he is looking down a well.

"Graham?" says Joe, and looks the young man up and down thoroughly. "What the heck are you doing up here in the stands? Your contract arrived today, and we've all been wondering when you were going to report. You're supposed to be warming up." He nods toward the players along the baselines.

Moonlight looks down at his glove, which is buckled to a belt loop. "Me?" he says.

"You came here to play ball, didn't you?" says Joe. "Manager's waiting to see you. Come on down and start warming up."

"Yes sir," says Moonlight and starts climbing quickly down the bleacher. He walks around the end of the fence, where Joe shakes his hand and puts him to throwing a ball with a ghostly substitute outfielder.

"What's going on here?" says Richard in a somewhat desperate voice. "What are you looking at? Who are you talking to?" He pulls at the sleeve of my shirt.

Richard can't see the players on the field as we see them. As I realize this, I become aware that instead of feeling sorry for him, I am highly elated. I know without asking that all he is aware of is the deadly silent park sitting in the cornfield, illuminated by one stark bloom of lights on a single standard. Richard's eyes are blind to the magic. There is finally a difference between us.

"Playing right field and batting seventh for the White Sox is Moonlight Graham," the announcer intones, and looking down we can see Moonlight standing in the dugout, smiling like a Halloween pumpkin. He has been clothed in a new uniform, and his chest now bears the White Sox brand, an O in the top crook of the giant S, and an X in the bottom.

"Catching and batting eighth is Johnny Kinsella," says the announcer.

My breath escapes like air hissing from a tire. I stare down to where he crouches, warming up the pitcher. My Class B catcher who played in the minors in Florida and California. My father. My dream has been fulfilled, my request granted. I have earned this favor by the sweat of my brow and the pain of my back. I should be ecstatic. Then why do I feel weak as a kitten? I feel as if I'm about to commit a crime.

Annie hugs my arm.

"That man has the same name as us," shouts Karin, running up the steps toward us.

"That he does," I say, and try to sound calm, for I have no idea how I will explain the situation to her if she persists.

Instead, she says, "Can I have a hot dog, Daddy?" And it is with relief that I cheerfully count change into her blunt little hand.

"Is this some kind of religion?" Richard asks. He has risen and stands a few feet away from me, his expression one of absolute bewilderment.

"It may be," I reply, trying to picture the world through his eyes.

"You're all crazy," he says with my voice. But we don't pay much attention to him. Annie is talking to Shoeless Joe, Karin has returned with a hot dog and a Coke. After the national anthem, I watch as Moonlight Graham trots to right field. If he is nervous he does not show it, for his stride is solid and his shoulders confident. He turns to face the infield and pounds his fist into his glove.

"Crazy," says Richard.

Salinger leans toward me. "And I thought I had a good imagination," he says. "I could never dream up a plot as bizarre as this."

"I'm going back into town," says Richard. "I was going to take the night off, but I'm darned if I'm going to sit around here with you people and watch the grass grow."

"Take the car," I say, tossing him the keys to the Datsun. I suddenly feel very benevolent toward Richard. "It will save you taxi fare."

"Ray's always been weird," Richard says in Annie's general direction. "He used to have imaginary friends when he was a kid. I don't know if they were people or animals, but he called them Rags and Sigs, and he used to have conversations with them and play games with them. I thought he'd outgrown it." Annie looks his way and smiles disarmingly. "I thought *you* were all right," he says to Annie.

"I am," says Annie. Her conversation with Shoeless Joe over, she steps back and sits down beside me, resting her head on my shoulder.

"And I thought the kid was okay," Richard persists. "I thought when she talked about games and baseballs and things, she just had an imagination like her dad when he was a kid."

"Kid?" says Eddie Scissons, suddenly attentive.

"Not you, Kid," says Richard in exasperation. Then to Karin he asks, "What do you see down there?"

"I see the baseball game," says Karin, taking a bite of her hot dog.

"Rags and Sigs?" Annie whispers into my ear. "Rags and Sigs?" She giggles prettily.

Richard glowers at Karin. I guess he thought he had an ally. When he is around Karin follows him as if she were a puppy and he had a pork chop tied to his ankle. He has taught her his carnival spiel, and she has learned it well.

"I thought I'd met some freaks with the carnival," says Richard, "but, but . . ." Words desert him momentarily. "A guy who's gonna be buried in a Chicago Cub uniform, somebody else who wears a baseball uniform day and night—where did he go anyway? Somebody who claims he's J. D. Salinger. And my own brother, who's too busy building a baseball field in the middle of nowhere and driving around the country collecting weirdos, to notice that his farm is being sold out from under him." He stops for breath.

"Go to town, Richard," I say. "I'll wait up for you and we'll have a talk. Sell lots of whatever it is you sell."

"The world's strangest babies are here. See the famous Siamese twins. The gorilla baby. The baby born to a twelve-year-old mother," Karin singsongs as Richard stomps down the green painted bleacher, muttering.

"And I swear I saw Archie, Moonlight, whatever, walk down these steps and disappear, quick as if somebody switched off a light," he says.

"Stay as long as you like. Come out when you're ready.

This is a family show. Mothers bring your daughters. Fathers bring your sons..."

"Shhh, honey," says Annie, and Karin goes back to watching the game.

"Oh, lord," says Salinger from behind me. "I was still in my crib when all this happened. These *are* the White Sox. After the scandal." When I turn to look at him, he is staring at me, his face rapturous.

"There are racing cars spinning gravel all around my ribs," he says, and rubs his chest. "It's like the day I held my newborn son for the first time."

I only smile.

"This is too wonderful to keep to ourselves. You have to share."

"With whom?" I say. "How many? How do we select? And first, how do we make people believe?"

"I'll vouch for you."

"With the rumors there are about you! I think not."

"You're difficult to convince."

"The pot calling the kettle names. But don't you see, we have little to do with this. We aren't the ones who decide who can see and who can't. Wouldn't I let my own twin brother see my miracle if I could? But more important than that, the way you feel now is the way people feel who react to your work. If I share, then so must you."

Salinger flops back on his seat.

The Sox go down in order in the first two innings. Moonlight Graham leads off the third. He has been swinging two bats in the on-deck circle. As the loudspeaker booms out his name, he drops the weighted black bat and advances on the plate, slashing the air with a brand-new white-ash bat the color of vanilla ice cream. He jigs a little in the batter's box, then cocks the bat, the top end of it trembling as if he were stirring something, and waits, tense.

The pitcher fires and Moonlight takes a curve ball for a strike. As he throws again, Moonlight snaps the bat forward and the ball sails in a high arc to right center. The center fielder backs up a couple of steps, lops a few strides to his left, and makes the catch. Moonlight runs it out, and as he curls across the diamond from second base toward the dugout,

I'm quite certain he gives us the high sign. I think of my visit with Doc Graham and our conversation about a baseball wish. And I feel as if there is a hot-water bottle pushed against my heart as I watch Moonlight Graham take his seat in the dugout.

I phone my mother to tell her of Richard's return. I've made sure to do it while he is away in town, in case he might bolt at the thought of any more lead being inserted in his boot soles.

She is very happy to hear the news. We talk for a long time, begin reminiscing about my childhood. I feel closer to her than I have in years.

"Remember the sparrow?" I say to her. And I don't give her a chance to reply, but rush on. I retell the story. "Mom, you've got to come and see what I have here. What I've brought to life." And I charge on, telling her the story of the baseball park—everything except about my father. But I hint, oh how I hint. I can only imagine her excitement.

When I stop for breath, though, she says, "I'm almost sure it was Richard with the gun that day. In fact I'm certain of it. You must be mistaken, dear."

I turn away and hand the phone to Annie. She is very good at talking with my mother.

I prance out into the yard and bay at the moon, as if I am possessed, until Jerry appears at the back door, and eventually Eddie Scissons hobbles around the corner of the house to see what is going on.

Moonlight is no longer with us. The moment he walked around the corner of the outfield fence and shook hands with Shoeless Joe Jackson he ceased to be one of us, if he ever had been, and became one of them. When the game was over, he laughed and joked with us and accepted our congratulations on making the line-up, on making his first hit. But then he drifted to the gate in center field with the other players, his duffel bag miraculously transported from the house to his hands.

Late that night, as I sit at the table looking at my bank books and bills, Jerry comes padding downstairs. His hair is disheveled and he is wearing a white shirt with the tail hanging out over his jeans. He is barefooted.

Without a word, he pulls up a chair and sits across from me.

"I don't want to offend you, Ray," he begins, "but as you may know, I'm not exactly poor."

"Okay, you can put in twenty dollars toward the groceries," I say.

"That's not exactly what I had in mind."

"I know. And I thank you, but I've got to wait this out. If I let you help, I'll feel like the rich kid who owns the ball and bat and makes people pay to be on the team. Anyway, I like to think I'm being put to a test of some kind."

"Maybe the reason you came and got me was so I could help you out of your financial jam."

"Maybe. But to use one of my mother-in-law's favorite terms, this seems like such a worldly problem. Surely there was a more important reason."

"What if you're wrong? Your brother-in-law and his friend will have the ballpark plowed under in a matter of minutes, after they get control of the farm. They'll bulldoze the house, sell off the equipment . . ."

"Don't remind me."

"Just let me bring the mortgage up to date. That will hold them at bay for a while."

"No."

"Why be so damn stubborn? Everybody needs assistance once in a while. I'd consider it a privilege to help."

"Promise to publish, and I'll let you."

Salinger's friendly but persuasive expression suddenly turns to one of indignation.

"One has nothing to do with the other," he shouts.

"I know." And for some reason I cannot fathom, I am smiling.

"You're not only ungrateful, you're stupid too," says Jerry.

"I know."

"What do you think you are, some kind of mystic?" He digs in his jeans and flings a quarter down on the table. "In God We Trust, and all others pay cash."

"Hang in with me, for a few weeks."

"Stick with you, and I'll end up in irons," says Jerry, the anger gone from his voice. He even half smiles as he adds,

"I'll help you and Annie look for an apartment after you get evicted."

Then he rises wearily and makes his way toward the stairs.

"There really is something out there, isn't there?" are Richard's first words as he comes through the door. There is a faint odor of popcorn and sawdust about him.

I nod.

"I know you're not really crazy, Ray. I wouldn't put it past you to put me on, though." He smiles my most charming smile, the one I use on my mother-in-law on holidays and her birthday. "But why can't *I* see?"

"Very few can. None of Annie's relatives, or anyone who just drops in casually, can see anything more than what I've built. I chose Jerry, Moonlight, and Eddie. But it wasn't exactly my own doing. It was like walking out in front of a full grandstand, the breath of thirty thousand faces on me, the throng clapping, cheering, stomping, whistling, reaching out to be chosen; but it was also like having my hand guided to pick out the *right* ones."

"But I didn't come here by accident. I didn't start reading phone books as if they were manifestoes, for no reason. Something guided me to you. Something made me move in here to be near you. You should hear me explaining *that* to my lady."

"As unsatisfactory as it may sound, we'll just have to wait and see," I say, thinking that I sound like Shoeless Joe Jackson sounded over the long months I waited for my catcher to appear. But earlier tonight, when my catcher was out there on the field whistling the ball to second, calling out which infielder should take charge of an infield fly, I sat as tightly in my seat as if I were glued there. I made no effort to go down to the field after the game to talk to the players, as I often do, until he was safely on his way to the center-field exit.

I was scared. There is no other word for it. How can I walk up to this man who will one day be my father, and treat him like any other ballplayer?

Perhaps Richard *has* been drawn here by something other than curiosity about a long-lost brother.

* * *

The next afternoon I go into Iowa City and stop by the change booth at the midway. It is just large enough to hold two women, sitting back-to-back on high stools and dealing out quarters, dimes, and nickels to the sparse afternoon crowd.

I stop and look up at the one I know must be Gypsy.

"My God. He told me he had a twin, but I didn't really believe him," she says. "Thought maybe he'd latched on to some local fluff and was taking a vacation from me these nights."

"How did you know it wasn't Richard in a change of clothes?" I ask.

"The eyes. The eyes. Richard's are harder than yours: His look is like jade that might crack at any second. Yours are warmer, wittier. You've probably loved somebody very much."

"And are you a fortuneteller, too?"

"I have been. You do whatever you have to do in this business. I want to look you over. Hey, Molly, I'm taking a break," she says to the woman behind her, who nods the back of her blond wig to acknowledge the statement.

"I'm Gypsy," she says, sticking out a small brown hand. She is tiny and wiry with straight black hair that looks like an untidy pile of shingles. She is wearing a black T-shirt with a silver picture of an unfamiliar rock singer on the front, blue jeans, and black cowboy boots. She has a small tattoo on her left forearm. Her mouth is thin, her smile ironic.

"You haven't seen the show," she says, waving her hand toward a twenty-foot trailer partially hidden behind canvas banners, splashed with garish pictures and lettering. "We have a truck with a camper that we live in and use to pull the trailer from town to town." In the background, Richard's voice emanates from a chipped black speaker wired to the rod holding up the canvas banners: "Stay as long as you like. Come out when you're ready. You owe it to yourself to see these strange babies. You've read about them. Heard about them. Now come in and see them . . ."

"Can I?" I nod toward the trailer. Gypsy takes a pack of Winstons from her T-shirt pocket, shakes out a cigarette, and lights it. She grins up at me, smoke leaking through her teeth.

"Why not? Richard and me bought it from the grandson of the owner. Old man died two years ago while we were wintering in Florida."

We climb a ramp that leads to the door of the trailer, where a sad-looking black man in a greasy jacket and baggy overalls sits on a backless chair.

"Hey Owen," Gypsy says to the man, "going on a cooks' tour." She parts the faded blue-velvet drapes, which are decorated by amber watermarks. The man, Owen, scarcely nods. If he sees me, he assumes I am Richard.

Inside, Richard's voice, my voice, becomes indistinct and mixes with the midway sounds. The trailer smells of dust and rose-scented room freshener. The floor is covered by cheap brown-brindle tiles, and one or two have their corners sticking up like marked playing cards. The walls are draped with faded blue velvet, and about a dozen glass containers, like built-in fish tanks, are inset at intervals. Each one contains a photograph of a deformed fetus and a small typed card describing the origins of the photo, with a few clinical details. The photos are black and white, faded, curled around the edges. Some of the explanatory cards have fallen face down or lay at odd angles. The bottom of each container was at one time covered in fuchsia-colored velvet, but in places it has faded to a pale pink. Dust, grit, and dead insects cover the bottom of most of the containers.

"Is this all?" I ask.

"What did you expect, live babies?" says Gypsy, blowing smoke. "This is a seventh-rate carnival. The posts are bigger than the rings you toss at them. There's lead in the milk bottles. The darts are made of bamboo, so if you breathe as you throw, they drift a foot. This is a carnival. People pay to be disappointed."

"I guess from hearing the pitch I expected more. At least a specimen floating in alcohol."

"You've lived in the country too long, Ray," she says with a good-natured smile. She closes one eye when she smiles.

"How much does it cost?"

"Seventy-five cents. Best moneymaker on the midway. No overhead."

"If it's profitable, why not clean it up?"

"What do you want, a science lab? People expect scruffy stuff. They don't go in there because of scientific curiosity. They go because they want to be shocked. They want to come

out and say how awful it was, how scummy and sickening—
something they can talk about to all their friends, and when
the friends think nobody is looking, they'll sneak in and see
if it was as bad as they heard."

"Would you tell me something, Gypsy?"

"I might."

"Your first name."

"Want to get one up on your double?"

"It will be our secret, I promise."

"But why? What does it matter?"

"Can't tell you."

She looks at me, figuring the angles and the odds, the tiny
lines around her eyes and mouth fanning out as she flexes her
facial muscles without smiling. "Our secret," she says, holding
out her small dark hand for me to clasp.

"Our secret."

"Annie," she says, smiling through her teeth.

On the drive back to the farm, I recall our childhood, and,
as I do, I realize that it was I and not Richard who was fascinated
by carnivals and midways. I believe it was the Laughlin Midway that used to come to Great Falls for a week each summer.
When we were little, Dad used to take us on the rides and feed
us outrageous amounts of ice cream, hot dogs, burgers, and
cotton candy. We would tour the midway and listen to the
spiels of the pitchmen. He would take us to see the freak show,
the dancing waters, and even the girlie show—"Harlem in
Havana," it was billed—which, in retrospect, seems as tame
as a dancing class.

The year we were nine, my father decided we were capable
of traveling the grounds alone, and gifted us with enough money
to make our usual tour. Richard, however, chose to accompany
my father to the horse races, while I ambled off to explore the
midway on my own. The carnival was set up in an open field
at the edge of town, and the ground had been generously covered in sawdust, and iced with cedar shavings. It had rained
during the night, and the shavings and sawdust had mixed into
the ground to form a firm and pungent base. By midafternoon
I was walking along game row, which consisted of two dozen
booths where you threw balsa-wood darts at half-inflated bal-

loons, or tried to knock three plaster bottles off a milking stool, using balls soft as rolled-up socks.

I stopped to listen to the spiel of the barker at the milk-bottle booth. He had a crooked arm that he used to attract attention and wave people in, and I followed the arm as if it were hooked around my neck and gently easing me forward. There were a dozen or so people around the booth, and the carny and his assistant, a brush-cut youth with eyes tiny as black peas, gently baited the customers and kept them trying again and again to not only knock the bottles over but clear them from the top of the stool. The carny, his hair tufted, face square and scruffy-looking as a tomcat, would set up the bottles, take a ball, bend over, and fire it between his legs, and the bottles would fly off in different directions. Then he would taunt his audience.

"Look at that! If an old one-armed side-hill gouger like me can do it backwards, you big strong fellows should be able to do it frontwards! And you get three tries to do it! Only three for a quarter!" And the big farm boys and squinty-eyed cowboys in denim would step forward, plunk their money down, and fire wildly at the bottles.

I worked my way forward, mouth hanging open in fascination as I listened to the carny and watched the balls smacking into the canvas behind the target or hitting the bench and ricocheting about the tent like trapped birds. There was a row of trunks across the mouth of the booth. The white balls rested on the battered green-and-brown surfaces. As I watched, I imagined the carny and his assistant packing the trunks full of green-and-vermilion-feathered monkeys-on-sticks, which were the prizes, and heading out for a new town.

I moved in until, pressed forward by the crowd, I sat down on one of the old, mistreated trunks at the far right of the booth. I must have been there a half-hour when the crowd thinned out, the big-shouldered farm boys walking stiffly away, ignoring the carny's entreaty to "Try it one more time there, Sonny. You almost won last time. Look! I'll show you how it's done." There was one man in a dirty suit coat playing, and two or three gawkers, when the carny noticed me.

"What are you doin' there, kid?" he said loudly, moving toward my corner of the booth. I was startled and jumped down from where I had been sitting. He could see I was scared, and pressed his advantage. "Look what you done to my trunk!" he shouted. "Look at the dents you put in it." I looked at the battered metal. It was difficult to see where one dent started and another finished.

"You're gonna have to pay for it, kid," he said, and I could feel my eyes getting larger. I shuffled my feet nervously in the dry shavings at the base of the trunk.

"How much money have you got?" the carny asked, moving over in front of me. I dutifully reached in my pocket and pulled out a dollar and a few coins. I counted it carefully. There was $1.80.

"Kid, you done twenty dollars' worth of damage to that trunk. You're gonna have to make it up some way." He was close to me. His face was scarred and craggy, like a map of Montana, all mountains, lakes, and plains. He smelled of sweat and cigars. He had a black canvas apron tied around his waist, and his good left arm was brown as an Indian's. I could imagine him calling my father and making him pay for the damage I had done—and then the long, silent ride back to Deer Lodge in the pickup truck, my father furious, my brother nudging me in the ribs and laughing.

"A dollar eighty," he said scornfully. "Is that all you've got?"

I looked at him wide-eyed and nodded.

"Okay, kid. Listen. I tell you what I'm gonna do. You can work it off." I felt like a car had just been lifted off my chest. I stood eager as a dog waiting for a stick to be thrown.

"You know where the freak show is?" I nodded that I did. "Well, I want you to run down there and tell the barker that I sent you to get the left-handed glass stretcher. Then you bring it back to me and I'll let you off the hook." He smiled, showing short yellow-stained teeth.

I sprinted off across the sawdust, the shavings crinkling around my ankles. At the freak show, the barker was in the middle of a spiel. A beautiful girl in a bathing suit with a red-satin cape over her shoulders stood to his right, looking tired and bored, while behind them, just inside the flimsy brown curtain, stood a man in formal outfit complete with top hat and white gloves, holding a black-handled handsaw that was at least four feet long. The barker was telling the crowd that in just a few moments, the Great Mancini—who was making a special appearance with the Laughlin Midway, direct from performing before all the crowned heads of Europe and Asia— would dazzle and mystify them by sawing this very-alive young lady in half before their unbelieving eyes. Mancini bowed slightly and raised his hat, revealing slick black brilliantined hair. The girl ran a hand languidly across her belly, to show where the wicked-looking saw was going to do its work, and the barker began his pitch to sell tickets. I snaked my way through the crowd until I was at the stage, which came up to the middle of my chest. I stood on tiptoe, reached forward, and tapped the barker on the toe of his run-down black loafers. He glanced down and continued with the spiel. The Great Mancini and the caped girl stood like wax dummies. I stretched up and tapped again, harder, like knocking at a door after receiving no answer. The air smelled strongly of cedar shavings, and as I glanced down I saw that I was buried ankle deep in the red-and-white curlicues. The carny swung his microphone away from his body and hissed down at me, "What do you want, kid?"

"The guy down there"—and I waved vaguely in the direction of the game booths—"wants the left-handed glass stretcher."

There was a long pause as he at first looked puzzled. Then, as a light began to shine in his eyes, he smiled. "Just a minute, kid," he said, and parked his microphone on its stand. He walked back past the catatonic figures of Mancini and the girl, and dug into a wooden chest that was painted a pale battleship-gray. The people up close who had been listening to the carny's spiel were now looking at me.

"You old enough to be working?" a man said to me.

"Should be in school," grumbled another.

"His parents are probably show people, and you know what *they're* like," said a bulky woman wearing a blue print dress and a matching bonnet.

The barker returned and thrust into my hands as wondrous an object as I have ever seen: shiny as a hubcap, small as a can opener, able to turn in my hand like a chrome frog. I have never seen anything like it. Perhaps it was indeed a left-handed glass stretcher. The barker bent down and spoke into my face. "Run this right back to the guy who sent ya," the barker said, but to his shoulder, as if he still had his mike under his chin. "This is the only left-handed one in the whole carnival, so tell him to guard it with his life. Ya sure ya know where you're goin', kid?"

I nodded dumbly.

Clutching the wonderful silver-jointed object in my hand, I whipped through the crowd and back down the midway to the bottle booth. I sat my treasure delicately on top of the very trunk I had damaged, and looked up into the face of the carny, who seemed genuinely surprised to see me.

"What have you got there?" he said, and lifted up the object as he might pull a hair from his breakfast cereal.

"It's what you sent me for," I said. "The guy at the freak show gave it to me. He says to tell you it's the only . . ."

"Kid, you just can't do nothin' right, can you?" he said scornfully. I could feel my mouth drop open.

"Kid, I sent you for a left-handed glass stretcher. Any fool can see this is a right-handed one." He held the object up as he might hold a dead mouse by its tail. Then he dropped it in the side pocket of his stained plaid jacket. "Now you go back down there and get me a left-handed one like I sent you for, and hurry up about it." I pushed through the crowd and began running again, but about halfway to the freak show a strange feeling, like bees buzzing, began low in my body and gradually moved up to my stomach and chest, leaving me feeling empty and foolish. It began to dawn on me that I had been the butt of a joke. I stopped and looked around. The carnival buzzed all about me. But what if I was wrong? What if the man from the bottle booth came after me, made my father pay for the damage to his trunk? I looked down at myself and cursed my choice of clothing. I was wearing a bright green T-shirt with horizontal white stripes. I stood out like a large green apple. Looking over my shoulder all the way, I skulked to the exit and made my way to the parking lot, making certain I was not followed. When my father and Richard returned from the races, they found me asleep in the truck box, my T-shirt carefully covered by a sheet of canvas.

Later, while the game is on, while Moonlight Graham patrols the right-field grass as Salinger watches contentedly, while my catcher, whom I haven't been able to approach, crouches behind the plate, while Eddie Scissons sits alone in voluntary exile about five seats from Karin and me, I hear a car cross the cattle guard and head up the gravel lane to the house. Moments later, Mark and Bluestein appear at the corner of the grandstand. Mark waves his arms animatedly to attract my attention, Bluestein holds a clipboard on which he is making notes.

The game stops. The players politely move out of the way as the interlopers move toward left field.

"I thought I made it clear that you weren't welcome here," I holler down.

"Can you come down here? We want to talk to you."

"Do you like it here?" asks Bluestein, his eyes glittering amber like a dog's. I can feel the cold winds of winter peeking over the horizon as I stare around at this piece of land that I love more than anyplace else on earth—this place where I have been happy.

"Yes, I like it here," I reply, "but I won't grovel for you. You blackmailed Eddie into selling me out. I want to enjoy what time I have left here without you snooping around and gloating."

"We want to make a deal," says Mark.

"So you can stay on the land," adds Bluestein.

"We'll leave the house. You and Annie can live in it free for as long as you like. No rent. It will make your responsibilities lighter while you find a new job."

"And the baseball field?"

"This?" says Mark, waving his arm around to take in the whole field.

"You have to leave it, too."

Mark nods to Bluestein, who scribbles on the clipboard.

"Do you realize what this land is worth?" says Mark.

"Over twenty-two-hundred dollars an acre," I reply.

"Isn't it about time you grew up?" Mark explodes. "You sit up there," and he points toward the bleacher, "like the world can't get at you. You build this whole stupid . . ." His face reddens as he struggles for words. "You're virtually bankrupt, and we're offering you a way out—because I love my sister."

"Because you're afraid of your sister."

"You're totally ungrateful," booms Mark. "No. This monstrosity will be the first thing to go, and I'll drive the bulldozer that levels it myself."

Behind him Bluestein draws a large *X* over the calculations he has made on the clipboard.

"Then we have nothing more to say," says Mark, and I feel cold, as if I have just pronounced my own eviction notice, which indeed I probably have. I also feel the wind from the cornfield pushing against my back. I stand up, and, with a fanning motion of my arm, spray my orange drink out in an arc that the wind carries over Mark's and Bluestein's heads, stippling their $300 suits. They both yell in anguish. Then Karin, who has been sitting silently beside me, rises and tosses her own drink in their direction; but her arm is not strong enough, and the drink pours directly over the fence. Bluestein partially fends off the deluge with his clipboard.

"You'll be sorry," he shouts up at us.

Karin hugs my leg and I tousle her red curls. I laugh to think that I have just about reached my maximum level of violence by pouring orangeade on an accountant.

Then Mark's voice roars up at us. "And he's a fraud." He points at Eddie Scissons like a tent-meeting evangelist pointing at the devil. His mustache curls as he speaks.

Eddie has been sitting, leaning on his cane, his chin resting on his hands, which are cupped over the serpent head.

"He never played in the major leagues. Not only that, but he hardly played in the minors—one year, part-time, for a Class D team in Montana, over sixty years ago. And he's been passing himself off around here for forty years as a Chicago Cub, the oldest living Chicago Cub.

"You're supposed to know all about baseball," Mark yells, turning his wet wrath toward me again. "I don't even follow the game, but ten minutes in the U of I Library and I found out *all* about *him*." He points accusingly at Eddie again.

Eddie is shrinking before our eyes, as if he were an inflatable toy and Mark's words were pins. I can almost hear the air escaping.

"You promised you wouldn't tell," says Eddie, in a bland, defeated voice. "You said if I sold you the mortgage you'd never tell Ray, or anyone."

"You're a joke," Mark rages. "Everyone knows about you, except Ray here. They humor you because it would be too embarrassing to call you a liar to your face. 'Crazy old Eddie,' they say, 'he likes to think he played baseball for the Cubs.'"

Eddie turns his face away.

"It's all right, Eddie," I say. "I knew. I've known all along, and it doesn't matter to me. It doesn't matter to your friends." I wave my hand to take in Jerry and Karin, and then, with a more expansive motion, I take in the whole ballpark.

"You promised," Eddie says hollowly.

I remember my own indignation after I discovered Eddie's secret. After I'd talked to him on the street in Iowa City that windy March afternoon, I had hustled off to the nearby Iowa City Public Library to find a copy of the *Baseball Encyclopedia* and check out Eddie's statistics. I'd had an uneasy feeling that something was not right, for he had spoken of playing in Wrigley Field in 1908, '09, and '10, and I knew without looking it up that that was at least five years before Wrigley Field was built, and that in those years the Cubs would have played in West Side Park. It seemed like a natural-enough mistake, though, if Eddie was indeed as old as he said he was.

But I marveled at the idea of the oldest living Chicago Cub. It was like finding a mummified baseball in an attic, yellow as if varnished, hard with age, but with a long-dead star's signature staring out, bright and real as the day the player signed it. I felt as if I'd stumbled onto a priceless autograph, something I could cherish, hold on to, hold back from other baseball fanatics as if it were a 1932 Smead Jolley baseball card with an advertisement for Turret Cigarettes on the back. Something as elusive as the perfect game, or a .400 lifetime hitter. A collector's dream.

At the library, I took the *Baseball Encyclopedia* from the shelf and turned to the Pitcher Register, and I remember the disappointment and then the anger I felt as I found that no one named Scissons had ever pitched in the major leagues. I tried the Player Register, in case I had misunderstood about his being a pitcher. But I also drew a blank there. For whatever reason, Eddie Scissons had been lying to me. I closed the book sadly and headed for home.

I told Annie about him, but mentioned only that he had a

farm for rent, not that he was a fraud when it came to playing for the Cubs.

But I understand Eddie Scissons. I know that some of us, and for some reason I am one of them, get to reach out and touch our heart's desire, like a child who gets to pet the nose of an old horse, soft as satin, safe as a grandfather's lap. And I know, too, that when most people reach for that heart's desire, it appears not as a horse but as a tiger, and they are rewarded with snarls, frustration, and disillusionment.

I imagine Eddie Scissons has decided, "If I can't have what I want most in life, then I'll pretend I had it in the past, and talk about it and live it and relive it until it is real and solid and I can hold it to my heart like a precious child. Once I've experienced it so completely, no one can ever take it away from me."

"How can you let him get away with it?" Mark shouts up at me, his fists clenched like a politician making a damning point. "You claim to know so much about baseball, claim it's so pure and wonderful. How can you let him worm his way into your game? How can you tell him it's all right? How can you forgive him for all he's done?"

And I wonder how I can. But I know I can. Fact and fantasy swirl together. "Worse men than Eddie have been forgiven by better men than me," I reply.

Much later I hold Annie in my arms, loving her, experiencing a whole separate world that makes me think of the thrilling isolation I feel when I walk through our cornfield between the high whispering rows.

"Whatever happens, I'm with you, Champ," she says, and erases my anxiety with her soft, sweet love.

The days pass, and each evening, as if time is controlled by a computer, perhaps in some distant dimension, the phantom baseball park superimposes itself on my labor of love as the sun dissolves into the horizon, tinting the clouds flamingo pink.

We watch the games, our usual group. Not one of us has said a word to Eddie about what happened. It is as if we don't mention it because to do so will make it real. Eddie is paler and more silent, his hands tremble noticeably even when clutched tightly on the head of his cane. Some evenings Richard sits with us a while—"Like watching a TV screen full of shadows and static," he says—and eventually walks away, a perplexed expression on his face, like that of a pagan watching, but not comprehending, a religious ceremony.

The catcher has been on a hitting rampage the last few games. He is more than adequate behind the plate. "He'll be with us for a while," says Joe, grinning happily. "You have good judgment when it comes to catchers."

But I still can't bring myself to face him. As with most of life, anticipation has been nine-tenths of the actual event. I sense that the catcher has some reservations about me, because after each game he exits through the gate in center field almost before the stands begin emptying. Breathing a sigh of relief each time the confrontation has been delayed, I walk across the field with Joe Jackson, Happy Felsch, and Swede Risberg, and a number of us end up squatting, or sitting Indian style, on the magic grass of left field.

Salinger tells the ballplayers the story of how I am soon going to lose the farm. "What would happen to all of you if this ballpark is razed, leveled, planted in corn?" he asks.

They exchange knowing glances, but remain silent.

"Some of us waited a long time for this chance," says Shoeless Joe.

Joe was the first of the Unlucky Eight to die. He was sixty-four in December of 1951, when his heart finally gave out. Freddy McMullin went in '52; Buck Weaver in '56; Lefty Williams in '59. Happy Felsch died in '64 in Milwaukee; Eddie Cicotte in Detroit in 1969 at eighty-four. Chick Gandil lived to be eighty-two, and Swede Risberg outlived Gandil by nearly five years, dying in Red Bluff, California, in 1975, at age eighty-one. The Swede was indeed a hard guy.

"Why can't you make a living on a farm like this?" someone asks, and I explain that I am equipment poor, and interest poor, and that my income has not kept pace with the price of land or the price of fuel, which has tripled while my income has remained stable.

"What can we do to help?" says Lefty Williams. "I was born on a farm in Missouri. I got a strong back and I'm pretty handy with my hands."

Several others nod. "I farmed some, too," says Buck Weaver.

"I've hoed a few acres of cotton myself," says Shoeless Joe with a smile.

"It's not the work that's killing me, it's paying for the equipment," I begin, but am cut off by Lefty Williams.

"How about horses?" he says. "Your machines do the work of ten men with horses, but here you sit with more men than you can use. Sell off your machines, pay off your loans, buy up a few horses, and we'll do your work for you."

"I remember horses," says Eddie Scissons. "I grew up on a corn farm in Nebraska. This used to be my farm. Harrowing, disking, plowing, planting, picking. I've done them all."

"Johnny, the catcher, he was raised on a dirt farm in North Dakota," says Shoeless Joe, looking right at me. "Bet he'd be willing to help out."

My head is filled with a wild vision of these men, these spirits, out in the dew-cool Iowa dawn, breaking the land, seeding and harrowing, the black reins wrapped around their wrists, cussing their teams on across the black fields, each man still dressed in his baseball uniform.

I see them rumbling in on wagons, the setting sun behind them, the wagon boxes overflowing with golden corn. I see them tending the fields by day, like members of some religious group who are forbidden to use worldly machines, and at night filing into my baseball park for a rendezvous with stalled time.

Their voices are ripe with excitement.

"It would be like rent," says Joe. "You done this for us. We'll pay you back." There is a current of assent.

"But can you do that?" I say. "I've never seen any of you anywhere except on the field. What do you become when you walk through that door in center field?"

The silence that follows is long and ominous. I feel like I have just stomped across an innocent children's game, or broken a doll.

"We sleep," says Chick Gandil finally.

"And wait," says Happy Felsch.

"And dream," says Joe Jackson. "Oh, how we dream..." He stops, the look of awe and rapture on his face enough of an explanation.

The magic has been broken. The other players edge toward the gate in center field.

"I remember horses," says Eddie again. "You fellows have a right good idea."

"Let's go to the house," says Salinger, taking Eddie's arm and turning him around.

There is an aura of mystery, a definite difference about the game to be played tonight. The opposing team, gray and ephemeral as dandelion fluff, does not consist of the usual opponents, who often appear to be identical to the players from the previous game, with only a change of uniform and adjusted batting stances.

Fittingly, it is Eddie Scissons who first notices the difference.

"That's Three Finger Brown!" he says, pointing to the shadowy pitcher warming up on the sidelines. "Check his number! Check his number!" he shouts. Eddie forgets that players didn't wear numbers in Three Finger Brown's era.

"Look at the infield!" Eddie crows. "Tinker-to-Evers-to-Chance. Do you boys have any idea how lucky you are?"

It does seem to me that the cloudlike infielders have the bear-cub insignia grinning from their ghostly uniforms. But what kind of game is it?

Shoeless Joe avoids my questions when I lean down to talk to him. He doesn't reiterate what I already understand—that there are things it is better not to know—but changes the subject, discussing, among other things, Moonlight Graham's .300 batting average since he joined the team.

As the game begins, Eddie gathers us around him like a group of disciples and regales us with the history of each Chicago Cub. He launches into baseball stories of all kinds, as if he were playing a game of free association.

"Got a daughter living in Seattle, I have. When I visited her, she took me to a game—sent me to a game is more like it. She convinced a neighbor boy to drive me there and back by giving him a free ticket. That Kingdome in Seattle is like playing baseball in your cellar. Why, they'd hit the ball toward first or third base and it would hit a seam in the AstroTurf and skip off into a corner, while the runner went tearing around the bases. And the sound doesn't carry. You can't hear the bat make contact, and even when the fans cheer, you can't hear them. It was like looking at a TV game with the sound turned down." He stops to chuckle, and his eyes take on their now-familiar faraway expression.

"We had a shortstop when I was in the minors, can't remember his name, but he used to carry twelve rocks in his hip pocket—scatter them out when he left the field, and he'd pick them up when he came out for the next inning. He'd sit on the bench and watch the face of the shortstop when lazy grounders suddenly hopped over his head like pin-pricked frogs. Stony! That was what he was called! I should have remembered.

"When I was growing up," Eddie goes on, "why I used to watch a catcher named Gordon Sims; played for Omaha in, I think it was a Class A league. My uncle used to take me up there once or twice a summer. Oh, but that catcher was great; built low to the ground and hard as a locomotive. They used to tell stories about how once the pitcher forgot to duck a throw to second and Sims threw the ball right through him, and got the runner out. It might have been true, 'cause I've never seen anybody rifle the ball the way he could. My uncle said he was gonna be in the Bigs in no time. But he never made it—just disappeared. The next summer when we went to Omaha we stayed in the same hotel as the Kansas City team, and my uncle buttonholed the Kansas City manager and asked if he knew what happened to Gordon Sims. 'You mean Crazy Sims,' said the manager. 'He developed a thing about throwing the ball back to the pitcher, or to second base for that matter. He'd catch the ball and then he wanted to hand the ball to a bat boy and have him walk it back to the mound. You can guess how long he lasted with that attitude—not that they didn't try to talk him out of it. The Omaha team even paid to send him off to the Mayo Clinic in Minnesota for a week. He was back planting corn on his papa's farm in Iowa, last anyone heard of him.'"

Going into the eighth inning, the Cubs are ahead by four runs, but after a walk, a single, and Swede Risberg's double off Three Finger Brown, the lead is reduced to three. A walk to the catcher loads the bases, and Frank Chance, who manages as well as playing first base, dispatches Three Finger Brown to the dugout and signals to the bullpen for a left-handed pitcher.

"My God," says Eddie Scissons as he watches the new

pitcher lope in from right field. Eddie stands, whacking his cane on the edge of the bleacher. Karin, who has been dozing in my lap, springs to life.

"Now pitching for the Chicago Cubs, Kid Scissons." The words reverberate around the stadium, as if it were a hollow gourd.

"I told you," Eddie says. "Didn't I tell you?" He looks around. "Where is that brother-in-law of yours now?"

In front of us, Kid Scissons, a swath of blond hair cascading over his forehead, his body solid, pure, and hard as birch, warms up on the pitcher's mound.

His style is awkward, his left arm whipping out toward first base like a shepherd's crook when he delivers the ball. As I watch, I remember Eddie telling us how left-handed pitchers came to be called southpaws. "Back in the early days, Chicago's West Side Park, as you might expect, faced west, so anyone who pitched left-handed was doing so with his south-most hand, or south paw. And that's all there was to it. Most mysterious-sounding things have simple explanations."

I look over at Jerry and assume he shares the tingly feeling that dominates my senses.

On the field, Eddie runs the count to 3–2 on Buck Weaver, then walks him. The lead is narrowed to two. I stare at Eddie Scissons, sitting, clutching his serpent-head cane, mouth open in awe like an orphan sitting in front of a clown.

Kid Scissons throws two balls to Shoeless Joe.

"Throw a curve," says Eddie. "Throw the curve, dammit, it's my best pitch."

Kid Scissons does throw the curve, and it hangs over the plate as big as a cantaloupe, and Joe swats it over the third baseman's head. It lands soft as a balloon along the foul line, and lies there while the third baseman races back and the left fielder charges in. When the dust settles, Joe stands on second, Buck Weaver on third, and the score is tied. Chance instructs Kid Scissons to walk Fred McMullin, to load the bases.

"Buzzard's luck," says Eddie. "He can't kill nothing, and nothing will die for him."

For a second, it looks as if the strategy of loading the bases, to make a force play possible at every base, has paid off. With the count 2–2, Chick Gandil raps the ball sharply, but it takes one hop and ends up in Kid Scissons's glove. Noisy Kling, the Cub catcher, stands solid as an iron statue on home plate, his glove extended, waiting for the ball and the force out, waiting to double up Gandil at first. But Kid Scissons is not thinking. He has already turned to look at second, where he has a play, but, instead of throwing, he looks back at first, then to second again, where it is now too late to force McMullin. He looks desperately at first again, and throws, but too late to catch the speeding Gandil. Everyone is safe and the Cubs trail. The catcher is still standing on home with his glove extended. He kicks the dust disgustedly and yells toward the pitcher's mound. Frank Chance says a couple of words to Kid Scissons, and the pitcher's head snaps straight, as if he has taken a jab to the chin. On the bleacher, Eddie pulls his cap lower over his eyes and concentrates.

The next batter, Happy Felsch, drives the ball deep to left center field on the first pitch.

"Go for it! Damn you, stretch your legs," shouts Eddie, who stands suddenly, his hair escaping from under his cap. The hair is yellow-white like an old dog's. The center fielder can't reach the ball and it rolls to the wall as Happy Felsch slices around the bases, pulling in at third standing up.

Kid Scissons stands dejectedly on the mound. He has not even backed up the play at third. Frank Chance does not walk to the mound; he just signals for a right-hander from the bullpen and points to the dugout. Kid Scissons walks off the field, head bowed, amid occasional boos and a smattering of half-hearted applause. As Kid Scissons slumps onto the bench in the dugout, Eddie Scissons sinks slowly to his bleacher seat, looking devastated.

After the game, Eddie disappears into his room and does not come out until nearly noon the next day; and then his voice is hollow as he asks me if I will drive him to Iowa City. As he gets in and out of the car, his body makes dry sounds like pages of newspaper in a breeze. We make two or three stops in Iowa City, ending up at his apartment, where I expect him to say goodbye. Instead he goes in, and returns with a shopping bag crammed with clothes, carrying his overcoat over his arm.

* * *

Dusk and the trappings of magic have not yet lowered onto and around my ballpark. The Iowa wind dominates today: The cornstalks bend ominously, rustling like plastic pom-pons. The wind is stroking, gusting, warm, living, a pervasive sign.

As I approach the field, I see Eddie Scissons standing alone on the bleacher. He has taken off his cap and is facing into the wind, his hair blown back like snow drifted against a fence. He is speaking, gesturing alternately with his free hand and the hand holding the serpent-headed cane.

Even though the wind is dry and toast-warm, I see that Eddie is wearing the same sleet-gray overcoat he wore when I first met him on the street in Iowa City. But under the coat he is wearing his Chicago Cub uniform, the material new as white envelopes, the blue stripes looking as if they have been freshly drawn by a felt pen.

I stand along the left-field line and stare up at him. He gestures broadly, making a point, but the wind floats his words away. Suddenly, as if the park has been inundated with butterflies and flower petals, the scene changes. The grandstands and floodlights appear, and the players file in through the gate in the center-field wall. They materialize out of the cornfield, as if from some unseen locker room. The sounds and smells of baseball are all about me. I peek over my shoulder and see that Richard has been trailing me, that Jerry and Annie and Karin are crossing from the house to the ballpark. Eddie leans down and whacks his cane on the edge of a board, to attract Shoeless Joe's attention. He speaks briefly with Joe, who in turn calls the other players closer. Eventually, we all gather on the left-field grass, staring up at Eddie standing on the bleacher, wild and windblown, looking for all the world like an Old Testament prophet on the side of a mountain.

"I take the word of baseball and begin to talk it. I begin to speak it. I begin to live it. The word is baseball. Say it after me," says Eddie Scissons, and raises his arms.

"The word is baseball," we barely whisper.

"Say it out loud," exhorts Eddie.

"The word is baseball," we say louder, but still self-consciously. I look down at Annie, who shrugs her shoulders. Karin claps her hands as the rhythm of Eddie's voice flows into her blood. The baseball players exchange aggrieved glances.

"The word is what?"

"Baseball . . ."

"Is what?"

"Baseball . . ."

"Is what?" As his voice rises, so do ours.

"Baseball!"

He pauses dramatically. "Can you imagine? Can you imagine?" His voice is filled with evangelical fervor. "Can you imagine walking around with the very word of baseball enshrined inside you? Because the word of salvation is baseball. It gets inside you. Inside me. And the words that I speak are spirit, and *are* baseball."

He shakes his head like a fundamentalist who can quote chapter and verse for every occasion.

"The word healed them, and delivered them from destruction. The word makes the storm a calm, so that the waves thereof are still." He looks around wildly.

"Your mother should be here," I whisper to Annie. She digs her small, pointed elbow into my ribs.

"As you begin to speak the word of baseball, as you speak it to men and women, you are going to find that these men and women are going to be changed by that life-flow, by the loving word of baseball.

"Whenever the word of baseball is brought upon the scene, something happens. You can't go out under your own power, under your own light, your own strength, and expect to accomplish what baseball can accomplish.

"We have to have the word within us. I say you must get the word of baseball within you, and let it dwell within you richly. So that when you walk out in the world and meet a man or woman, you can speak the word of baseball, not because you've heard someone else speak it but because it is alive within you.

"When you speak the word, something will begin to happen. We underestimate the power of the word. We don't understand it. We underestimate all that it can accomplish. When you go out there and speak the word of baseball—the word of baseball is spirit and it is life.

"I've read the word, I've played it, I've digested it, it's in there! When you speak, there is going to be a change in those around you. That is the living word of baseball."

The players shuffle their feet. Some move away a little, but then it is as if Eddie's voice pulls them back in.

"As I look at you, I know that there are many who are troubled, anxious, worried, insecure. What is the cure? Is it to be found in doctors and pills and medicines? No. The answer is in the word, and baseball is the word. We must tell everyone we meet the true meaning of the word of baseball, and if we do, those we speak to will be changed by the power of that living word.

"Can you say the word?"

"Baseball," we chant, and our voices rise toward Eddie Scissons like doves on the warm Iowa wind.

"The word is what?"

"Baseball."

"Is what?"

"Baseball."

"Praise the name of baseball. The word will set captives free. The word will open the eyes of the blind. The word will raise the dead. Have you the word of baseball living inside you? Has the word of baseball become part of you? Do you live it, play it, digest it, forever? Let an old man tell you to make the word of baseball your life. Walk into the world and speak of baseball. Let the word flow through you like water, so that it may quicken the thirst of your fellow man."

Late that night, I am sitting in the dark at the kitchen table when Eddie joins me. He wears a nightgown that looks as if it may have been made from a Chicago Cub road uniform.

"You're afraid to talk to him," he says, pulling out a chair, leaning heavily on his serpent-head cane as he takes a seat.

I know immediately that he is talking about the catcher.

I nod to show Eddie that I do indeed know who he is referring to, and that I am indeed afraid.

"I heard somebody say once, 'Success is getting what you want, but happiness is wanting what you get.'" He lays one of his large hands out on the oilcloth-covered table before me. "You saw what happened to me. I got what I wanted, but it wasn't what I needed to make me happy."

"But you still . . ."

"Believe." Eddie finishes the sentence for me. "It takes more than an infinite ERA to shake my faith," he chuckles, not unhappily.

"It's just that the implications are so immense," I say.

"They don't have to be, Ray. I know I'm sounding like I'm trying to be the wise old rascal, and I suppose I am. But you were so excited when you told us about the idea of your catcher appearing. Since he has, all you do is sneak around your own ballpark looking at your shoes.

"Just go up to the man and tell him you admire the way he catches a game of baseball." Outside the window, the moon is whitish and hangs like a sickle of ice. "Share what you've got in common," he goes on. "Talk about the small ballparks he took you to as a kid, where kids played with mongrel dogs under the bleachers and farmers scuffed their boots on the boards and kept one eye on the sky. Tell him your name is Ray, and introduce him to Karin—for her sake, not his, because someday she'll be old enough to understand and appreciate what you did.

"The right chemistry will be there, it can't help but be. You both love the game. Make that your common ground, and nothing else will matter." Eddie smiles at me, the cool summer moon reflected in his pale eyes.

"But how can I do it and not give away what I know?" I think of a picture of a group of baseball players standing in front of a bleacher in a small town in Montana. It was taken by my mother with an old-fashioned Kodak box camera made of heavy black cardboard. The ballplayers in the picture are all but indistinguishable, but my mother used to point one out and say, "That's Daddy," and if I looked closely, I could see the square cut of his jaw, could recognize him by the way he liked to stand with his left hand resting on his hip.

"Of course you can do it," says Eddie. "You're awfully good at keeping secrets. I should know." But I hardly hear him, for I am thinking of the man I knew in Montana, John Martin Duffy Kinsella—a name as Irish as shamrocks, a name that derives from the word *peninsula* and was, until the mid-1800s, O'Kinshella. He was an affectionate, sentimental man who sang songs about The Wearin' o' the Green, and about the patriot he was named for, John Martin Duffy.

"Of course you can do it," Eddie says again. "You have to do it. How many people get a chance to do it? I've got a sneaking feeling that the magic has been here all the time, that *it* was what drew me out here from Chicago, not the teaching job. But I was like a key with one tooth missing. I didn't have what it took to let the genie out of the bottle. Maybe that's why I stopped you on the street."

Spikes of moonlight decorate the table as Eddie reaches across and clasps my hand. "I'm counting on you. And in more ways than one. I guess you know that there weren't any baseball boys. That was all malarkey, like everything else I told you . . ."

"I understand," I say. And I hope I do.

"Once you meet him, it will be like the last inning of a perfectly played ball game—you'll pray for extra innings so you'll never have to go home. You'll see." He rises and makes his way to the stairs, and seems to float upward into the moon-spangled darkness.

I sit alone, recalling a conversation I had with Salinger.

"That catcher's good. Look at how fast he comes up with the ball," Jerry said one day. "He has an arm like a catapult. Is he really? . . ."

"He is."

"Does he know?"

"Of course not. He's a young man from North Dakota named Johnny Kinsella, who has just broken into the majors with the White Sox. I'm not even a glint in his eye."

"And you can't tell him?"

"That's why I haven't even approached him. I'm afraid I'll give myself away."

"It must be painful for you."

"You're a master of understatement. But if you were him, would you want to know what I know?"

"No mere apple could equal the temptation. But no, I wouldn't. It would destroy anyone to know his own future."

"I know I have to put what I'm aware of in perspective. He's young and rugged and unafraid and full of hope. It should be enough for me, to see him doing what he loves best."

Salinger nodded his head in agreement.

"But I saw him years later, worn down by life. Think about it. I'm getting to see something very special."

It was after noon when Salinger decided to ask Eddie if he wanted to play hearts. When he got no answer to his knock, he opened the door and found Eddie dead. Eddie must have had a premonition, for he had changed into his Chicago Cub uniform. His cap, glove, and brand-new spikes were laid out beside his bed.

It is more difficult than you might expect to dispose of a dead body, especially when you find you know virtually nothing about the deceased. We knew that Eddie's daughters were scattered about America in Seattle, Boston, and Phoenix, but we did not know how to contact even one of them. Some kind men from the Johnson County Sheriff's Department finally took charge of the situation, after asking me a number of pointed questions about why I had the body of a ninety-one-year-old stranger in a Chicago Cub uniform in my guest bedroom. Eddie's body ended up at Beckman-Jones Funeral Home in Iowa City. His daughters were notified by the proper authorities, and each dutifully booked passage to Cedar Rapids Airport. I could picture the flight paths of their airplanes sectioning a map of the United States into triangles and rectangles as they rushed home.

Annie and I make a duty call on them at Eddie's tiny apartment, where the three of them have holed-up on arrival. They are middle-aged women, severe as suffragettes, who inspect us critically and ask our religious affiliation. I tell them only that Eddie was homesick for the farm and that we had invited him to spend a few days with us. They sniff disdainfully each time their eyes land on one of Eddie's baseball artifacts that line the mantel and windowsill, or when they see one of the Chicago Cub programs that are thumbtacked to the walls of both living room and bedroom. I don't mention my interest in baseball, but tactfully inform them of Eddie's desire to be buried in his Cub uniform.

"I know," replies one who is wearing a crocheted hat. "He wrote each of us at least a dozen times to tell us that." She scowls and sniffs.

"The coffin will be closed, of course," says a second daughter, whose hair looks as if it has been stained with blueberries.

The following day the phone rings.

"Mr. Kinsella?"

"Yes."

"This is Gladys Vickery speaking."

"Yes."

"I used to be Gladys Scissons. We met briefly yesterday."

"We did."

"Well, I'm calling from the lawyer's office. My father added a strange clause to his will—just last week, in fact. I think it is preposterous, but Mr. Embury says I should at least check with you . . ."

"Go on."

"At the end of his will, he added, 'I want to be buried in Ray Kinsella's cornfield.' Just like that. No explanation or anything."

"No one else would understand," I said.

"Do you understand?"

"We had a mutual interest in baseball."

"Oh," she says in a knowing voice. "Did he fill you full of his awful stories? You know, he never played for . . ."

"It's all right. I can afford the space. Your father can be buried here."

"I'll have Mr. Embury draw up a contract. We'll pay you the same as the cemetery."

"That won't be necessary."

There is a long silence, then I hear her aside to the lawyer. "He says he wants him buried there. Must be as crazy as Daddy was."

The daughters decide not to attend the burial. I am able to convince them that they would not want to muddy their shoes in a cornfield. The hearse that delivers Eddie's coffin is painted an apple green, with black stripes along the sides like swaths of ribbon. The two attendants, who could easily serve as mannequins in a formal-shop window, are anxious to see the body planted. We let them wheel the coffin as far as the baseball stadium. Their eyes race back and forth in gloomy faces, and it takes great self-control for them not to ask questions. They place the coffin on the ground beside the grave. Jerry and I insist that we will lower the coffin into the grave at a more appropriate time. The dolorous attendants, who speak like English butlers with midwestern voices, reluctantly agree.

We are not dishonoring Eddie's last request. Yesterday, as Salinger and I headed for the cornfield behind left field, shovels in hand, we saw to our surprise that the ballplayers were holding a workout.

"We'd like to be part of it," Shoeless Joe Jackson said with great sincerity. "He loved the game as much as anyone can, and we'd like to pay our last respects."

"But out there you can't?" I said, nodding toward the spaces beyond the fence, where the corn rustles greenly.

Joe nodded. The others were behind Joe, silent and subdued.

"What happens to you when you go through that door? It's not fifty yards to the gravesite," I said. But Joe and the others only smiled sadly, enigmatically.

"If you can't come to the grave, then suppose we bring the grave to you?" said Jerry.

"That would be most considerate," said Shoeless Joe, and the others nodded solemnly.

I looked at the blade of my nearly new shovel, the black paint barely scratched, and I thought of the labor, the love, the passion I'd expended to make the field. I looked in horror at Salinger for suggesting such a thing.

But he looked back at me with a level brown gaze, and the players stared silently at me, and Shoeless Joe walked wordlessly across the outfield, slowly, his magnificent bat, Black Betsy, wavering in front of him like a metal detector, like a divining rod.

And the place where he stopped was in deep left field, where the grass is most lush, the grain of it like expensive carpet, the color dark and luxurious as ripe limes.

The wind whispered through the empty stands, and heavy clouds roiled across the sky. Salinger had lowered the stars and stripes and the Iowa flag to half-mast on the flagpole in center field. Both flags snapped crisply in the breeze.

"All right," I said resignedly. And as I did, I felt the greatest tenderness toward Eddie Scissons. He may have exaggerated a little, but he did it with class. I hope people will be able to say the same about me after I'm gone. "But let me make the first cut," I said, and placed the shovel on the ground and stepped down on it. I felt it slip into the earth easily, as if I were spading chocolate pudding.

Now, as the varnished coffin sits beside the grave, I recall the service that afternoon in Iowa City—a closed-coffin service in which a minister from a church Eddie had never attended ranted and chanted and raged over his coffin. His words were, I suppose, in some way a comfort for the daughters who had engaged him, but he said not one thing about Eddie, except that he had lived a long life and produced three fine God-fearing daughters.

Well, old buddy, I think, whatever happens, whether you stay buried here beneath a baseball field or whether it all gets leveled out and planted in corn, there's no finer resting place in the world.

"I think we should open the coffin," I say aloud. No one objects. It takes Salinger and me a while to find the hidden snaps with which the undertakers have fastened it. Inside, Eddie, capless, his white mane trimmed and hair-sprayed into place, the cosmetics of the dead making him look younger than I have ever seen him, lies resplendent in his Chicago Cub uniform. His cap rests on his folded hands, his feet are encased by his new cleats, his glove lies at his side below his right hand. One of the daughters must have remembered that he was left-handed.

"Yes, it's Eddie Scissons," I say.

"Dead as Billy-be-damned," says Salinger, playing his part.

"It's all right to bury him now," I say, as the players file by the coffin, caps in hands. "There *are* baseball boys, Eddie. There always have been." And as I look around me, I have the feeling that if I were to go to Iowa City tomorrow, go to the public library or the university library, find the reference section, and pick up a copy of the *Baseball Encyclopedia* and turn to page 2006, I would find right at the bottom of the page, right after the entry for Hal Schwenk, who played for the 1913 St. Louis Browns, and right before the entry for Jim Scoggins, who played for the 1913 Chicago White Sox, a listing under Eddie's name that would look like this:

KID SCISSONS   Scissons, Edward Sebastian — BL TL 6'2" 195 lbs.
                        B. Nov. 12, 1887 Kearney, Neb.
                        D. July 28, 1979 Iowa City, Iowa

And under that would be the details of Eddie's three seasons as a relief pitcher for the Cubs: his won-and-lost record, number of innings pitched, ERA, strikeouts, bases on balls, and batting record. I have the feeling. I have the feeling.

When it is finished, when the coffin has been lowered by the ballplayers, and the ropes retrieved, the grave filled in, the excess earth, which was piled on tarpaulins, removed, the top of the grave convex as a pitcher's mound, I look at Joe Jackson and start to speak.

"I've played on worse," says Joe, reading my mind, and I picture him hopping over the gopher-riddled outfield of one of the Textile League ballparks in South Carolina, one of the fields where he began, and where he ended, his playing days.

It is late afternoon when the Fargo one-ton, pulling the cream-colored twenty-foot trailer, clangs over the cattle guard and parks beside our driveway, out near the highway.

"Uncle Richard's brought the carnival with him," squeals Karin. "I looked at the pictures in the trailer when we were in town. They're icky! It's the song I like." She chants bits of the incantation that Richard uses to draw the public to his exhibit.

"The midway has moved on to Cedar Rapids," says Richard. "We'll catch up with them in a couple of weeks. We haven't had a holiday in years."

"He claims he heard a voice that told him to come here, and bring me and the exhibit," says Gypsy in a stage whisper as she hops down from the cab. I look sharply at Richard, but he seems very interested in the ground.

Gypsy skips around the farm, exploring like a cat that has just been dropped at a strange location. "That really is a baseball field, isn't it?" she says, smiling her tight-lipped little smile as she spies the fence, the bleacher, the light pole.

"The world's strangest babies are here," sings Karin.

The garish canvas banners and loudspeakers are trussed to the top of the trailer.

After supper I keep pestering Richard. "What kind of voice did you hear?" I ask as we make our way toward the baseball field, where the brilliant lights of the stadium reflect off the high, clear sky.

"She was teasing; I don't hear voices," says Richard. He is taller than average, and his hands, like mine, are long and thin. He wears a cap with a long red bill. The cap advertises Turfco Fertilizer. Gypsy and Annie trail along behind us. They are virtually the same size and might have been cut from the same pattern, though on opposite sides of the earth.

"Oh, wow!" says Gypsy as we walk along the third-base line. "It's all there, isn't it? Just like the big leagues. I saw a game in Minneapolis once. This could be the same stadium."

So Gypsy sees. I turn to find Annie grinning with approval.

"There's nothing out there but an empty ballpark," says Richard, "and it's a little one, like the place in Montana where we went when we were kids." But we ignore him. Annie and I and Jerry are joyous as children, welcoming Gypsy to our special fraternity.

As we sit down on the warped bleacher, Richard looks for a long time at Gypsy, at her tough but beautiful face with the laugh lines patterned around her eyes and mouth like spider webs. And I think I know what he is feeling. That somehow he sees her slipping out of his arms, moving further and further away from him though remaining perfectly still.

"Ray," he says to me, looking wildly around him. "Ray, teach me how to see."

Several days later, as we are all watching a game, I imagine Eddie Scissons sitting to my right, his hands cupped over the head of his cane. His veins are so blue and bulging that his hands might be backed with spruce bark. On the other side of me, Jerry leans forward, engrossed in the game, his chin cupped by his left hand. The humid air surrounds us like a cocoon. Karin, in a green-and-gold sunsuit, sits between Richard and Gypsy, sipping Coke from a frosty green bottle.

I seem to possess magnified sense perception, where the

protection of my miracle is concerned. Over the hum of the crowd, I hear a car crossing the cattle guard, then a door slamming, feet climbing the steps to the house, a knock, the creak of the door opening, voices, the door slamming, feet descending. The voices get louder.

Then I see them behind the backstop: Mark and Bluestein, walking right through the grandstand, oblivious to all but themselves. In the distance, I hear the screen door slam and Annie's light footsteps tattoo down the stairs.

Mark and Bluestein are talking and gesturing to each other as if no one else were present, as if the lights weren't blazing, as if a flamingo-pink sunset were not painted on the right-field sky.

Annie rushes past them, disregarding the crowd.

"Mommy," says Karin, standing and pointing, slopping her orange drink and making puddles on the dark green boards at her feet.

"What?" says Jerry as Karin's voice brings him back to reality.

"Ray, they've got an order of some kind," yells Annie from below. "They have temporary control of the farm."

On the field, the action is suspended. The White Sox, who are on the field, relax, as if a pitching change is taking place. Happy Felsch drifts over to right field to talk with Moonlight Graham.

"Go back to the house," says Mark, grabbing Annie's arm.

"The hell I will. You thieving..."

"I don't know what you're complaining about," says Mark. "We'll see that you're taken care of. You and..." He has never been able to remember Karin's name.

Like an irate manager, Annie kicks dirt all over Mark's shoes and the cuffs of his expensive suit. He grabs her and picks her up by the arm. Annie knees him. He drops her. We lose sight of them for a moment as Jerry and I scramble down the bleacher and walk around the end of the fence. We stay outside the foul line as long as we can, but then cut across the field to where the others are standing. They are in shallow left field, Annie shrilling like a blue jay at Mark and Bluestein. Bluestein is carrying an ax.

"What's going on?" I demand of Bluestein, who is wearing

a wide-shouldered green corduroy suit that makes him look like a gangster.

From the inside pocket of the suit, probably from a leather holster, Bluestein produces a sheaf of papers that I suppose are as deadly as any weapon. I hear him explain that they have some kind of court order giving them what amounts to protective custody of the farm. If the mortgage payments are not brought up to date within seventy-two hours, the farm belongs to them. "But while we have custody of it," Bluestein says, his malevolent black eyes coming close to smiling, "we're going to knock down that eyesore of a fence and that pile of rubble you call a bleacher." He waves the ax, the blade sparkling dully under the lights.

I try to imagine how Bluestein and Mark must view the stands. Their eyes are as blind as newborn kittens'. All they can see is the single battery of floodlights behind left field, and the empty stadium cooling in the sunset.

"Who are they?" Bluestein says, pointing the sheaf of papers toward the spot where Richard, Gypsy, and Karin sit on the bleacher. When I don't answer, he says, "Tell them to get down."

"Tell them yourself," says Annie.

He looks at me, but I'm not going to make things easy for him. The three figures on the green bleacher have moved closer together.

"Hey you!" Bluestein shouts.

Richard looks up, a mildly startled expression on his/my face. He still cannot see. He still will not admit to me that a voice of unknown origin has spoken to him. Sometimes he claims to see things—shadowy outlines, perhaps of the stadium, perhaps of players—but I suspect it is only because the rest of us have told him so often about what is there. The ballpark remains shadowy to him, he says, as if it is obscured by leaves and foliage.

"Get down off there!" bellows Bluestein.

Richard and Gypsy stare down at the group of us standing in an uncertain pattern, like chess pieces knocked off their squares.

"Why?" says Richard.

"Never mind why. Just get down."

"I don't do nothing unless Ray or Jerry says it's okay." I notice that Gypsy is holding a green furry monkey on a fuchsia-colored stick.

"I've got a court order," Bluestein insists.

"What do you say, Ray?" asks Gypsy, pointing the monkey in my direction.

"Stay where you are," I cry. "Everybody." I bolt for the yard and my car. I recall Annie's words to me as I left on my odyssey a few weeks ago: "Ray, it's so perfect here. Do whatever you have to, to keep it that way." The stands part magically, as if I am running into a television picture. Behind me, I hear Bluestein saying, "Then I'll chop it down with them on it. The court is with me."

I feel my cap ripped from my head as I crash through the honeysuckle near the house. As I yank the keys from my jeans, I break the little beaded chain that holds them together, and they fall silently into the warm dust.

I retrieve only the one for the trunk of my car, slam it open, and rip my gun from a scuffle of rags, where it has slept since I purchased it in Des Moines. In my hand the gun is heavy, but warm as a sun-toasted rock. Its oily smell surrounds me as I race back to the field.

Everyone is still, seemingly arranged in a tableau, and I am reminded of the soldiers raising the flag over Iwo Jima. Richard, Karin, and Gypsy still sit in the stands, but their backs are a little straighter, Gypsy's monkey-cane pointing downward like a magic wand. Jerry stands with his back to the bleacher, facing Bluestein. He has his arms folded across his chest and is nose-to-nose with Bluestein—nose to chin, rather, for Bluestein is a full foot shorter than Salinger, even with his platform shoes. Behind them, Mark keeps grasping at Annie's arms, holding her at bay as she aims and kicks at his shins. The ballplayers congregate in groups of two and three, patiently waiting, seemingly unaware of the drama being enacted around them.

Then I come running out of the stands, like a character leaping fully alive from an oil painting, holding the gun over my head like a starter's pistol.

I intend to fire a shot in the air, to let everyone know I mean business. I squeeze the trigger, slowly increasing the pressure, as I read somewhere you should do. Nothing happens.

I keep trotting forward, trying to disengage the safety; but not having handled the gun for months, I have forgotten exactly how to do it.

Then there is a loud pop like a fast ball hitting a catcher's mitt, followed by the smashing of glass and the whang of metal off metal. My hand feels numb, as if I've been hit a sharp blow on the elbow. I see fragments of one of the floodlight bulbs from my own light standard drift to the ground slow as feathers, sparkling orange and blue. The tableau freezes. At least I have captured their attention.

Annie stops kicking, and Mark releases her arm. In the stands, Karin fastens on to Gypsy's denim-covered leg like a baby monkey clutching her mother. Bluestein steps away from Salinger and faces me.

"What do you think you're doing?"

The gun feels hot in my hand, as if firing it has raised its temperature. I imagine it turning a rosy hue like the lids of my mother's wood stove did, long ago, when I was a child in Montana.

"I'll shoot again," I say, my voice cracking. "Get off my property!" I yell at Bluestein. I lower the gun and wave it unsteadily in his direction. Everyone makes an effort to get out of the line of fire: Salinger moves a few steps to his left, Mark moves closer to Annie. Only the threesome in the bleacher remains stationary. I concentrate on waving the gun at Bluestein, who is still babbling about having a court order, and is pushing the papers toward me squashed tightly in his clenched fist.

"Does it say we have to leave the land?" I ask.

"Not yet," says Bluestein, "but we have control of crops and equipment and buildings. You can't sell or move anything."

"The only thing that's going to move is you and him," I say, and I point the gun toward Mark, who moves closer to Annie, so I have to point back toward Bluestein.

"Be careful with that thing," says Jerry, and he is about to say something else, perhaps to remind me of my mechanical incompetence, when a sound and movement from the stands attract us.

Gypsy, Richard, and Karin have risen. Gypsy taps her black cowboy boot on a green board to give them a beat, and, waving the monkey-on-a-stick as a baton, she conducts the three of them. Richard, with the bill of his cap pulled down so far his face is invisible, and Karin, in her green-and-gold sunsuit, dancing like a cheerleader, waving her half-eaten hot dog— they look like a surreal rock group about to assassinate the national anthem. "The world's strangest babies are here. This gallery of human oddities. You owe it to yourself to see these strange babies. Mothers bring your daughters. Fathers bring your sons. See the baby born to a twelve-year-old mother..."

"You're crazy," Bluestein rages. "You're all crazy. You build baseball fields in the middle of nowhere. You... you dress funny... and you sit around with your weird friends and stare at... nothing."

"I'll count to three..."

Bluestein and Mark begin backing slowly toward the house.

"One!" They begin backing a little faster.

And then it happens. I see everything out of the corner of my eye. Seeing me advancing and Mark and Bluestein backing away, Karin apparently decides to join us. As she takes her first step down, her foot skids on the spilled orange drink and she is falling forward as if she is diving from the side of a pool. I feel as if I have a steel egg stuck in my chest as I watch helplessly. She appears to fall in slow motion, and it takes forever for her body to come down with a sickening sound on the hard green boards. Her hot dog flies off, the bun and wiener separating in midair. One small sandal bounces end over end and lands at the foot of the bleacher.

Seconds later, everyone is standing around her where she lies on her back on one of the bottom rows of seats. Jerry is staring down at her, his long face as white as his hair. Annie hovers, her hands opening and closing, reaching in close, then moving back. Mark and Bluestein are rooted to their spots at the foot of the bleacher, as if they've been driven into the ground like pins in a map. Bluestein's ax leans impotently against his leg. We are all afraid to touch her.

"Should we move her?" We each say the words, all of us looking around wildly, hoping for advice from some non-existent authority.

"You can use my car," says Mark, all the arrogance and pomposity gone from his voice. I look at my hand and find

I'm still clutching the gun. I turn and hurl it in a high arc and watch as it disappears over the back of the bleacher, landing somewhere in the soft earth of the cornfield.

Annie and I reach our hands out toward Karin, then withdraw. She is unconscious, fighting for breath. Our eyes meet, and the anguish I see in Annie's expression chills me. I hope the terrible fear that grips me like steel bands around my middle does not show in my eyes, but I know it does.

I curse myself for not knowing anything about first aid; for not knowing any medical techniques, for not even having read about any. Initials like NBC, FDS, CPR, STP flash across my brain like subliminal advertising blurbs. One of them is a rescue technique, or mouth-to-mouth, or at least for heart attacks. I don't know. My brain is numb as a piece of liver.

"We'd better *not* move her," I hear myself saying. "They never move anyone on TV shows." I realize as I say it that it must qualify for the inane-statement-of-the-year award.

Karin's lips are bluish and her eyes are open, the pupils rolled back to reveal a bloodshot whiteness ugly as beef fat. She gasps for air, and it seems to me that she is convulsing.

"Call an ambulance," I say to Annie, and she sprints for the house, happy to have a task to take her mind off the tragedy. Gypsy follows along behind her. Richard stands silently beside me.

"How long?" asks Jerry.

"It's a twenty-minute drive from town."

In the silence, we can hear the corn rustling behind the fence. What if I am wrong? What if I've made a decision that will kill my daughter? I look furiously at Jerry, who reads my face.

"You had to make a choice," he says quietly.

Most of the players have gathered below us on the left-field grass and stand staring up, silent, as if waiting to hear a speech.

I kneel on the step below Karin, my hands wavering above her in indecision. Her nose and one side of her face have been severely scraped by her fall. Blood trickles from her nose, across her cheek and down her neck. She is becoming bluer and her cough is faint, as though she is in another room. Her arms appear pale through her tan, her freckles look as if they are resting on snow.

I glance over my shoulder to see that Bluestein has taken off his $300 pale-green velvet corduroy jacket and is wordlessly holding it out toward me. Our eyes meet, and for an instant we share the grief of losing a beloved child; our other pursuits, whether they be baseball or land acquisition, become insignificant. Jerry takes the jacket and covers Karin gently, as if she were made of flower petals.

Though it seems like hours, only a couple of moments have passed. Annie is probably only now reaching the phone, may at this moment be calling the ambulance. I am beginning to feel that I have made the wrong decision, and consider clutching Karin in my arms and running for the car, starting on a mad drive to Iowa City.

Then I feel compelled to look at the baseball field. In order to do that, I stand up and walk a few steps up the bleacher. What I see is Moonlight Graham loping in from right field, lithe, dark, athletic: the same handsome young man who played that one inning of baseball in 1905. But as he moves closer, his features begin to change, his step slows. He seems to become smaller. His baseball uniform fades away and is replaced by a black overcoat. His baseball cap is gone, supplanted by a thatch of white hair. As I watch, his glove miraculously turns into a black bag. The man who without a backward glance walks around the corner of the fence—a place where none of the other players will venture—is not Moonlight Graham, the baseball player of long ago, but the Doc Graham I spoke with on that moonlit night in Chisholm, Minnesota, when I flew softly across the dimensions of time.

As he walks toward us, I recall how a former nurse of his said that he *never* carried his black bag when they went on a call, but insisted that she carry it.

"What have we got here?" he says matter-of-factly.

"She fell," we all say together, even Bluestein.

"This child's choking to death," says Doc, and picks her up with one hand under her shoulders and the other under her knees. He seats himself on the bleacher, shaking himself a little to get his coat out of the way. He turns Karin face down, with her head pointing toward the floor. He supports her chest with one hand, while with the heel of the other he delivers a series of sharp blows between her shoulder blades. Annie and Gypsy come running back.

"Who?" says Annie.

"A doctor," I reply. I can see some of the pain retreat from her face.

Doc repeats the process, and I can suddenly see Karin's diaphragm expand as she sucks in air. Doc reaches around and pries her mouth open, releasing a sizable piece of hot dog and bun.

As he turns her over, I can see the blueness disappearing from her face as she continues to breathe deeply. Doc peels back each eyelid in turn, stares at the pupil for a few seconds, and lets the eye close.

"Looks to be okay," he says. "She should be coming around in a minute or two." He re-covers her with Bluestein's jacket.

"The ambulance?" says Annie.

"Won't do any harm to have her checked, but I'd bet she'll be fine."

The relief that washes over me is like a flood of warm water.

His medical work done, Doc looks around him. He scratches his head. His eyes light on me and hold. "Why, you're the young fellow who was waiting outside my house the other night!"

"Ray Kinsella," I say. "My daughter." I point to Karin, whose eyelids are beginning to flutter. "My wife." I point to Annie. Then, for no reason I can fathom, I introduce everyone, even Abner Bluestein.

"Well now, it's lucky I happened on the scene, Ray Kinsella. That little girl wouldn't have lasted very much longer." I look at him, smiling from ear to ear, and I recall someone saying of Doc, "He was always the first at the side of an injured player in any sport." But I wonder how much he has sacrificed to save Karin's life. It seems to me that he will never be able to walk back onto the ballfield as Moonlight Graham. He has violated some cosmic rule that I vaguely know exists, and do not even attempt to understand.

I reach out and take his hand, holding it with both of mine. "Thank you," I say.

"Now you were the fellow who was talking about a baseball wish, weren't you?"

"I was."

"You drop down to the school one day, Ray Kinsella, and we'll talk some more about that. Not that I believe you could do it at all. I'd best be getting back," he goes on. "Alicia will be expecting me." He walks briskly around the corner of the bleacher, into the dark summer cornfield.

Karin blinks her eyes and raises a small brown hand to rub at her head. "Oh, honey, we're so glad you're okay." Annie and I are both kissing her small freckled cheeks.

"Boy, Daddy, you counted at that fat man just like you do when I don't eat my turnips," she says excitedly.

I have spent close to two hours explaining to Richard what has happened to me since the voice of the baseball announcer first boomed out, "If you build it, he will come."

But finally I arrive at the spot where I become bogged down like a car stuck in sand. "Richard, what would you do if you... You know, Dad played some semipro baseball... in Florida and California. What if he made the big leagues?"

Richard sits on the other side of the insect-legged table in his camper. The tension lines between his brows are deep as ditches as he frowns at me in the orangey light.

I stumble on. "What if you had a chance to meet Dad—to meet our father?"

"You mean you've brought him back to life, like you brought Shoeless Joe Jackson back to life?"

"Not me, but somehow... but he's out there, Richard. Not like we ever knew him. He's twenty-five years old and he's catching for the White Sox, and he has his whole life in front of him and doesn't know about us."

"But I can't see it—your ballfield," says Richard, "though Gypsy can, and I know she wouldn't put me on about something like that."

In the front of the camper, the part that rests over the cab of the truck, I can see Gypsy's slight form curled up on the bed like a child, like the remnants of a thirteen-year-old who ran away from her parents' home in Kellogg, Idaho, and discarded layers of her identity in secret places all across the face of America, in the process becoming very wise.

The silence is long, and I am beginning to feel ill at ease

when Richard says, "I'd go to him. I don't know what I'd tell him, but I'd become his friend. Ray, people toss around the phrase 'Heaven on earth,' but it seems to me you've gotten a lock on it. Play it for all it's worth."

Heaven on earth, indeed. I think of virtually nothing else for the next day. Karin is home, a bit subdued, her bruises and scrapes still visible. The near loss has affected us all; we each seem to be more concerned about the other, after having had our mortality waved in front of our faces.

At the ballpark, Annie snuggles against me, her small hand inserted flat inside my shirt, her fingers warm on my chest. Gypsy leans close to Richard, whispering to him a play-by-play of the action taking place on the field. Often she jumps delightedly and cheers, then slides back down next to Richard and stares up at him with her ironic smile, so full of love, and tells him what has happened.

Salinger has appeared preoccupied all day, and his eyes are far away tonight as he sits and hums absently, tapping one large white hand on the knee of his jeans. What he is humming makes me smile, for it is the tune Richard and Karin use when they chant the song of the carnival: "Mothers bring your daughters. Fathers bring your sons. The world's strangest babies are here. Buy your ticket and come on in."

Late in the game, Salinger suddenly taps me on the arm. "I've had a dream," he says when I turn to look at him. "I know how things are going to turn out."

"Things?" I say.

"The farm. Listen! It will be like this . . ." He moves down and sits in front of us, his back to the game, so he can deliver a lecture, like a professor with five graduate students who has been assigned an amphitheater for a classroom.

"It will be almost a fraternity, like one of those tiny, exclusive French restaurants that have no sign. You find it almost by instinct.

"The people who come here will be drawn . . ." He stops, searching for words. "Have you ever been walking down the street and stopped in midstride and turned in at a bookstore or a gallery you never knew existed? People will decide to holiday in the Midwest for reasons they can't fathom or express.

"They'll turn off I-80 at the Iowa City exit, drive around

the campus, get out and stroll across the lawns, look at the white columns of the Old Capitol Building, have supper at one of the tidy little restaurants, then decide to drive east for a while on a secondary highway. They'll watch the hawks soaring like Chinese kites in the early evening air. They'll slow down when they see your house, and they'll ooh and aah at the whiteness of it, the way it sits in the cornfield like a splotch of porcelain. They'll say how beautiful it is, and comment on how the flags snap in the breeze. At this point, they won't even realize that the flags fly over a center field. They'll be hypnotized by the way the corn sways in the breeze.

"They'll turn up your driveway, not knowing for sure why they're doing it, and arrive at your door, innocent as children, longing for the gentility of the past, for home-canned preserves, ice cream made in a wooden freezer, gingham dresses, and black-and-silver stoves with high warming ovens and cast-iron reservoirs.

"'Of course, we don't mind if you look around,' you'll say. 'It's only twenty dollars per person.' And they'll pass over the money without even looking at it—for it is money they have, and peace they lack.

"They'll walk out to the bleacher and sit in shirtsleeves in the perfect evening, or they'll find they have reserved seats somewhere in the grandstand or along one of the baselines—wherever they sat when they were children and cheered their heroes, in whatever park it was, whatever leaf-shaded town in Maine, or Ohio, or California. They'll watch the game, and it will be as if they have knelt in front of a faith healer, or dipped themselves in magic waters where a saint once rose like a serpent and cast benedictions to the wind like peach petals.

"The memories will be so thick that the outfielders will have to brush them away from their faces: squarish cars parked around a frame schoolhouse, blankets covering the engine blocks; Christmas carols drifting like tinseled birds toward the golden wash of the Northern Lights; women shelling peas in linoleum-floored kitchens, cradling the unshelled pods in brindled aprons, tearing open corn husks and waiting for the thrill of the cool sweet scent; apple-cheeked children and collie dogs; the coffee-and-oil smell of a general store; people gliding over the snow in an open cutter; the dazzling smell of horsehide blankets teasing the senses.

"I don't have to tell you that the one constant through all the years has been baseball. America has been erased like a blackboard, only to be rebuilt and then erased again. But baseball has marked time with America has rolled by like a procession of steamrollers. It is the same game that Moonlight Graham played in 1905. It is a living part of history, like calico dresses, stone crockery, and threshing crews eating at outdoor tables. It continually reminds us of what once was, like an Indian-head penny in a handful of new coins.

"I'll bet some of the men will be dragging along little women in flowered housedresses and high-heels who will see nothing and whine about sitting on a backless bleacher seat for two hours. And, occasionally, a woman will pull along a pale, sink-chested husband, or one squat as a rosebush who looks like a bulldog with a cigar clenched in his teeth, who gave up the sports page for the Dow Jones Average when he was twenty-one; and while she watches and thrills, he'll read the financial pages of the *Times* or the *Trib* and be soothed as a pacifier soothes a baby. But mostly, the arrivals will be couples who have withered and sickened of the contrived urgency of their lives..."

As Jerry speaks, a car turns off the highway and, in the twilight, zippers up the long driveway toward the house. It is a black Chrysler with the scorched-gold license plate of New York State.

"You talk a good dream," I say to Salinger.

Behind me I hear cars. Richard and Gypsy will be there selling tickets to the ballpark. Near their trailer, farther up the driveway, Karin will sit at a child-sized table, her orange cat curled around her ankles, chanting the carnival litany, and above her will be the garish canvas signs. She will offer the newcomers passage to the exhibit, but they'll shake their heads tolerantly and walk on toward the baseball stadium, where the lights blaze furiously.

"I dream of things that never were," says Jerry.

I spot a car with Ohio plates; in the dusk, its occupants resemble Wandalie and Frank, the holdup man and the waitress from Cleveland.

I am smiling convulsively. Whoever controls the strings must be chuckling, treating me like the heroine in the *Perils of Pauline*. By midnight, if the cars keep arriving, I'll have more than enough money to bring the mortgage up to date.

"I'll go and see what those cars want," says Gypsy.

"What cars?" says Richard.

The game tonight has been a double-header, and, when it is finally over, Richard and I walk out on the field. My fists are clenched, my tongue a piece of rock chipping against my teeth. As we make our way toward the plate, I feel like a schoolchild commanded to an audience with the principal, who, until now, has been only a rumor. Richard and I stand close together, side-by-side like the figures representing the Gemini astrological sign.

The catcher has been talking to Chick Gandil. He looks at us and smiles, and I can feel my heart shatter. But I do not die. Richard's hand grimly holds my bicep, his knuckles white.

"I admire the way you catch a game of baseball," I say, my voice sounding like thunder in the nearly empty park.

I don't hear his reply, which is spoken in a gentle voice and accompanied by another smile, Richard's smile, my smile, just a little off-center, showing teeth crammed together like passengers in a crowded elevator. I'll have Richard's fingerprints bruised into my arm for weeks. I stare at Richard's face, his eyes wide as those of a kid who's just had a coin pulled from his ear by a magician. All evening I have been peeling gauze from his eyes—Jerry and I have taken turns, actually, Jerry eulogizing about the lost past and the purity of baseball, and I counting the cars, looking at the fans that accumulate around us on the bleacher and fit into the phantom stands like baseballs tossed into a sea of baseballs. I feel as if I am watching a war movie in which a nurse is removing the last feet of white bandage from a soldier's eyes. Will he see?

My father stops speaking and looks questioningly at Richard, who is squinting at him as though he is at the far end of a microscope.

"He's been having a little trouble with his eyes, but I think it's clearing up," I say.

"It's true," says Richard, air exploding from his lungs.

"It is true," I reply.

"I admire the way you catch a game of baseball," he says to the catcher, slowly, hesitantly, his voice filled with awe.

As the three of us walk across the vast emerald lake that is the outfield, I think of all the things I'll want to talk to the catcher about. I'll guide the conversations, like taking a car around a long, gentle curve in the road, and we'll hardly realize that we're talking of love, and family, and life, and beauty, and friendship, and sharing . . .

And I think of Gypsy waiting for us, clutching the handful of bills that will act as the cement to keep the stadium solid and permanent as the game it houses.

V

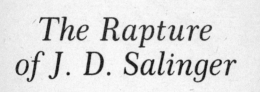

*The Rapture
of J. D. Salinger*

No one asked me. It was instinct that caused me to build that door in the right-center-field fence, a very ordinary door that, from a distance, looks as if it was created by sawing the shape of a door into the finished fence. The door opens out and is held in place by a silver bird-beak latch.

When a game ends, the players, both those with substance and those without, amble across the field, visiting with each other, gloves hanging limp in their hands, bats resting languidly on their shoulders. The bat boys and equipment men drag brown sacks of bats and balls across the outfield, leaving a quavering wake behind them on the bright green grass. The last to leave pulls the door closed behind him, and, as if this were a signal, the lights that whiten the baseball field snap off, glow eerily from yellow to orange to gray, and then vanish altogether, along with the other accoutrements of wonder: the stands, the fans, the vendors. Often Karin and I are left alone on our perch, the one weak battery of floodlights sizzling above us. We make our way across the cool, moist outfield grass, Karin sometimes walking, sometimes being carried. With my help, she latches the gate, pushing the silver bird beak through the silver circle.

Then we walk toward our home, our shadows long and black behind us. On the porch I switch off the lights, and the ballpark sighs in the silence, a frog shrills, the fence creaks in reply.

I try not to wonder what is beyond that gate, to speculate on what kind of limbo my ballplayers lay in. Do they smell of mothballs, like dolls packed away in an old woman's trunk for fifty years? Are they stored on shelves? Is there a warehouse full of ancient baseball players packed away in bales, brittle and dry, faces full of eggshell cracks? Or do they merely move on to another ballpark, another town? Are there other ballfields like mine, other players, other magic farms? Are there layers upon layers of dimensions, like coats of varnish on fine furniture? Or do my players go back to a phantom hotel, change clothes, and head out to shadowy restaurants, bars, and nightclubs?

I do have hope. I think cunning thoughts. My hope is that if I serve them well, I may someday be told their secrets, may even be invited to walk through that door with them after a game.

That is why I am at first surprised, then envious, then angry when I overhear a conversation in the outfield among Shoeless Joe Jackson, Salinger, and Happy Felsch.

"How would you like to go out with us after the game?" says Joe to Salinger, while Happy Felsch nods his approval. It is early in the evening. We are on our way to the stands, the outfielders have been shagging flies. Everything seems so . . . normal. It is as if they are unaware of the uniqueness of their situation, the import of their suggestion, the stardust that is their lives.

"I'd be delighted," says Jerry, smiling warmly.

In the bleacher I am as silent as if I am being rained on. I remember that once, as a child, I invited two friends over to play with a board-game I had been given for Christmas. In a short time, they discovered it was more fun with only two players. They played. I watched and was outraged at their betrayal, which they seemed not even to realize.

The same is true tonight. Salinger pretends nothing unusual is happening.

By the sixth inning, I can no longer control my seething anger.

"Why you?" I demand of Salinger.

He is very interested in the action on the field. He refuses to look at me.

"I built this damn field," I shout. "I carved it out of my cornfield. It's been like creating a giant work of art, like birthing a child. It's mine." I stop as the words pile up on top of each other in my throat. Whatever I may say will be inadequate to express my rage.

"I didn't ask them to," says Jerry.

"*I* built this field. They wouldn't *be* here if it weren't for me. I brought *you* here because I wanted to renew your life. *I* don't want to be replaced."

"Nobody wants to be replaced," Salinger says quietly. "But you didn't think this up. You told me yourself that you were told to come to New Hampshire and find me," he says logically. But I am not at the moment interested in logic.

"Oh, you've already rationalized it until it's okay. I should have known I couldn't share without being taken advantage of."

"There is a reason, I assure you," Salinger says with quiet dignity. It is as if he is speaking to a stranger, after all I have done to make him a friend.

"It's not fair," I say, knowing that I sound like a pouting child. But am I really so wrong? This is my creation. If I can't play, then I'll take the ball home.

Salinger studies the backs of his large hands, the hair on them bristling white as phantom willow stocks. He locks his fingers together, twisting them tightly until the nails become ice-colored.

I picture myself in the quiet, air-conditioned cab of the high, dark-green John Deere tractor that sits, bulky as a weapon, in the machine shed. I could drive right through the fence, time and again, and smash the bleacher with two or three careful runs. I could gather up the pieces, tie them in bundles, white splinters grinning out of the dark-green boards, drag them off to the woodpile, and use them in the fireplace at the house. Then I could hook up the plow and chop the field up, as if I were cutting salad with a glittering French knife; bury the bases, erase the baselines. The single beam of light from the tractor would circle the field all night, and the beam would play across the corn each time I turned the wheel, driving my ghostly players away like fugitives. By dawn, there would be only a plowed field, level as a black sea.

If Salinger says "No one ever promised you life would be fair," I'll do it, I swear. My stomach hurts. I can feel cold sweat trickling down my sides.

But Salinger remains silent, thoughtful. Karin has fallen asleep in my arms. Salinger reaches over, takes one of her tiny hands in his. Her small nails are blunt, her freckled fingers scuffed.

"All right," says Jerry, and he looks me squarely in the eye. "All right," he says again. "I gave the interview."

"What interview?"

"You know damn well what interview. The one about baseball. The one about the Polo Grounds. The one that charged you up and sent you all the way to New Hampshire to find me. That one."

"You lied."

"Back then I couldn't let anybody get that close to me." Karin stirs slightly as Salinger closes his hand over hers. "I've thought of telling you, but I was saving it for the right moment."

"Well, I think this is definitely the right moment," I say indignantly. "I was just contemplating destroying the field."

"I thought of turning them down," says Salinger. "I really did. Telling them it was you who created them—you who deserves to be first. But then I thought, they must know; there must be a reason for them to choose me, just as there was a reason for them to choose you, and Iowa, and this farm."

Yes, there are obvious reasons why he has been chosen, and they wash all around me as I see Salinger staring tenderly down at Karin. And as he does, he nods toward the house, toward where Annie waits with her brilliant love.

"If you can package up your jealousy for a few minutes, you'll see that I'm right. I'm unattached. My family is grown up. And," he says, smiling sardonically at me, "if I have the courage to do this, then you'll have to stop badgering me about the other business. I mean, publishing is such a pale horse compared to this. But what a story it will make"—and his voice rises—"a man being able to touch the perfect dream. I'll write of it. I promise."

"You really gave the interview? You really said those things? You really wanted more than anything else in the world to play at the Polo Grounds?"

"I did."

"I apologize for everything I've been thinking."

"No need."

" 'I saw myself grow too old for the dream. Saw the Giants moved across a continent, and finally they tore down the Polo Grounds in 1964.' You really said that!"

"I did!"

As if on cue, Annie appears, skips up the bleacher, and sits beside me. She rubs her denimed thigh against mine. She is warm as sunshine, Annie is.

"Jerry's been invited out with the baseball players after the game," I say, trying to make it sound casual, the way ten years from now I'll say, "Karin's going to the drive-in tonight—with one of the Kowalski boys, the one whose fists drag the ground and who was arrested for reckless driving last month."

"Out?" says Annie.

"Out," I repeat, pointing toward the door in the right-center-field fence.

"Well, be careful," says Annie, smiling brightly.

Jerry nods.

"What do you think is out there?" he says to me. "Are there other places like this, people like you?"

"I don't know. You're asking the wrong person. I'm the one who's always one play behind, the last to know—if you know what I mean?" But as I say this, I, too, am smiling.

"Ray, do you think the Polo Grounds just might be floating around out there? Do you think I might get to play, or, like Eddie Scissons, get to sit in the stands the way I am now, and watch a twenty-year-old kid, with a smooth face and black, pompadoured hair, try out with the 1938 Giants? I think that's what I'd like to do."

"Well, I hope it works out," I say. "I hope you won't be disappointed."

The game ends and the players begin to drift off toward their exit. Jerry places Karin's hand carefully on my chest, breaking the chain by which the four of us touched. She curls her fingers into a fist, and tucks it under her chin.

Jerry climbs down the bleacher and walks around the end of the fence. Below us, Shoeless Joe Jackson has been waiting in left field.

"Take care of my friend," I call to Joe.

He salutes, claps a hand on Jerry's shoulder, and they walk across the outfield to where Happy Felsch and the catcher wait by the gate.

Joe, Happy, Salinger, and the catcher are the last ones through the gate. The lights dim, making cooling sounds like icicles breaking. The rest of the mirage retreats slowly, like a boat sailing into a fog bank. The voices of the ballplayers merge with the silky rustling of the cornstalks.

I place Karin on my shoulder, like a small sack of corn. Annie hugs my waist, her face against my arm, and we make our way first to the gate, which Annie and I lock by forcing the silver point through the silver ring, and then on toward the house.

On the porch, we turn to look at the silent, satiny green of the field. I press the switch, and, like a candle going out, the scar of light disappears. Above the farm, a moon bright as butter silvers the night as Annie holds the door open for me.

ABOUT THE AUTHOR

W. P. Kinsella has published four short-story collections to great acclaim in Canada. His stories have been widely published in U. S. and Canadian magazines and have been included in many anthologies, including *Pushcart Prize V (1980–81)* and *Best Canadian Stories: 1977*. In 1982, he received the prestigious Houghton Mifflin Literary Fellowship Award for *Shoeless Joe*.

His home is Calgary, Alberta, Canada, where he teaches fiction writing at The University of Calgary. He spends his summers, however, touring U. S. baseball capitals in a beat-up Datsun with his wife, Ann.